ANCIENT LOVERS

H E N R Y   D .   W I N G F I E L D

ANCIENT LOVERS

CITI OF BOOKS

CITIOFBOOKS, INC.
3736 Eubank NE Suite A1
Albuquerque, NM 87111-3579
www.citiofbooks.com
Hotline: 1 (877) 389-2759
Fax: 1 (505) 930-7244

Ordering Information:
Quantity sales. Special discounts are available on quantity purchases by corporations, associations, and others. For details, contact the publisher at the address above.

Printed in the United States of America.

ISBN-13:   Softcover   979-8-89391-875-5
                eBook   979-8-89391-876-2

Library of Congress Control Number: 2025945390

TABLE OF CONTENTS

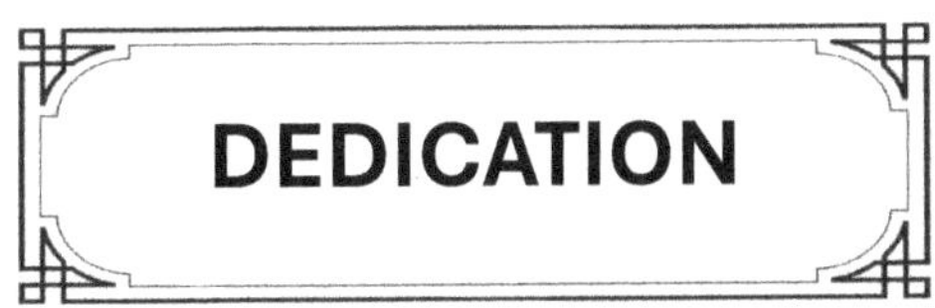

To all of my relatives; to all of the creatures on this earth, underwater and in the sky (both alive and in the other world); and especially to my divine, longest female friend and editor, Peggy Marquiss, whom without her expertise of the English language, Ancient Lovers would still be a dream in my head. Because of Peg. it is now in print.

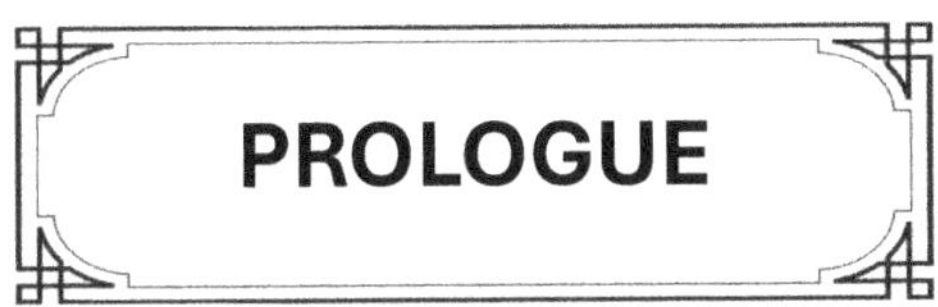

PROLOGUE

Ancient lovers entwine as one, and one becomes the other. Ancient lovers meet again-some other place, some other time.

It was 21 centuries ago this couple was together. His time alive was a mere 31 years by the Roman calendar. She was on earth for 40 years. They were entwined together in love for only 15 years. So short... so maddening... so sensuous... so erotic... so passionate so short. His name was Argos, hers Felicia. They settled near Rome after migrating from their birthplace in Greece. They did not know for knowing. They did not care. It was love, undefined, unconditional and boundless. Love energy became their manna.

In those short 15 years, they made vow after vow to each other committing to carry on and find one another after their deaths in some other place, some other time. Vows were made every sacred day of their lives that, when apart temporarily, they would always be together in thought. And this love that was so nurtured became entombed in a spiritual web, and today was reborn again.

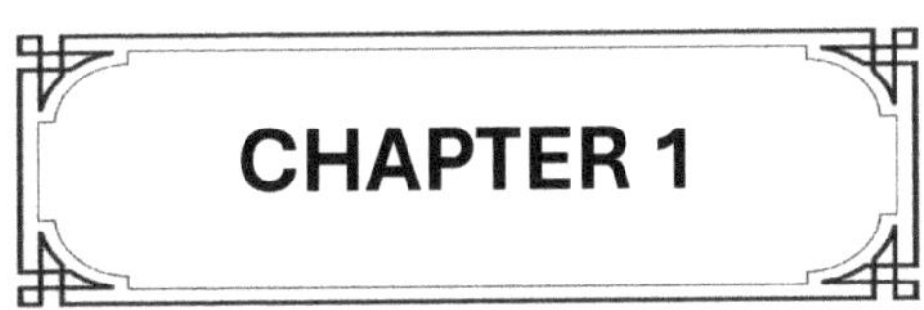

CHAPTER 1

7 BC: Felicia stood and stared, moving her head like a beacon in a lighthouse, scanning the horizon for survivors. She knew it was useless. She knew no one could have survived the plague once it was upon you, yet she had one ounce of belief remaining, and she called it "hope."

The fever had been with Argos for 10 days and it weakened him to nothing. For that whole time, Felicia nursed him but did not know how to make him well. This was horrible for her to accept. The last hours were the worst. The hallucinations sent Argos into delirium. Then, with the most aware consciousness, he came out of his daze and told Felicia they would meet again, some other place, some other time. Argos passed away in her arms yesterday and, with his last breath, whispered, "Take care, my love, and carry on with Artemus. Hopefully, we shall meet again." She took in his last breath, and he was finally at peace.

Felicia's entire family had succumbed to the dreaded plague except for herself and little Artemus, the only child she and Argos bore together. She was pregnant by Argos one other time, but the baby was stillborn, and they had never tried again. It nearly killed her.

In 17 BC, people were not married. They were united in a common, mutual love embrace exchange. Not much can be said before the recording of documented history; therefore, we do not know much about Felicia and Argos except whatever we gather in 1997 from a man named Pedro and a woman named Abby. The peculiar thing is Abby's eyes and how Pedro sees a movie of their past lives playing in them. Pedro had never met Abby before January 22nd, 1997.

1997 AD: This rebirthing took place yesterday, in Pedro's medical clinic in Callebocca, Guatemala. It was now, but it could have been then. It was today, and Pedro was perplexed. Under tragic circumstances, Abby lay on a cot in a jungle in Guatemala in a coma. She was transported to some other place, some other time, and the movie reels playing in her head were seen by Pedro, a doctor, when he peered into her eyes to check for consciousness.

One can transport oneself in time simply by moving energy. Reading is another time machine, just like going to the theater. Ancient lovers meet again and unite in ceremony just as before, entwined as they once were. This cannot be broken with words. But what is it really? Is it fair to imagine that an indian brave killed in battle cannot have another chance at life or that an elder of a tribe who has passed on cannot come back as an elk or a buffalo or some other visionary life form?

The giant oak grows simply by producing a seed and dropping it to the ground. Suppose a porcupine ingests that acorn and digests it, then excretes it and the defecation decomposes. The wind blows, and suddenly the acorn becomes a willow. Suppose another varmint re-ingests the acorn, reproduces with its mate and its seed becomes fertile, is transformed into an embryo within the female, and she gives birth. The oak lives, and so does its seed, but it does not necessarily have to come out the same way it went in. Death is just another form of birthing. What does our energy become when we pass on our last breath at the end of this life?

Ancient lovers become one, and one turns into the other. Centuries pass, and Felicia and Argos' energy is picked up after their deaths and implanted into the DNA of Abby and Pedro when their parents conceived them in the 1940s.

Pedro was a beautiful, dark-skinned native born in Livingston, Guatemala, who grew up working on his parents' successful family farm where orchards produced a variety of fruits that they bottled and sold as refreshing drinks.

Abby was born in 1949 in Boston, Massachusetts, but her family moved a lot because her father was a regional manager of engineering with Dupont Chemicals and was required to relocate from city to city, mainly on the East Coast, to get other plants up and running.

Twenty-one hundred years later, after Argos and Felicia had long been gone, Abby and Pedro spiritually entwine, but do not physically become one. They remain separate, yet unite in memory and recall by watching this movie playing in Abby's eyes. They are happy to be together again and share what once was. There is a completeness here, a fulfillment that elates them both knowing they have found one another as predicted in their vows of 17 BC. So they carry on spiritually, and energy is exchanged in thought- kind, gentle, loving thoughts that get transported through the air.

It is too soon for them to realize what is really going on, especially since Abby is still in a coma. Pedro is praying for her consciousness so he can discuss this phenomenon with her.

For now, when he examines Abby's eyes, their thoughts become one. Her nakedness is etched inside his eyelids. His touch is engraved inside her palms. Her scent is laced inside his nostrils. His hunger is tantalizing to her tastebuds, and their hearts beat as one. They could be apart and still be together. Their love will last forever. This was Argos and Felicia being transcended unbeknownst into the beings of Abby and Pedro.

As it was then, it is now. They embraced the same, conjuring up dreams just to give them something to remember.

17 BC: "Here, Argos, you take my heart and beat it into yours," Felicia said. Argos said, "Here, Felicia, take my dream and let it be a start of forever inside your heart." They sensed right then and there that what one experienced, the other shared in feeling and sensation.

Explosive love is boundless and, cast into the sea of all possibilities, will be washed ashore someday to be discovered by ancient lovers who find the cord, like Abby and Pedro did in Guatemala.

Argos commented during his delirium in 17 BC, "I do not care, so long as I am doing sign language with the wind, and I know she will appear once again in time. I view death as a beautiful happening, like birth. Yet, as we do not know what either is like at that moment of experience, if viewed as beautiful, then so be it. Little empty pockets full of wisdom." Felicia continued her vigilance not understanding what he was mumbling.

(Author's note: You work at your life, with your life and, hopefully, become your life. It is everyone's destiny to seek it, though many don't know where to start. The importance lies in resignation. I resign myself to live fully within myself, to know myself and be committed to myself with love, and live for no one else. All visitors are welcome, and I will share the most intimate with whomever I choose, so long as it is reciprocated. If life comes from within me, then I know life has its own destiny. My mother had life within her. She birthed me, and I became me. Therefore, one must seek ones own destiny, and I am but a mere image of this newness, this freshness, this oneness that I choose to give birth to. There is loss. There is abbreviation. There is judgment. Life is created and life goes on in whatever realm for which it is destined. Death, as we know it, is just another beginning. Death may end a particular life, but does it end a love energy two people share and commit vows to pursue in another passing? Can two new people recognize themselves as ancient lovers who meet again in this time?)

1997 AD: Because of her psychic abilities and powers, when she awakens from her coma, Abby accepts meeting Pedro for the first time as a reunion. Her communication skills are precise and loving, fully aware that she does so without the spoken word. When she has something to say, she thinks it. Her thoughts are always clear and pure at the moment which makes her an angel in her own right.

Pedro, the doctor she meets in Guatemala, is her ancient lover. He does not realize this just yet. At his clinic in Cailebocca, Guatemala, he is only treating her for injuries she sustained in an automobile accident.

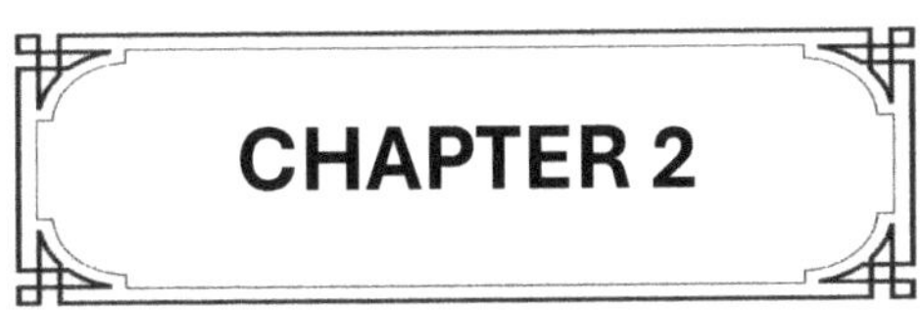

CHAPTER 2

Abby and Stephan, her husband, had been vacationing in Central America since January 1st, 1997. Their jeep overturned January 22nd in Guatemala, and Stephan was killed. They were madly in love with one another and shared a bountiful life together, but had no children. Abby did not know the long-range ramifications of what was about to transpire with this dreadful, fatal single-car accident.

Abby suffered a broken leg, cuts and bruises and a concussion. She was transported to Callebocca, Guatemala, on the east coast near the Caribbean Sea to a small public medical clinic. She was unconscious for five days while under Pedro's care and supervision. He took an unusually special interest in Abby. Something touched him with her beauty. He could somehow see a past life from deep inside her eyes. Pedro checked them every day for consciousness or awareness, but instead saw into her past like a movie flashing before his eyes. He recognized a main character as himself in someone else's body. It was, in fact, a movie he was watching inside Abby's eyes. He was fascinated by this, not freaked out or scared. He fell deeper into the plot, but really did not know where it was going.

All of her vital signs were stable, but Pedro wondered what the news about Abby's deceased husband might do to her when she awakened from her coma. He would find out soon enough, because Abby was beginning to stir after five days of stillness.

She was achy and groggy when she finally opened her eyes on the sixth morning. The first coherent sentences out of her mouth were, "Where's my husband? How is he? Where am I?" Then, "What happened?" Pedro was there. He had been since day one. performing a vigilance for her recovery. Now he consoled her with more than medical jargon. In his fluent English, he told her she had been involved in an automobile accident and that she was in a clinic in Guatemala. He was holding her hand as if they were lifelong friends, although he had never seen her before January 22nd. 1997. She appeared to show no real stress, but she wanted some answers to her questions. After Pedro expressed concern for her, he introduced himself. "My name is Pedro and I am a doctor treating you." Then he asked, "What is your name?" "Abby," she whispered, with a quaking note. Pedro proceeded with more questions. "How do you feel? Can you wiggle your fingers? Good. Do you remember the accident and how it happened," Pedro asked. From her responses and what appeared to be a calm, rational state, Pedro assessed that she could handle the bad news directly. No beating around the bush trying to pad a falling anvil directed toward one's head.

Pedro ran the gamut of probings and proddings until he was certain that there was no further damage to her delicate body other than the cuts and bruises-but no stitches-and, of course, the broken leg, now in a cast. He felt assured of her recovery.

Pedro possessed a natural attitude when it came to his medical practice. His ethics and scruples, therefore, became his entire philosophy and approach to life. He had graduated from the Harvard School of Medicine in 1983, took his medical boards, and was awarded his certificate to practice medicine. He had then moved back to his home town in Livingston, Guatemala, to help his own people. He established a family clinic 20 miles from Livingston in Callebocca. He knew he had to devote his services to those less fortunate. He was 41 years old when he moved back home in 1984 and carried that certain Latin-American look in his skin that women seem to melt over. His eyes were warm, clear and conscious, and he was open and easy to get to know.

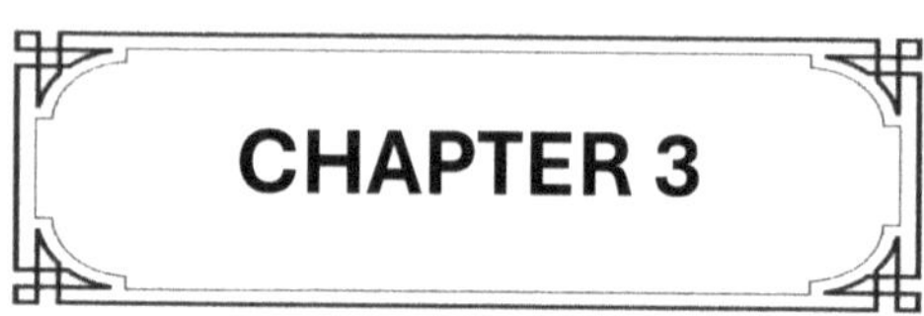

CHAPTER 3

Pedro's parents, Juan and Margarette Salvarez, were wealthy business people who owned, operated and managed citrus orchards. They produced a variety of fruit trees. They picked the fruit and made a commercial juice called "Fruit Flows." They packaged and bottled everything on the farm. They were well known throughout neighboring villages and towns surrounding their thousand acres of orchards, and they were highly respected and adored by all.

Juan and Margarette raised Pedro to revere all living creatures, to respect others and try to understand things he didn't comprehend. But most importantly, they taught him to realize that there is no weapon on earth that can combat and defeat love felt from the heart.

The Salvarezes distributed Fruit Flows around the world. They could have retired today and been well off, leaving a fortune to all of their children, but they were devoted to their work, loved their private life, and found time to enjoy the pleasures they deserved without being too consumed in greed. It really was not a matter of finding the time for it was never lost-but, rather, making the time, because they created the moments and what they did with them. If work was fun, then you enjoyed what you did without hostility, and you did the best you could, providing for your workers, giving back what you reaped for all to enjoy. "Health is wealth." was the family motto. Therefore, all of those employed by the Salvarezes were happy and content.

Fruit Flows was a variety of delicious, all-natural juices. It was said they had medicinal value, but there was no verification of this. Kids loved it, and adults proclaimed that it had healing properties because it tasted so good. And isn't this what good feelings are for, to make you feel better?

Though Guatemala is noted for its banana and coffee production and exportation, the Salvarezes knew the earth could support other crops as well. And so, years ago when they first started planting, they experimented with mango, papaya and cardamom. All of them took to the earth like a fetus to an umbilical cord. Hence, 40 years later, their orchards and herb fields flourished with life and healthy blossoms yielding a prolific harvest annually. They had never used a dangerous pesticide on their crops. Juan, an amateur scientist, had studied the indigenous insects and their attacks on fruit trees. He had learned to be harmonious with the immediate environment and did whatever it took to co-exist and commingle with all of nature and her inhabitants.

Juan introduced natural predators, like bats and hummingbirds, to their plantation to combat the destructive insects. Along with this special ecosystem, he introduced a plethora of wild native plants and flowers to support the bird population, but also to naturally ward off the invasion of certain insects due to their repulsion of aromas from these plant blossoms. They also supported a small colony of native bees which had no ill effects on the hives when the "killer bees" migrated from South America in 1995. There was no reason, no explanation for this. "Don't ask," Juan would say. "Just leave it to Mother Nature."

Margarette played a very important role in the family production of Fruit Flows. She was acting vice president of the Salvarez farm. She and Juan risked everything to get started in 1942. They had Pedro in 1944. Pedro was one of five children. In chronological order, there were Migel, Florencia, Roberto, Pedro and Juanita. All of Pedro's siblings participated in the farming and production of Fruit Flows.

Pedro showed exceptional talent and skill in school. Though all of the Salvarez children were smart and passed all of their studies, no one desired to go on to college more than Pedro. Juan and Margarette would make sure all their children achieved what they wanted in life.

Pedro wanted to go to college. He knew he wanted to study medicine-modern medicine-because he sensed this would be at perfect combination with his native medical background he had acquired from "the people with knowledge" working on the farm growing up. He first applied to the University of Costa Rica Medical School in 1960, was accepted and graduated with honors in 1964. For the next 20 years, he built his medical practice in his small clinic in Callebocca hoping to one day go to med school in America. He was affixed with this notion.

He finally got accepted to Harvard in 1980 after writing a dissertation few professors on the review board could fathom. One did, and she was responsible for his acceptance. She addressed her review board colleagues and influenced them on the grounds that she found his writing to be "remarkable, exceptional." Her name was Sophia Wordsworth, and she agreed to be his overseer, proctor and mentor. She had obtained a doctorate in medicine, but never took her boards. She raised a family instead. She was considered a genius among her peers. She had a demeanor that no one challenged. She was humble. She was generous. She lacked all ego, yet she seemed to acknowledge others and called them on it as if she were that person and understood the ego involved. She had the deepest blue eyes, like the middle of the ocean, that penetrated your own vision and perceptions. Everyone who spoke with Sophia felt forced to listen, but listened with focus and comprehension, not just watching her lips move.

After Sophia graduated from Cornell Medical School, she married, birthed three children, supported her loving husband with all of his worldly endeavors, raised her children to be scholars, and decided she wanted to teach at the college level when her kids were grown and gone. Harvard snatched her up in a heartbeat. She had her choice of the top medical schools in America to staff the review and acceptance boards of applying students. To her, this was perfect. She saw that this was teaching at its essence, to be able to choose prime students for acceptance and watch them grow with their quest for higher knowledge. It was also an opportunity for her to take personal interest in the special ones and to tutor them. Everyone adored Sophia, both the students and the administration.

Pedro could not have been in better hands. But he already had a degree in medicine and had been in practice for 20 years. "Why go back to med school again?" was the campus query. Call it fate, but he knew he was destined to graduate from an American medical school of international credibility, his lifelong ambition.

Sophia saw to it that Pedro excelled in his studies. She was correct in her prognosis that this doctor was extraordinary. He graduated from Harvard in three easy years. He had an innate desire, a quest, an insatiable thirst to learn everything that interested him and learn it well. Naive he was not, but he could not understand why others did not behave as he did when it came to a worldly view and universal love for the planet. Could it be a "product of the environment" influenced by parental upbringing. and then realize that there is a Harlem, and "Harlem is Harlem," and there is a Watts, and "Watts is Watts," and there "is what there is" and that "that is what that is"?

"Challenge nor and ask not why, for it will only lead to controversy, leading to discrepancy, leading to an argument ending in a fight." Pedro was taught this by his father, though this was one of the things Pedro found to be a flaw in his father's thinking. The only way to learn is to ask and sometimes asking may lead to a difference in opinion, yet not necessarily end in a fight. Pedro's philosophy was: "If you ask. I will take a bullet for you. If you don't ask, I will step out of the way-but you have to ask first."

Pedro could not have had a wiser childhood, and he respected his parents and all of their viewpoints. He just didn't have to agree with them. Pedro knew he had to challenge that which was before him in order to grow. Less than this would have meant to stifle himself.

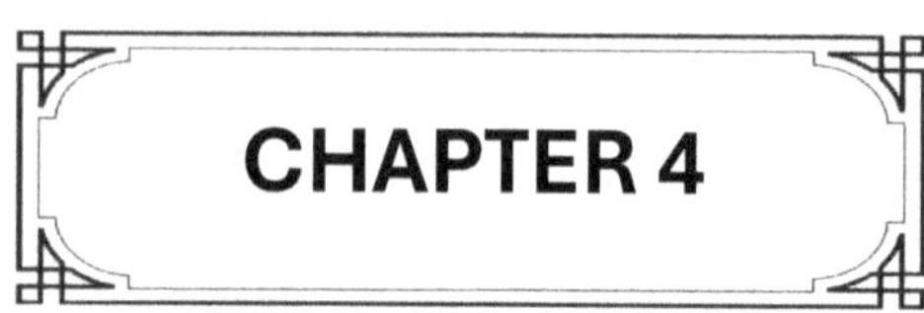

Pedro's focus was now on Abby and her movie-projecting eyes. He was spellbound by the first entrancing image of himself starring in her eyes. What got him even more was this sense-this calming sense, this sense of well-being-near euphoria-when he gazed into her eyes.

Abby was still in a daze, confused and wondering about her husband, though she knew the imminent answer was death. There was no other reason Pedro was withholding telling her the status of Stephan. Therefore, she put it boldly to Pedro, "My husband is dead, isn't he?" Pedro responded that he had probably died instantly. His neck had been broken and both carotid arteries severed.

No one found the wrecked vehicle for approximately two and a half hours. Three local farmers came upon the scene and realized something was dreadfully wrong. When they got to Stephan, he was cold and motionless. When his pulse was taken, the person knew he was dead and his spirit gone, vanished into thin air. Villagers around Livingston did not know how to handle such situations with outsiders. Death was common with old and young, usually relatives. So the spirit of the deceased was very, very important to witness. When grandfather was on his death bed, everyone gathered in the room until his last breath was expelled. All present could share the omnipresence of the holy spirit the dead were said to possess for that instant, and then let it go. If the dying have it, then the living must, too. It just lies dormant until it comes to fruition. And this is why they call death "a passing on." Few are privileged to be present and take in that last exhalation. Yet, the final breath exhaled becomes one with the weather patterns of the universe.

The Salvarezes abstained from any formal religious belief, unlike the rest of Central America. When the missionaries invaded the natives and thrust Jesus down their throats in the form of communion wafers and the devout word of God, the Salvarezes' ancestors challenged this one-god theory and it never took hold with them. The wise leaders of the family believed there are many gods, one for every occasion, and this is what they passed down from generation to generation. Whatever was going on around them didn't concern them unless it meant participating in a group effort to rebuild a barn, help a neighbor with some advice, or go to a social event for communal dining. Other than this, their focus was family, good clean living, honesty and hard work. They believed in creation of life, soul and spirit enveloped in love.

The "people with knowledge" simply felt "death is a conception yielding birth over and over again." So when they came upon Stephan's lifeless body, cold and without spirit, they knew it was too late to witness his departing breath and turned their attention to Abby's body which still had breath and life. The three local villagers were all male and kept their composure in dealing with Abby's delicate situation. They managed to free her from the jeep and carry her up to the road where they would wait for another vehicle to pass by and would hopefully flag it down.

It was not too long before a friend of Pedro's was cruising by from Livingston. He was headed to his home in the jungle 20 miles further down from the wreckage. He was hailed to stop and did so. Realizing the accident was serious, he willingly rushed the woman back to his friend's clinic in Callebocca. Pedro's clinic was 25 miles the other way, but that was no consideration for Fidel. He knew the immediacy of Abby's injuries versus wellness. Abby lay unconscious the whole way in the back seat of his car. None of the farmers could spare the time to travel along and assist. Fidel reassured them that this would not be necessary.

Pedro's clinic was there to serve all of the neighboring villagers for miles and miles. Locals would walk to his place with any ailment, sometimes carrying their infants on their back. It was the only place to receive medical services, and Pedro turned no one away.

This was his only mission in life, his crusade to help his friends, family members and visitors..

So there Abby lay in an unconscious state for five days. Pedro, mesmerized with every glance into her eyes, fascinated by the show of regression deep into a past life and recognizing himself as a different person with this woman from centuries ago, but not the woman lying in his clinic, allowed himself to go with the flow. He wanted desperately for her to awaken just to see if she would recognize him standing before her or be able to look into his eyes and see the same movie. He figured it did not work that way, but who could say?

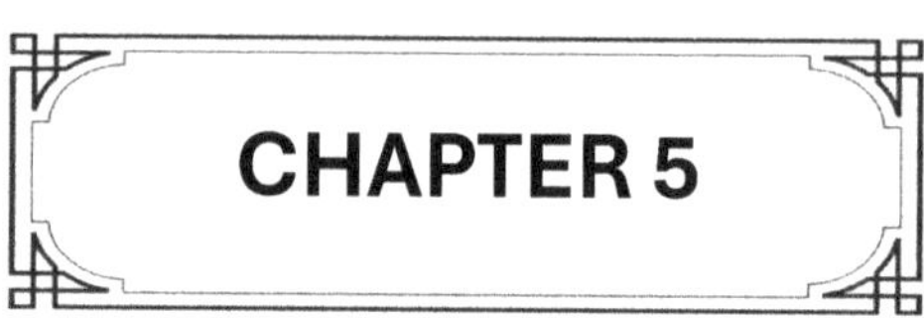

CHAPTER 5

Abby accepted the news of her husband's death and held Pedro's hand with tender loving anguish. She cried and cried, tears streaming down her face, soaking her pillow case. Pedro said, "Go ahead and cry. Don't hold back. Cry for the love of your husband. Tears are how the oceans were formed." Her crying lasted what seemed like an eternity, then turned to sobs and moans for another, much longer time. Pedro leaned down and cradled her in his arms, letting her rest gently in the crux of his shoulder as her tears moistened his shirt.

He laid her back down to rest, her eyes open and appearing now somewhat calm and very, very exhausted. She started to whimper, "It was a terrible accident. I remember it now. It was raining miserably, and Stephan swerved to avoid a huge rut in the road. He drove the right front wheel off the shoulder of the road and down the steep embankment, flipping and rolling uncontrollably. All I remember after that was the thrashing about inside the Land Rover. I must have been knocked unconscious before we came to a stop."

Abby reached out for Pedro's hand and asked him not to leave. His hand was soft and gentle like a surgeon's. Abby held on for dear life, but not squeezing out of fear, more out of some strange and curious love and compassion she felt inside her living flesh.

Lolita, Pedro's wife, heard voices and came in to see how the patient was doing. Pedro gestured for her silence and to come closer. Abby was just falling asleep when she glanced up into Lolita's eyes and gave her a sincere, warming smile, thinking, "What a lucky, beautiful woman to be married to such a wonderful man," then nodded off into sweet slumber. Pedro crossed Abby's arms upon her abdomen and walked Lolita out of the room.

Lolita was Pedro's nursing assistant, office manager, and also his wife. She, too, was gorgeous, "to drop dead for," when they were seen in public. They met in Costa Rica when both attended medical school. Lolita knew she did not want to go beyond a nurse. practitioner certification and fell madly in love with Pedro. She stayed by his side until he left for Harvard. The clinic stayed open while Pedro finished his lifelong ambition to graduate in medicine from an American university. Lolita did what she could to treat minor ailments, diseases and typical jungle crud so that the clinic would not lose its purpose to serve the locals. When more serious complications arose, she had the patient transported to a hospital in Livingston, or even Guatemala City 200 miles west. She had that loving touch that seemed to be the healing cure for many of the illnesses she came upon. Many think it was because of her beauty that the sick felt better simply by looking at her.

Pedro and Lolita had no children. They decided they were too dedicated to their mission and did not want to take on the responsibility or commitment of raising a family. They were married in 1975. They were revolutionary in thought, liberals at heart, and always kept an open door for those in need. "And besides," they mused, "to be childless is a simpler way of life when your services are directed toward wellness and serving the public." They were very happy together, both very strong, independent individuals, and when apart from one another always couldn't wait to be together again, yet managed all right when separated.

Abby slept for 12 hours, awoke rested and not too achy, but starving. Pedro was there with cereal and fresh fruit, deciding she should have something light and nutritious. He asked her what she liked to eat. "Strict vegetarian, semi-veggie or just about anything, including meat?" She indicated, "Anything, including meat," with a half smile. And she said, "You should know." This startled Pedro. He queried, "Why did you say that?" Abby said, "I don't know. It just came out that way. I guess I just figured you being a doctor and all should kind of know these things by looking at someone." Pedro replied, "Yes, but I have no idea of someone's eating particulars. I can help them with diet if I know what their eating habits have been. I must admit, when I looked into your eyes when you were unconscious, I saw a lot more than what you should be eating."

Abby was curious. "What did you see?"

Pedro suddenly became intense. "Please try to understand. What I am about to tell you is bold and forward. Do not take it lightly, nor with underlying meaning. I saw into your eyes as if I was watching a movie, and that movie starred us, together, as lovers from long ago, but we did not look like ourselves today. I have never met you before six days ago. I cannot explain it, and I do not know if it is necessary to even try. But I am not afraid of it. Can you give me some insight into this phenomenon, or should we just disregard it and move on?"

Abby became like a teacher. "You're right. What you saw in my eyes was a movie. I dreamed it when I was unconscious. It was playing in my head. Real or not is irrelevant. I sense we were ancient lovers, too. I feel it in my heart. To love you today would be unfair and unreal at this time. But to acknowledge what we once had as a mutual relationship is very real and very enlightening. I've always dreamed like this, but never put it together with a living partner. In my unconsciousness, the movie reels rolled and it was almost like being entertained. Do you realize the rarity, the oddity, of these two energies of past lives reuniting together with mutual compassion in this lifetime as two different people?"

Pedro exclaimed, "Extraordinary-phenomenal but do you realize what you are suggesting?"

Abby, scholarly, said, "Of course. I practice this daily. It's part of my psyche. I just never went this far with another person who could relate or see it through my eyes. Tell me now, where is Stephan's body?"

Pedro, "I knew you were going to ask that. He was brought to the clinic shortly after they brought you here six days ago."

Abby, directly, "You see, you knew I was going to ask that. There is a lot more to this movie than just watching a show of past lives. Did you sense anything else while I lay in that unconscious state?"

Pedro, "Yes. I had this tremendous sense of familiarity. I held your hand like we were best of friends-more than friends. We were lovers, ancient lovers from some other time and place a long, long time ago."

Abby took a big sigh and whispered with confirmation, "While I was supposedly unconscious, I felt love, true love from my heart- in my heart. I even felt a strong wave of sexual energy, near arousal. Isn't that strange? Lying there in pain and feeling aroused. What really does happen in that unconscious state? I sensed feeling. I was aware of love and desiring sex. But I didn't sense any sadness. Did I sense Stephan was dead and yet still feel these erotic feelings? Was this because your energy was plugged into the movie you saw and we were both transported together back in time to when we were ancient lovers? Is the human touch this powerful? We need to explore this further, if you are willing. Are you? That nurse is your wife, isn't she? I can tell. You don't have to answer. You two look like you belong together. Our explorations together will not jeopardize your relationship as far as I am concerned."

Pedro, "Her name is Lolita. We are madly in love with one another. We have been married 22 years. No children. She would completely understand our conversation, but I would just as soon not involve her with our movie. Somehow she is not in it, and this is very personal to us only. Suffice it to say, she would understand and respect our privacy. This is not a secret. There are no secrets, just as there is no place to hide. Yet certain things need not be divulged. It protects the innocent, as we all are. What could possibly be wrong with two people in 1997 discovering they were ancient lovers and mutually agreeing upon the circumstances that what was, was, and what is, is? Wow, where are we going with this?"

"I know. But first I must see Stephan's body. Is this possible?" Abby asked.

"I knew you would want to see him. He was badly mutilated. Rigor mortis naturally occurred within five hours. I had to embalm him after the first day, and you weren't showing signs of consciousness. We kept his body refrigerated in one of my father's old, retired fruit refrigerator bins. You will probably want to bury him in America at your discretion. I just need you to identify him and sign the death certificate to suffice our policy and procedure in Guatemala under such circumstances. The officials already declared his death an accident, so they released him to my clinic under my custody until you gained consciousness and would direct us what to do. I am so sorry for you to have to deal with this now. You are safe here. No one will bother you any further about this issue."

Pedro guided her from her room to the backyard of the clinic. Abby hooked Pedro's arm and said, "Thank you. I'm all right. I think I can handle it."

Pedro spoke as they slowly walked toward Stephan's resting place. "My father gave me this old refrigerator unit after it exhausted its cooling capacity. I had a friend put in a new motor, and now it works perfectly fine for our needs, basic storage of medicines and an occasional corpse. If you can manage on one crutch, you may stay linked to my arm and I will show you the way to our warehouse. The walkway is safe. You shouldn't have any trouble with me holding onto your arm."

Abby replied, "Thank you again. I may need you. You feel most secure to me, but let's go slowly."

They arrived at the warehouse cooler unit and there Stephan was in a body bag, stretched out on a table with rollers similar to a gurney. Pedro watched as Abby approached the table with trepidation. Abby reached out for the zipper, held it in her fingers and paused. Stabilizing herself on her crutch, leaning onto the table, she took a deep mournful breath while Pedro held her arm for balance and reassurance. The silence was deafening. Abby exhaled and unzipped the body bag to reveal the cold, white. petrified face of Stephan Brooks Schumaker. That was all she needed to see. Abby left it unzipped at his neck and stared. Pedro, feeling her pulse, kept hold of her arm. Abby took another deep breath, and with a long, slow exhalation, sighed for the entire out-breath, taking it to the limit of near borderline exhaustion and fainting. She then bent down, slightly wobbly-Pedro there to steady her and without missing a beat kissed Stephan on the forehead and whispered for Pedro to hear, "Take care. go now… and perhaps some other place, some other time, our spirits will reunite."

Pedro gasped and slightly increased the pressure on Abby's arm, saying, "I have heard that before. This feels like a deja vu. Do you believe in reincarnation, Abby?"

Abby, straightening up and looking at Pedro, said, "Of course, and so do you, but you don't have to remember to go there. It's almost like two ships passing in the foggy night, blowing their horns to acknowledge one another, and then a captain of one vessel wondering, 'Did I blow my horn?" She continued, "It is so incredibly rare when you can place yourself in a past life, and almost unheard of to recognize someone from that past time, present in this time, in some other form, and then for that person to acknowledge the same familiarity of a past connection as well."

Pedro asked, "Why did my hearing what you whispered to Stephan give me the chills as if I had heard that phrase before?"

Abby. "Because you said that to me 2000 years ago when I was holding you in my arms. You were dying and told me we would meet again, 'some other place, some other time,' and for me to take care of myself and Artemus."

"Will you look into my eyes and tell me what you see?" Pedro asked.

"Sure," Abby quickly responded, positioning herself to fulfill the request. "I see a kind, gentle, loving soul. The eyes are the gateway to the inner spirit and the doors of perception. For some people, you do not go there. This is why Native Americans look. over your shoulder when talking to you. They will seldom look into your eyes for fear of blocking the spirit of vision and interrupting the flow of the truth. And they are observing over your shoulder, or surrounding your body, what psychics have labeled your 'aura.' This will warn them of friend or foe."

Pedro, "Do you get flashbacks into a past life looking into my eyes, as if you were there? Or do you see a movie? Do you see me in that past life?"

Abby, holding onto Pedro's arm and hobbling with her crutch, guiding him over to a sofa against the wall. "Let's sit over here. Are you okay being here? Are you chilly?"

Pedro, "No, this is fine. Don't stop now."

Abby, "I do not see a movie in your eyes, and I don't get flashbacks of a past life. I see only you as you sit before me, but I did get a tingle, a sense of familiarity. It was comforting, but I didn't get such vivid visualizations as you did when you looked into my eyes. Maybe it's just a calmness I'm sensing. But my husband is dead and I don't know what's in store for me now. Shouldn't there be sadness? Shouldn't I be forlorn? No. Instead I am content, safe and glad to be here in your clinic with you. So don't be concerned that I don't see the same thing in your eyes. Look into mine again and tell me what you see. Then I must go call our families and tell them about Stephan and make arrangements to fly him home."

Pedro and Abby sat next to each other. They held hands. Pedro turned and fell into Abby's eyes. This time she concocted the results. It was mesmerizing. Pedro again was hypnotized, entranced. Almost a minute passed, but what Pedro saw he knew lapsed back 2100 years. He blinked and withdrew his stare from Abby, expounding, "It is absolutely, spellbindingly unbelievable to me. I have no other way to express it. I do not understand it. What I just saw was us-you and me-but we were different people in a different time, in a different place, and we were lovers. I knew that. In fact, we were together as a couple. I want to say 'married,' but I know we were not because they did not have that back then, and somehow I just know that. I do not believe this is a form of reincarnation, although I do believe in reincarnation. This is something else. I am watching a movie of ancient times in your eyes, and we are the actors. I see myself in the form of some other body with what appears to be a burlap sack on my body as clothing. I might be 15 years of age, but I feel older. You are plain and yet stunning because I love you so much. Your complexion is olive and your eyes are different than what I see now, but they are just as beautiful. You are so gentle and full of love-new love, fresh with every breath. You are very happy. You might be 13 or older. Can I go back there again?"

Abby, quickly, with sincerity, "Not now. We should go back to the clinic. Will you take me? I need to rest. We'll explore again soon."

Pedro. "Of course. How insensitive of me. You must make those arrangements."

Abby was escorted back to her bed in Pedro's clinic. Lolita was making her rounds. She was taking the temperature of a young man in the waiting room. She saw Pedro and Abby enter Abby's room. She went to offer a hand to her husband. She was too late. Abby was just being placed on her back in her bed. Lolita, with utmost sensitivity, said in perfect English she had learned from her husband, "You must have come from the viewing. I am so sorry for your loss. How do you feel?" Lolita felt it was beneficial to speak English fluently. Pedro had been a good teacher.

Abby responded lazily, "Slightly weary, but I'm glad to have seen Stephan one last time, if for nothing else a personal sense of completion. I now have the dreaded task of contacting his parents and my family to make arrangements. I'm very close to all of my family, in-laws included. Stephan's mother and father, two brothers and sister will want to have him flown home and buried in his hometown. I should escort his body home and be present at the funeral, but something tells me not to go. Something is holding me here. Stephan and I both discussed in our seven years of marriage that funerals were just a formal proceeding, and we agreed burial is senseless. We felt it was far more important to remember that person alive, vibrant and full of love, not dead, stiff and lifeless. I only wanted to see his body because I didn't see it when we crashed, and I had something to tell his lifelessness. So that part of my life with Stephan is over, yet the memories, the fun, the conversations will be with me until I pass on, and then maybe our energies will meet again in the form of spirits or, who knows, maybe even another life form."

"Ancient lovers," Pedro said softly.

"Entwine as one and one becomes the other," Abby followed poetically, almost as if filling in the blanks.

"Sometimes I wonder about that," Lolita said.

"Abby, do you remember anything else about that poem?" asked Pedro.

"Only the ending. 'Ancient lovers meet again, some other place, some other time,' but i don't remember who wrote it," she recited beautifully.

"Very interesting," Pedro whispered as Abby was slipping into sleep. "Let us leave you so you can sleep."

"I will want to make a few calls when I wake up. May I use a phone?" Abby asked, half asleep.

"Of course," Lolita said. "There will be one by your bedside when you awaken."

The clinic had three beds and one examining room. It was not unusual for a patient to spend the night for observation. Pedro kept mild narcotics and antibiotics on hand in the refrigerated bin where Stephan's body lay in eternal rest. They never had a problem with break-ins and theft. The clinic was far too valuable to the public.

Closure of the clinic due to there being no medicine would be crippling to the villagers who came to rely on the competence of the results they garnered when serious illness struck a family member, especially a baby. The clinic employed two helpers aspiring to get into some aspect of medicine, should the opportunity ever arise. They were paid well and given free medical benefits for themselves and their immediate family members. The doors to the clinic were seldom closed. When Pedro and Lolita went on vacation together, they attempted to bring in a doctor friend from one of the surrounding villages to at least oversee the practice while they were gone. Their two helpers could manage the simple cases of colds, flu's, cuts and scrapes. If a close-by doctor could not come for an emergency, the staff had numbers to call in larger cities where it might be possible to send a resident physician or helicopter for a life-or-death situation. This seemed to work and enabled Pedro and Lolita to get away together at least twice a year.

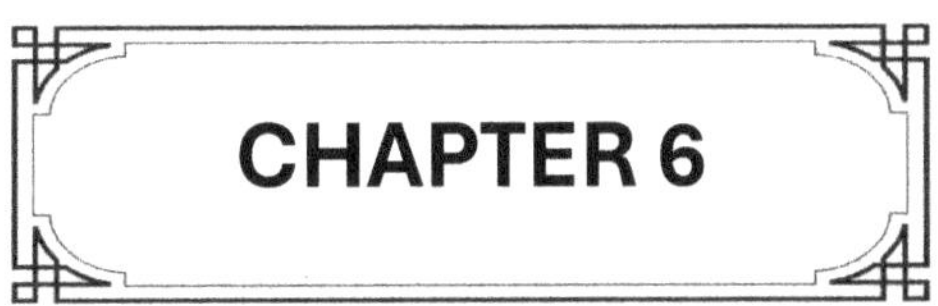

bby awoke from her nap two hours later. She got her bearings, scanned her room and focused on the telephone by her bed. This immediately reminded her of what she had to do. She took a sip of water, then dialed an international operator. She knew exactly how to do this from the calls she and Stephan had made thus far in Central America. Abby spoke enough Spanish to get by, no matter what the dialect.

"Mom, it's Abby."

"What's wrong? Where are you?" Abby's mother questioned with precise motherly instinct.

"I am safe in a clinic in Guatemala outside of Livingston. You can find it on a map, but you probably won't find the village of Callebocca, where I am now. Please don't ask any more questions until I finish. We had a terrible accident six days ago. I have been unconscious for five and a half days. I am getting around now on crutches. I only broke a leg. Stephan is no longer with us, Mom. He died in the accident. MOTHER, he is dead! My Stephan is gone. I can't talk much more. I think it's now starting to hit me hard. STEPHAN IS DEAD. Oh, my

God. Mother, he's gone. It was raining so hard. Stephan was driving too fast. He tried to avoid a rut in the road. All I remember is the tire going over the edge and then the car rolling down a steep embankment to a ravine. Three men found the wreckage and pulled me out after determining Stephan was dead. They carried me to the top of the hill and flagged down the next passing vehicle. I was unconscious the whole time. I was driven to a clinic, and that's where I am now under good loving care in a family-run clinic. Stephan's body is here, too. I saw him a few hours ago. I'll probably have him flown home according to the Schumakers' desire. Believe it or not, I am fine and recovering comfortably. Pedro and Lolita are well trained, English-speaking doctor and nurse. I should be able to travel in a day or two. It's important for you and Daddy to realize how safe and in good care I am here. I'll probably stay for an extended time here. I don't want to attend the funeral."

"Honey, you know that would be wrong. You must come home. Do you need anything? We must get your exact whereabouts. Your father and I will come immediately and bring you both home. The Schumakers will expect you to be there for Stephan's funeral," Abby's mother said lovingly and with the utmost of delicacy.

Abby, "No, Mother. Don't you or Dad or anyone come down here. You would serve no purpose except to console me, and I am okay for now. You can do all of that when I'm home. I can manage all of the details the transportation, the expenses, everything. Just don't come yourselves, PLEASE."

"Does this mean you'll be coming with Stephan?" her mother asked.

"Yes. You were right. I just now made that decision. I realize now that it would be a terribly rude and insensitive act for me not to come. It's just that Stephan and I discussed death so often and our stance on funerals and all. I just thought it would be hypocritical of me to go through with the ceremony, but I wasn't thinking of others. Mom, I've got to hang up now and call the Schumakers. Please tell Dad. I just can't manage explaining and rehashing the story over and over. Once more will be hard enough. Good-bye, Mom." Abby said as she hung up.

Then, "Bob, it's Abby." Abby began, talking with Bob Schumaker, Stephan's father.

"Hi, Abby. How is everyone down in that rainy, sweaty, beautiful part of the world? It's gorgeous here in Salem. We haven't spoken to you young traveling lovers in two weeks. What's up?" Bob sounded jovial and excited.

"I'm in a hospital, sort of, more like a clinic in the jungle. We had an accident. Stephan rolled the jeep, and I was knocked unconscious for five days with a concussion and a broken leg which is in a cast now. No stitches. Bob, please be prepared for what I'm about to tell you because I will not be able to carry on much more of the conversation with the details you'll want to hear. Stephan died instantly from the crash." Abby began to cry uncontrollably. Suddenly, reality hit her like a ton of bricks falling on her head, like a full steam locomotive hitting her head-on, like the Titanic going down, like there were no more whales in the ocean. She had just told her father-in-law and friend that his son was dead.

Bob said, "My God... Abby, are you all right? What happened? I am flying down there immediately. Tell me what happened." Abby heard the emergency in Bob's tone as he called to his wife, Pat.

Abby wiped at her tears and took a deep breath. "Bob, maybe I should call back."

"NO! Where are you? Give me the phone number in case we lose contact."

Abby replied, "I don't know it. I'm in a hospital bed and they brought this phone in to me. There isn't a number on it." Abby. frustrated, continued, "I am in a village called Callebocca in Guatemala. It's about 25 miles south of Livingston on the Caribbean Sea. You don't need to come down here. I can make all of the arrangements, and I'm being treated and taken care of with the best of loving, healing attention. I just hung up the phone with my parents, and I convinced them not to come. I'll be here for about another week, maybe less, and you couldn't make that time pass any faster. There's nothing anyone can do now. I'm getting around okay and feeling better every day."

"Abby, this is Pat. What happened? Bob gave me the phone. He's white and speechless. He's sitting down now with his head in his hands. What's wrong with Stephan? Is he okay? Is he dead?"

"Pat, Stephan died in an automobile accident six days ago. I'm flying him home when I can travel-the doctor says maybe in a week or less. Please take care of each other and don't let Bob come down here. I have everything under control."

Pat. "Abby, are you okay? What happened?"

Abby, sobbing, "Yes, I have a broken leg is all. Stephan rolled the jeep on a wet road and we flipped and rolled down a steep embankment. It was raining so hard, and we were pressed to move on. We should have stopped for the storm to pass. He tried to avoid a rut in the road and lost control. Please, Pat, I can't describe much more. I'll answer all of your questions when we get home."

Pat, with composure, "I understand. Abby, I am so sorry. 1 won't let Bob go. It sounds like you are under good supervision and have control of the sad situation. Know that we are with you in thought, spirit and love. Do you need money?"

Abby, "No, I have plenty in travelers checks. I will need everyone's support when I arrive. I've been drained emotionally. My Stephan is gone! The people here are treating me with the best of care. My leg is healing rapidly. I may come back here. I feel there is something else for me here. Bye, Pat."

"Bye, Abby. Let us know what airline and flight number and where you are flying into. We'll be there to pick you up."

"As soon as I know, you will know. I'll probably call you from Guatemala City. I love you. Bye."

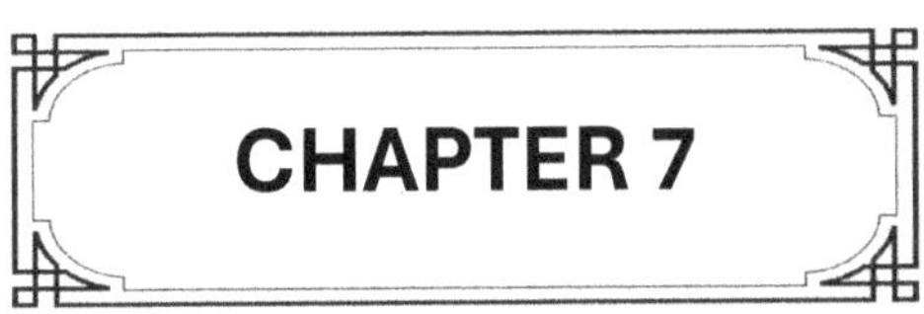

CHAPTER 7

The flight to Salem was gruesome. Abby had too much time to think, mourn, muse and ruminate some more. But she also had happy thoughts about her experience with Pedro in the clinic. This is why she knew she had to return to Callebocca as soon as possible. She had to find out more about this movie in her eyes and ancient lovers. Abby believed in predestination. She believed everyone has the power of choice, but the choices one makes have already been decided by a predetermined order. Every day is just another paragraph, another episode, another page in your life book. All one has to do is turn the page by experiencing each moment and get through that one, because the next one never happens. It turns into the one you are finishing and therefore becomes the one you are supposed to experience now. The choice is whether to go on, and this, too, has already been determined. Take the fatal accident, for example. A deluge of rain falling on a slick foreign road, pressured for time and realizing the dangers of pressing on. Query: Pull over? Turn around? Slow down? Switch drivers? Keep driving? Right or wrong, a decision was made. It was made before they made it. All

Abby and Stephan had to do was execute it, and so they did.

(Author's note: The exact same reasoning and philosophy holds true for birth. I did not decide to be born. It was predestined on a hot steamy night my parents made love-maybe it was a hot steamy day, or a wet, cold afternoon, or an early morning lovemaking just for a wake-up call, and I wasn't even thought of.)

Stephan was cremated. Bob and Pat Schumaker did not protest, much to Abby's relief. Abby knew it really didn't matter, though she and Stephan always talked about cremation. All Abby could pray for now was perhaps a reunion with Stephan, the way they talked about, when it was her time to pass on. Is this a continuation of ancient lovers, she wondered. Why not? The past is the past, and if one can somehow find the channel of energy to connect the cord, then ancient lovers can conceivably be brought into the present through two other living beings' DNA. But the wind must be just right to transport the messengers to deliver the message of the ancient lovers' DNA up the nostrils of the parents of the unconceived child. Yet this cannot be prearranged, arranged, nor programmed. The odds are greater that pollution will be eradicated, we will discover a cure for cancer and HIV, and overpopulation will dwindle as controlled by family growth agencies according to worthiness and competence of 'wannabe' parents.

Stephan's ashes were sprinkled slowly over Pat and Bob's family rose garden. Everyone was present. It seemed as though it took an eternity to perform this task, as every family member took a handful of Stephen and, in reverence, sprinkled it, saying what they wanted to in remembrance of him. Abby kept repeating, in her mind, "We will meet again as ancient lovers found, some other place, some other time, and we will entwine as one while one becomes the other."

And so, she felt true completion of her purpose. Time to move on with her life. Abby's parents, brother and sister, Bob, Pat, and Stephan's brothers and sister went inside for food and drink. It was discussed that everyone should stay in touch. Abby's parents live in Florida, as do the brother and sister. All of Stephan's remaining family lives within a 20-mile radius of Salem, where Pat and Bob live. Everyone was concerned for Abby, especially when they heard of her plans of returning to Guatemala immediately. No one could understand.

She reassured everyone, "Trust me. I don't know why yet, but I believe there is something there for me in this clinic where I rehabbed. Pedro and Lolita invited me back. They said I would be most needed in the clinic. He graduated from the Harvard School of Medicine, and she is a nurse practitioner. They've been married more than 20 years. They give medical attention to all in need. They have an amazing philosophy on life, and I feel that they can teach me something about humanity just when I need it the most. If I stay around here, I would be treated and pampered well, but I'd also fall into a deep state of depression and dependency. I have nothing here without Stephan to share it all with, and the close proximity of loving family would make my life miserable and restrictive. Please try to understand this. I must go back as soon as possible. Even more importantly, don't be offended. I'll stay in close touch with you all about everything going on with me. I love you more than you will ever know."

No one said a word. Everyone was in a state of shock, stunned and weeping.

Night was falling and slumber was right on its heels. Abby wanted to go to sleep in the bed where she and Stephan always slept when they'd visited Bob and Pat. Abby placed no stigma or spiritual weirdness on wanting to sleep there. She was not stuck in the notion that she could conjure up Stephan's spirit through some perversion of sleeping in his scent. She just wanted the closeness. She excused herself from the family circle, reminding them all that her leg was a little achy, and she needed to rest.

After completing her bath, she collapsed in the bed. She instantly fell into a deep sleep and entered her dreams. She woke up with the sunrise, wet, really wet, between her legs. She was wide awake, alert and euphoric as she lay on her back recalling her wet dream. She had dreamed that a man looked into her eyes and entered her body through them. She felt his presence in every living cell as he traveled and ventured inside her. The dream lasted perhaps 15 seconds, but took her back 2100 years to Argos. As she was wet and sexually aroused during sleep, her hand erotically fell to her vagina where she entered her body. Slowly and rhythmically, she pulsated her magic points and tripped into an incredible orgasm seconds before she woke. Spontaneously, with her waking and the dream ending, she slowly withdrew her finger, and at that instant she ejaculated the delicious juices of sex between her legs. This is the exact moment that this man in her dream exited her body. It was his enlarged penis tickling her that sent her into a frenzy of joy. She felt. There is no greater feeling next to godliness than an orgasm.

(Author's note: "Have you ever had a bad orgasm?" There, 1 got Woody Allen in my book.)

When she opened her eyes, she saw Pedro in her hallucination of excitement. Then he vanished. She felt between her legs for the magic juices and dipped her finger into the climax on her inner thigh. She had never emitted such a flow before during orgasm, be it masturbation, cunnilingus or intercourse. She recognized the smell as that of fresh cut hay from a wet meadow. She placed her sticky finger in her mouth and called for Argos. This "love glue" formed a link with the DNA of Argos directly to Abby's dream. She was elated. It was a wild, vivid experience that she thought was real. She felt the dream put her in touch with her ancient lover, and that is why she called for Argos. She had never met an Argos before this, so there was no real mistake in identity. She wanted to know more. She was beyond intrigue. She knew now that Pedro was really seeing a movie in her eyes and that he was her ancient lover, Argos. This confused her for a second, but then her psyche locked in and she knew that Pedro was real in this life as the person who saved her in his clinic. His body was not disguised as Argos, yet Pedro was reincarnated from Argos. Argos was short and skinny with shoulder-length brown hair. Pedro was tall and stately, with coal black hair. That is the spiritual connection. Argos' and Felicia's energies from many years ago became a part of Pedro's and Abby's DNA structures of today in their bodies as they were in 1997. It was predestined for this to occur. It is what energy is all about simply energy moving matter from cell to cell, place to place, on waves of energy we call air. Then enter in the weather patterns of the earth and you have movement unlike stillness which yields stagnation.

Energy can be explained as radio waves being transmitted from tower to tower, satellite to satellite. When a frequency has been interrupted, a tower may be down or a satellite knocked off course. A reasonable explanation for mood swings might be losing contact with an energy wave or someone disturbing its flow. Therefore, when you are in alignment and open to all possibilities, channels become clear waves of frequency. This is when one becomes "psychic." It is also the time energy waves may pass through two people at the same time. This is called a "contact transmission." and it is possible to have a "flashback" or "regression" to a past life. And so one may surmise that in our energy fields there are both transmitters and receivers. If you happen to be in perfect balance, with no disharmony between yourself and your immediate environment, then you might be considered psychic. This is how transmitters or receivers may at some point come in contact with a psychic and travel in time to a past life.

This was what happened to Abby and her immaculate wet dream. The transmission was in the form of an orgasm tripped off by Pedro, totally unbeknownst to him, which sent Abby back 2100 years to see Argos through Pedro. Mind-boggling.

True or not true is irrelevant. What is relevant is the experience… the feeling… the sensation. Reality? It is all real. Dreams versus waking. Abby entered her dream, participated in it, had proof from her orgasm, and now, in a waking state, related to Pedro as an ancient lover known as Argos. Unreal? Unbelievable? Believe it-it's real.

Abby had to get back to Callebocca. She certainly could have her cast taken off in Salem, North Carolina, but she wanted Pedro to take it off. Plus, there was a lot more research to be done concerning ancient lovers who meet again. She began making her travel arrangements: flights, connections, destinations and layovers.

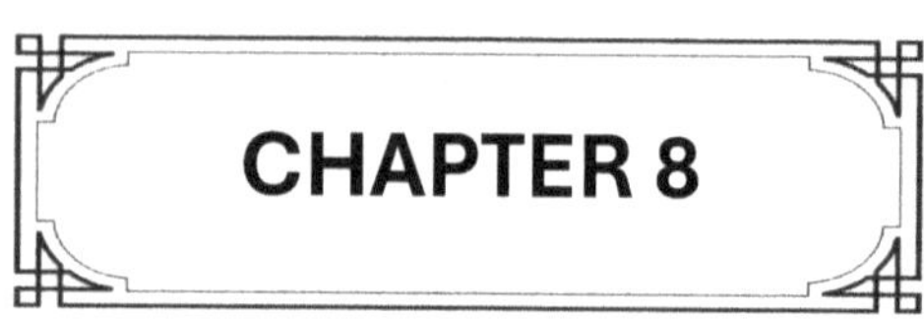

Pedro was conducting business as usual in Callebocca. He was also transfixed on this experience with Abby. Her eyes. The movie. Himself as Argos. Abby as Felicia. Their child Artemus. Pedro mused deeper and deeper as to the effects of this. He was sometimes paralyzed with emotion, joy, elation and mixed signals. Yet, what could be more profound than seeing it for real in someone else's eyes and having that person confirm what was playing in her mind while you were watching it in her very eyes? The mind conjures, swirls, creates, dreams and tries to make sense of it all. Work remained his focus, he was that well trained and disciplined. No distractions when dealing with other peoples' illnesses yielding wellness. So he saved his fantasy for more private moments like a buddhist monk during zazen.

He had not spoken a word of this to Lolita. The buddhist monk never discusses what happens during meditation with the head monk, unless, of course, there is a problem with discipline and achieving satori. Then the head monk will say, "You are distracted. You have fallen. You must suffer more and be desireless more." In turn, the student of zazen might say, "Yes, master. I do not understand. Why am I thinking these thoughts during meditation causing the distraction?" The head monk might say, "Well, then, there you have it. The question is the answer. Go and have your distraction so you can get on with meditation."

Pedro did not want to keep anything from Lolita. He simply wanted to know more about what was going on between him and Abby before making a decision whether to tell Lolita or not. A passing phase, like a gust of wind, need not stir up any more turbulence than necessary, he thought. A tempest could result.

The night of Abby's wet dream, Pedro left his body during sleep and took to subconscious flight. He began an incubus. He floated in what he thought was a cosmic liquid warmth within a mysterious cave full of pulsating life. It could have been a womb and he could have been experiencing a rebirthing, but he was too far in a deep theta state to relate.

When he woke the next morning, he was totally refreshed and had an erection as stiff as a totem pole, standing straight up. It was Sunday. Lolita opened the clinic every Sunday so that Pedro could sleep in. The clinic was a 15-minute drive from their house. Pedro lay there with his erect penis in his hand as all men do when waking. Usually men get a piss hard-on just before dawn. Pedro's was a combination of the need to urinate and arousal from his dream. He closed his eyes and created his own movie as if he were looking into Abby's eyes and watching her movie reel. All through this time, in his made-up script, he envisioned Abby naked as he jerked himself off with 75 incredibly rapid strokes ending in complete eruption of sperm gushing like a geyser onto his torso, then trickling the high viscosity dripping syrup into his pubic hair. He lay there while the euphoria slipped into its special vault where the mind stores good and bad, happy and sad episodes in our lives. Then he downshifted into a very pleasant state of now- ness and said to himself, Yes, I feel great. The powers of an orgasm, once again, proved themselves to be next to godliness. And fantasy is just a pathway to travel upon. Everyone has a magic carpet somewhere in their mind that they love to ride on from time to time.

Pedro did not lose sight of where he was, what had just happened, and what he had to do get dressed and meet Lolita at the clinic for a day's worth of work and mending others. He also realized that whatever this movie was in Abby's eyes was captured on film (her mind). He would have to wait for her return to see it again, and maybe this wouldn't happen in this lifetime if she did not return. It was all in Abby's hands now. Imagine this introduction to a past life, and then to miss the continuation because time pressed on in a different direction and energy waves shifted? Oh, well, Pedro shrugged.

His love for Lolita was never-ending. He did not feel betrayal because he was falling in love with another woman. He wasn't. His devotion to his wife was true. He would do nothing to hurt her. But there might come a time when he might ask her for her understanding and compassion with a complex, metaphysical cosmic phenomenon involving another woman, sensual arousal, orgasm--but no intercourse-and a regression into a past life with this same woman who was once his ancient lover as two completely different people than they were now. This might be too much for the ordinary person to swallow, not to mention accept. Lolita was the exception. There is always an exception, except no, the word is "accept." Expect the unexpected and life will unfold the way it is supposed to if you are willing to accept.

Since Pedro had not fallen in love with Abby and maintained that they were once together in a past life as far back as 2100 years as two completely different people-Abby concurred-then, in fact or fantasy, there is LOVE, and ancient lovers entwine as one, and one becomes the other. So how could this interfere with his real married life in the present time? Lolita would have to keep an open mind and work through acceptance and understanding of this scenario. For this was only an outline of two peoples' fantasies that coexist, commingle, and cohabit within a contact transmission high.

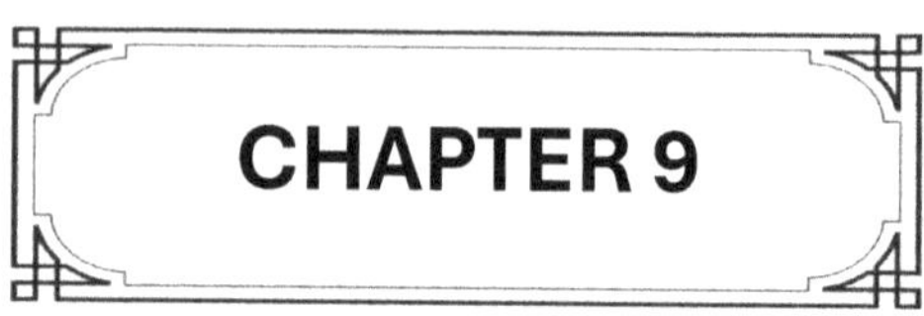

CHAPTER 9

Abby had a flight out of Charlotte, North Carolina, to Miami, Florida, at 8 a.m. Monday morning. She was leaving the next day for Guatemala City on PanAm Flight #305 out of Miami. She called the clinic and spoke with Lolita, telling her of her plans. Lolita expressed much excitement, welcomed her with an open heart and open door to her home, and told her Pedro would be even more excited to hear this news. Lolita and Pedro always extended this kind of hospitality to friends and visitors. They used this philosophy of hospitality within their clinic-which most people referred to as a hospital, a place to seek welcome relief from an illness. "Hospital" lives within "hospitality."

Abby bid her adieus to everyone in a very personal one-on- one, heartfelt way. It took all of that Sunday, but it was done with love and without haste. Monday she would be on her way back to the place where she lost her husband but found an ancient one. Stephan would remain a memory of unconditional love she would always keep in her heart and take with her for the rest of her life, and hopefully into the next. For now, it was Flight 305 and a return to the scene-a movie scene that might take her back 2100 years once again for another rerun.

The flight from Charlotte to Miami was uneventful. The flight from Miami to Guatemala City was a different matter. The takeoff from Miami International was smooth on a beautiful cloudless day in March 1997. Abby was sitting in the middle seat with a man to the left of her in the aisle seat and a woman to her right in the window seat. The man on her left was good-looking and probably Latin American from his gorgeous olive skin, just like Pedro wore so handsomely-and naturally. He was tall, with straight black hair, distinguished cheekbones and facial features with eyes that, at a glance, could entrance Abby, but she wasn't sure because she didn't want to be caught staring. Yet she could feel something and had to pursue it. It was just her nature.

When the time was right, she looked again, innocently. His eyes were so warm and inviting. She had this urge to stroke his face, caress it in both her hands and stare into his eyes. She wanted to renderly kiss his lips just for the pleasure of it. She wanted to excite him and let him know what a turn-on he was. She snapped out of it and quickly turned away before he noticed her. She realized he had the power in his eyes to perform a contact transmission because Abby felt love for him as a mother would for her newborn child. Yet she desired to kiss him differently. This confused her because the movie she saw in his eyes portrayed him as her son.

She was a minute away from kissing him, and he was 60 seconds away from hijacking the plane. Instead, they met in the middle, seconds from love and seconds from disaster. Things that never happen and things that might.

They never spoke during takeoff. Within seconds of being airborne, somewhere about a thousand feet off the runway, Abby asked, "Are you touring in Central America, or do you live in Guatemala City?"

His immediate response was short. He snapped, "We are all going to Cuba. That is where I am from, and your government will not let me go back there, so I am hijacking this plane. I do not know why I am telling you this because I should be taking you as a hostage for negotiations."

"Wait, please listen to me," Abby demanded, touching his arm. "Hold on for just another few precious moments that just might save your life. Pretend we are together," Abby whispered in his ear. "This way nothing will look out of the ordinary. So far you haven't hurt anyone, and I promise I won't blow your cover. I'll act as if this part of our conversation never happened."

Abby did not know what she was saying. She was driven by impulse. She had no idea what possessed her to even try to reason with this volatile man, but she sensed he was confused, disturbed, and did not really want to hijack this plane or hurt anyone. She felt as though someone was speaking through her with the utmost courage and nonchalance. She continued dominating the conversation, not letting him get a word in edgewise.

"First of all, let me assure you, you can trust me. You must begin with this trust," Abby said urgently.

The young man spoke quickly. "Why should I? Why am I even here? I should be up front commandeering the pilot to fly us to Cuba." He was calm, but with an edge.

Abby. "Please, I won't tell you what to do. I'll only advise you of the consequences. There is no way out. There's no place to hide and, most importantly, there are no secrets. So, you see, with me, no harm will come to you," Abby said with benevolence.

"Look, lady, I don't know who you are or why I am listening to you, but it ain't going much further," the man said decisively.

Abby, "If you do this act, you'll never get to hear my story, which is all I'm asking you to do. Simply listen. You just might be able to help me."

"I will help you in Cuba." He was weakening, she could tell. Abby said, with haste, "No, wait! Please. I told you I wouldn't attempt to tell you what to do. Please, just listen to me for one minute." She promptly continued. "There, that was a request, not a command. So far no one has noticed our differences, not even detected the slightest distress or uneasiness. We are just two passengers sitting here talking as if we were traveling companions." "What is it with you, lady?" He seemed agitated.

"My name is Abby. What's yours?"

"Carlos." He was almost compliant. Once again, like Pedro, a foreigner in the U.S. who spoke perfect English.

Abby, "Are you alone?"

"Yes. But I shouldn't be telling you this. I just want transportation to Cuba. I do not want to hurt anyone."

Abby, "And so far, you haven't. You're safe with me. Trust me." "Why? What do you have to offer me?" he demanded.

"I just want you to hear my story. I've been through a lot in the recent past. My husband was killed in Guatemala in January of this year. I was in the car when it rolled over, flipping every which way. I was knocked unconscious and suffered a broken leg and had a concussion. I was in a coma for five days, laid up in at clinic in the jungle outside of Livingston. Pedro, the doctor, and his wife, Lolita, helped me to recover. But Pedro says he can look into my eyes and see a movie being played. He says he sees himself as some other person starring in it and it takes place sometime before Christ. He goes on to say he sees me as his ancient lover in another body he calls Felicia. This can't be verified except to say that I know I have these powers in my eyes but never met anyone who could see into them like Pedro has. So I took Stephan-that's my deceased husband's name-back to Salem, North Carolina, to be cremated. It was a sad, yet joyous time for me. Don't ask me to explain. I don't know why. Now I feel compelled to return to Callebocca and the clinic where I spent time recovering. Nothing went on between Pedro and me except this energy exchange. I call it a contact transmission or regression. Do you understand?" Carlos was stupefied, baffled and speechless. He felt frustrated and yet intrigued. "Go on," he said, interested. "What do you want from me?"

Carlos had been stuck in America since 1982. He hid underground, protected by fellow Cubans legally in America on business. He always had a revolutionary attitude, but never acted on it. He did not want to get arrested in America and spend time in an American jail. He also knew he would never get deported this way, so he kept his nose clean, so to speak. He had a tremendous patronage to Cuba and wanted to return, although he only had distant relatives living there. His parents had both died in Cuba in the past five years. He could not attend their funerals, but he could go to their grave sites if he could get back to Cuba. He had one sister living in New York, legally, but they had stopped talking 10 years ago. Now his revolutionary attitude bubbled to the surface and he wanted to hijack Flight 305 to Cuba. He was acting with a sense of desperation, not thinking clearly, without a plan. He thought he was seeking sanctuary, when in actuality he was only escaping from a place he thought he did not want to be. And, lord knows, there are far too many people living where they don't want to be living and doing what they don't want to be doing, and it breeds hostility, not hospitality.

(Author's note: Just look at the state of things around you. "I HATE MY JOB. I HATE LIVING HERE." Because of this general pathetic attitude, people are starving to death and being slaughtered in the streets by the hundreds. Oceans are being depleted, the Amazon polluted, and the forests stripped for grazing cattle to feed the billions of mouths on this planet; political slanders and scandals, insurance fraud, and religious zealots committing mass suicide, freaks trying to catch a comet's tail and woo-

woos thinking some alien spaceship lost on a mountain is going to take off with them on board. The rain feeding the dry earth is rancid from industrial fallout. Fruit is already tampered with before it is picked. Acid rain is penetrating its membranes. Salmon have malignant tumors, and we grill them on charcoal. Be careful where you breathe, and do not drink the water...)

Carlos thought he could simply overpower the pilot and demand that the plane be flown to Havana. He did not anticipate meeting Abby. If you let people be, and do what they want to do, then freedom reigns-as long as you don't hurt anyone in the "doing."

"So where do I fit into this dramatic play of yours or is it a fantasy?" Carlos asked.

Abby said, "I want you to look into my eyes and tell me what you see."

Abby was dead serious, but she had an underlying scheme. She thought this just might be the perfect ploy for Carlos to become distracted. Time would go by, and then it would be too late to hijack the plane or he might be swayed by Abby to escape to Guatemala and perhaps travel with her or go on his own way. Abby was quite aware that she had persuasion over people with her eyes or with her voice. She had this certain intonation that people enjoyed listening to and, in fact, some fell into a trance. over it. She knew she was very articulate. She would think before she spoke, and therefore her words were chosen for effect. If you did not become entranced with her eyes, she used her voice. With her voice, she was able to get Carlos to at least listen, and this bought the flight some time. Now she could conjure with her eyes, knowing that she did this successfully with Pedro. No one before Pedro had ever expressed seeing a movie in Abby's eyes, but she knew she had the power. She closed her eyes, knowing Carlos could not refuse her, and aligned herself in her seat so that she practically faced Carlos. Then she opened her eyes, allowing Carlos to fall into them. Instantly she was aware that Carlos was falling in love with the experience. She knew he was not falling in love with her. She allowed it to go further. She opened her psyche even more. She shifted into the alpha state and was nearly unconscious, yet in a controlled subconscious state. She had never premeditated this act to this extent before. With Pedro, she simply let it unfold with some guidance. Now she was at the helm, but there was nothing to steer. Carlos would see what he saw. This was a movie where she simply allowed the reels to roll.

Carlos had no idea what was happening to him, how much time had elapsed, who he was or where he was. He had lost possession of himself. He took leave of his absence. Feelings and sensations were about the only things registering with him. He was, in fact, traveling through time on a contact transmission, seeing himself as a different person acting in the movie in Abby's eyes. Energy was moving matter, once again, being perfectly aligned for these two people at this time, in this place, for signals to cross, intermingle, entwine and become one- but not as lovers.

This was different than Pedro's portrayal as ancient lovers. Abby knew Carlos' role, but only while the reels were rolling, as she was attempting to interject thoughts for him. Carlos saw himself as a baby being cuddled by Felicia, his mother. This was so far-fetched for Carlos, but he could not stop to question it. He was too deep in theta. It was easy for him to be there. He had comfort and was being nourished. His thought processes as Carlos were not functioning.

When he blinked and turned his head, the movie was over. He also knew right then and there that he was not going to hijack this plane to Cuba. Something came over him like a tidal wave of new energy. He no longer had the desire to go to Cuba, nor did he feel the need for self-attention. He possessed a new self-image. It was as if a hypnotist had reprogrammed him to have a more pleasant outlook on life, a higher self-esteem and a greater value for life itself. Carlos regained composure of himself as Carlos, with his past veil lifted, but with the retention of what had played in Abby's eyes.

He was refreshed. He felt invigorated. And when he looked at Abby again, without a stare, he said, "Holy shit! Thank you."

She said, "You're welcome. I could only sense where you went, but I knew you were going, and I felt very happy for us in that other place. My breasts felt full of milk, and I felt I had a life full of love in my arms."

Carlos, "You were my mother. It was centuries ago. I know because everything was dirt, and the shelters were made of poles and thatch. Yet I felt I did not have knowledge of these things because I was an infant. But it was easy to watch the movie and see my life as a baby for just a quick glimpse. How strange. How do you do this?"

Abby said, "At least I'm not in control as a hypnotist might be, but I'm directing what's going on by allowing you to go further into the theta state while I'm in the alpha state-theta being deep sleep and experiencing the dream world as real, and alpha being in the subconscious state and somewhat directing thoughts to enter a dream world. I guess I've always had this ability. It's part of my psychic energy. My eyes become a movie projector for those people whose energy I want to direct in conjunction with the viewer who plays a character in the movie but doesn't know it at the time. I just never acted on it until Pedro discovered it for himself. But I truly believe my concussion and 5-day coma somehow brought me to my senses of directing him from a subconscious alpha state. This time I invited you in, but you were the one who transported yourself because we matched. Our energies synapsed together. This is incredibly rare. In fact, I don't think anyone would believe this unless they were 'believers.' Do you believe in bloodless surgery, Carlos? Do you believe in psychic healers? Do you believe in Shaman, or 'people with knowledge' like medicine men— or witches,for that matter? Do you believe e=mc2? You believe what you want to believe, you see what you want to see, and you hear what you want to hear. If you believe anything is possible, then you believe Jesus Christ walked on water, Newton discovered relativity just because an apple fell on his head, and Gandhi was the epitome. of unconditional love. So why can't someone see a past life by looking into a medium's eyes?" Abby asked with poignancy.

Carlos, his eyes bulging, said, "This is remarkable, to say the least. I came on board this plane planning to hijack it to Cuba. Now all I want to do is get off in Guatemala and follow my instincts."

It worked. Abby's intuition worked. She was able to not only divert Carlos' attention from time and a criminal act, but also to show him a different approach to life. She felt tremendous relief from impending danger to herself and the entire crew and passengers on board. She also recognized the gratification she had received knowing the power of her eyes and voice and how they could be directed.

The biggest reward came in her heart. She had found an ancient son from 2100 years ago. It all begins with the heart, the mighty muscle beating a rhythm of life and love for everyone. This was where Abby's work could begin, from her heart. She knew she must be true to it like Moses was to the message written in stone he found on the mound. Was he hallucinating? Did he carve that tablet with his own hands just to proclaim the commandments of a new religion supposedly sent to him by God? It does not matter. These questions are moot. The tablets are relevant and the words written on them, not just the messenger. Yet what is even more pertinent is the fact that Abby and Carlos were on their way to Guatemala. The flight was safe, and no one needed to know the potential disaster brewing on Flight 305. What transpired between Abby and Carlos was as real as what Hollywood could do on any movie set, except this movie was in Abby's eyes.

61

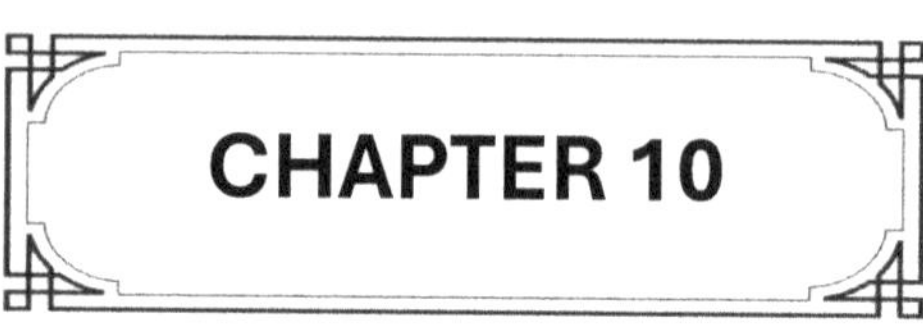

CHAPTER 10

As soon as they landed in Guatemala City 8 hours later, Abby called the clinic. Pedro answered and was ecstatic to hear Abby's voice. He had been told by Lolita that Abby was planning on returning to Callebocca. Now she was bringing another guest. She had wondered if this would be okay. She knew it would be all right to ask. It was the only way. She was not going to just appear with Carlos at Pedro and Lolita's doorstep expecting them to welcome him as well with open arms. Pedro shouted through the phone to Abby, "Of course, this will be all right with Lolita and me. We look forward to meeting this Carlos."

By the time Abby and Carlos drove to Callebocca, accommodations were made for both guests in separate quarters of the house. Pedro and Lolita kept four small bedrooms ready in their home for family and friends. They notified all family members that out-of-town friends were coming to give them fair warning not to plan a visit to their home for a while. This gave their guests a more comfortable time to stay and relax as long as they liked.

When Abby introduced Carlos to Pedro and Lolita, Pedro instantly felt warmth and a strong bond toward Carlos. Carlos expressed to Abby later that day that he recognized Pedro as someone in his vision in Abby's eyes, but it was not the man he had met today. He felt a family connection, a good, positive one between father and son. Abby reminded Carlos that Pedro was Abby's ancient lover and that Carlos was now recognized as her ancient son, and therefore Pedro is Carlos' ancient father. More had to be observed now that the three were together again.

Lolita had a nice dinner prepared for everyone. After-wards, they all adjourned to the outdoor patio to watch the galaxy of stars perform in the sky. Abby and Carlos felt at home since Pedro and Lolita were happy to provide them hospitality and a place of well- being. The discussions were quiet and subdued. Abby was tempted more than once to talk about how she and Carlos met, but each time she decided it was the wrong place, wrong time. Curiosity was there, though, as Pedro inquired of their relationship, "How long have you two known each other? Where did you meet?" The questions were answered by Abby, but did not go any further than the basics. No detail. "We met on the flight from Miami to Guatemala City. Carlos has an open agenda to travel, so I invited him to accompany me as far as is comfortable." She continued, "He's in search of himself and found a tiny aspect of it on the flight down here. But I'm very tired and need to catch up on my sleep. May I be shown to my room now?" Carlos concurred, and both were shown to their rooms. Pedro took Abby to her room, then pointed out to Carlos that his room was across the open courtyard under the breezeway to the casita, just 40 feet from Abby's sliding door entry to her room.

Sleep was deep for everyone and took Abby like a sinking block of cement into the middle of the ocean. Her dreams were wild and vivid, but Pedro's were beyond this world. He dreamed Abby was Felicia. They were lovers then united in what we would call 'marriage. They had a child they named Artemus. But now Carlos was Artemus- only he was Carlos. Pedro was called Argos by his friends during the time in his dream. As Argos, he discovered that he carved oars for fishing vessels and lived in a small village outside of Rome, Italy. Pedro had experienced a subliminal contact transmission when he had shaken hands with Carlos earlier that day. Carlos, upon shaking hands with Pedro, shifted gears and transported Pedro back 2100 years to when Pedro was Argos, Artemus' father. Pedro woke in a sweat, squeezing his erect penis. He was dreaming of Felicia the split second before waking, which prompted him to masturbate.

Lolita had gotten up and was fixing something in the kitchen. Pedro knew it was a realm of reality which existed within the physical body detonated by instinctual lust and a drive for self- gratification that all human beings masturbate. (Author's note: Don't ever ask one if they do, they just might lie. Trust me that they do. Masturbation is the most solo thing you will ever do, should you choose to. Everyone masturbates.)

Pedro's dream, beyond this world, gave him vision and insight, but also made him horny. He was driven to animism. Now he lay in his sweat and goo, thinking of Abby and her friend, Carlos.

(Author's note: We perform our destiny according to what we say. It is how the stock market crashes or soars, it is how we proclaim our vows to one another in marriage or religious conviction, and it is how wars are started and ended. Silence is the safest way to perform any action. If you want to keep what is inside the mind a secret, tell no one.)

Pedro felt great. He heard Lolita in the kitchen rustling around with the pots and pans, probably putting the coffee on and preparing breakfast for everyone. He slithered out of bed, limp, and into the shower. His thoughts were refreshed, clean and pure. His intuitive instincts were sharp-sharper than ever before. He knew age was the key factor to wisdom. He sensed that the reality of his present state of mind was focused on the here and now. He was married. He was a doctor. He had a purpose and humanitarian goal in mind. He loved his life. And he was aware of Abby's eyes and the movie playing in them featuring this other woman, Felicia, and her husband, Argos, of twenty centuries ago. He knew he was not in love with Abby, but rather he was infatuated by the flashbacks that transported him into this past life that she had shown him. He fathomed, Could we enjoy orgasm together without intercourse? Orgasms always worked like that for Pedro. He considered them next to godliness, just like Argos and Felicia did. Their sex life was real and bountiful and driven like animalistic urges to reproduce. The big difference between animal drive for reproduction and a man and woman's drive for orgasm was that they do not have to have intercourse to have orgasm. Therefore, Pedro and Lolita allowed themselves to explore with or without one another to reach orgasm. Even solo was acceptable and practiced at random.

There was something peculiar about Pedro's thinking on this matter in conjunction with his dreams, Abby's eyes, and his current real life in 1997. He was not confused; more disoriented for a brief moment. Then that passed and he seemed to accept this new viewpoint that this was just the way things were. New characters were added that changed the plot every day. Somehow, this offered him solace.

Pedro and Lolita enjoyed a marvelous, explorational sex life. They never openly talked about masturbation. It was a subject left open and untampered with, as it should have been. They both respected each other's privacy and let certain issues be as they were without interference. They had a certain trust level they both agreed on that it just did not need to be discussed.

Carlos, Lolita and Abby were sitting around the beautiful wooden table in the kitchen when Pedro appeared under the arched entrance from their bedroom hallway into the kitchen. He was vibrant and full of energy. Abby was instantly stimulated by his presence and became wet between her legs at her genitals. She felt the moisture between her labia and began to fantasize on coming right then and there by the mere power of thought and sexual energy. It was a powerhouse of emotion running like lava-but not orgasm. She withdrew the notion which dissolved the urge.

Their kitchen was huge, with pots and pans hanging from steel hooks over a butcher block. Pedro and Lolita loved to cook. Whoever got to the kitchen first prepared the meal at the time according to what the preparer was salivating for. To them, the kitchen was the heart of the house from which came a pulse that nourished the body and soul. And so it became the place for family and friends to hang out, socialize and communicate with one another, which was why they designed the kitchen to be big and roomy with lots of comfortable seating around the table.

Suddenly, Lolita realized the time and was up and out the door to go open the clinic. She told Pedro she would do this for him so he could spend some relaxing time with their friends, orienting them to the house, the gardens and the property. She said that if he was at the clinic before noon, this would be good. If an emergency came up, she would, of course, call him immediately.

Pedro was quite relieved at his wife's kind offer as he poured himself his first cup of coffee.

He addressed Abby and Carlos. "My house is your house. You are welcome in it. There are great gardens where you can sit and meditate, fountains to listen to, and hiking trails for short strolls."

Fresh off the plane from Florida. Abby and Carlos were slightly weary from travel excitement and not enough sleep, not to mention being in a foreign country where people and customs were different.

Abby looked ravishing to Pedro-in fact, voluptuous. He glanced into her eyes from across the kitchen table and immediately saw Argos. He recognized himself fresh from his dream, but blinked and quickly lost the image. No one else knew or saw this, yet Abby sensed it with a tingle between her legs. Eroticism came naturally to her. She couldn't quite figure it out, but she thoroughly enjoyed it. She was ecstatic to be in Pedro's home. She wanted to excuse herself and masturbate, dreaming of Pedro as Argos between her legs, but she didn't, as she savored the wetness from Pedro's glance.

Carlos was near oblivious as to what was transpiring between Abby and Pedro as he was enjoying his coffee. He said, "Well, friends, this is better than being in Cuba-or jail, for that matter." Staring at Abby, he said, "You changed my life."

Pedro said, "Now can you perhaps inform me of what is going on between you two? I sense it is a lot more than simply meeting one another on a flight and exchanging a few words that made you become best of friends and traveling companions."

Abby, "Your intuitive gut feeling is right, Pedro. In a nutshell, Carlos was assigned the aisle seat beside me and had every intention of hijacking that plane to his home country of Cuba. Instead, I lured him into my eyes as an experiment to see if he could see into them the way you could. Initially, I thought, if nothing else, it might distract him long enough that he might think it was too late to hijack the plane. At best, perhaps he could be persuaded that going to Cuba would incur major life changes for everyone on board and probably prison for him. Carlos had already told me that he didn't want to hurt anyone, and so far he hadn't. Now it was up to me to prevent a catastrophe. So I told Carlos I needed help, that all I wanted him to do was listen to what had transpired in my life in the past 60 days. I got it all out in two and a half minutes everything, including your role, Pedro. Then I asked Carlos to look into my eyes. Could I capture him? Would he see a movie as you did? Would Carlos be in it? What could he see? I invited the energy. I opened the channels and, sure enough, a contact transmission occurred. Carlos really was part of the show, but as a different character. He was transported back thousands of years to a small village. There he saw himself as an infant being cuddled by his mother. He says he felt tremendous love and comfort, but he couldn't really relate to the time or place except for the dirt floor and thatched roof shelters. When he came out of it, he then recognized me as his mother, a totally different person than who I am now."

Pedro, "Then what?"

Abby, "Carlos was so taken aback that his fascination continued and he lost any inclination to go to Cuba. In fact, he felt a revelation had occurred that was going to change his life for the positive, one of peace and tranquility. That's when I invited him to join me and expand his horizons in a different direction."

(Author's note: It was epistemology.)

Carlos, "There was no way I was going to pass up this opportunity, if nothing else, to explore this supposed flashback into a past life. The doors were open, and Abby's eyes became the vehicle. Then she brought me here. And I've got to tell you, Pedro, upon our first meeting yesterday, I felt a real connection to you- kinship, in fact. I think you were my father in that movie Abby was showing me in her eyes. It just came to me, the feeling, the flashback. You are-were-my father, but not as the person you are now. You were different then, but everything was. This is very confusing to me."

Abby, "Do you two realize how rare and unheard of this is? People get regressed to past lives through a neutral medium or psychic, but it's channeled through a trance and never involves anyone present during the session. But this, this is a true contact transmission whereby the person conducting the trance is, in fact, part of the play unfolding for the person who is in the trance. And then the plot thickens because, coincidentally, another character is introduced as a common affiliate with the other two parties. In essence, this is everything I practice and believe in. What is happening here is the distribution and absorption of pure energy, both past and present, from cloud to cloud, lifetime to lifetime. The scary thing is, there can never be any real scientific proof that this is happening between all of us."

Pedro, "Do you think this really matters? Aren't there supposed channelers who can regress people to past lives, and they have no real proof? You, the paying customer, walk away thinking you were Napoleon or Chief Sitting Bull or some bus named Priscilla, or some shit like that, and you are satisfied. Why do you need some sort of scientific proof for the unexplainable? Isn't this metaphysics, supposed natural phenomena that cannot be explained or rationalized?"

Abby, "Maybe you're right. Maybe this is supposed to be left alone or, rather, left to those who want to delve and explore into the unknown."

Pedro excused himself, but not before orienting Carlos and Abby to the house and grounds. Lolita was expecting Pedro before noon. It was now 10:50 a.m. He guided Abby and Carlos around the property and left them alone in the garden to fend for themselves. "The refrigerator is yours-so is everything here. Lolita and I should be home from the clinic by 6 tonight," Pedro called to them in a scurry to leave. He hopped into his truck and was off to the clinic.

The trust Pedro left in his trail was certainly reassuring to Abby that she and Carlos were welcome in their home. She felt it deep in her heart. She gave a great sigh of relief, knowing she wouldn't have to deal with the awkwardness of "gelling" personalities one usually encounters with first-time meetings with other mutual friends. They felt like they were instant family, pectin enriched.

Abby came from the bathroom looking to join Carlos in the gardens. The house was laid out like a maze of rooms, and one could actually travel in circles returning to the same room if the right door wasn't taken.

Therefore, it took a few wrong turns for Abby to find Carlos in the atrium connecting to the deck. Carlos said with a smile, "Hi there, savior."

Abby, "Hi. Isn't this an incredible place?"

Carlos, "Yeah, and I feel so content, comfortable and at home here. Pedro and Lolita are most hospitable. They go beyond that. I don't know if you feel it, but I feel like I have known them forever."

Abby, "Yeah, that's part of the script. It's really coming into the light now. I believe the stage is set, as it always was or is for everyone, although few people play it out. I remember this person once said to me a long time ago in a bar in Cambridge, Massachusetts, 'Be a light, not a lamppost. Illuminate the way for others to see. That's all she said. Now I know what she was referring to. She had this incredible presence about her, like she knew I was going to shine someday. It was almost like a blessing she placed on me. She covered me with a veil of prophetic destiny. I always wonder about her, because after she said that, she got up and left the bar. I never saw her again." Abby took a breath and finished, "Things like this ever happen to you, Carlos?"

Carlos, "Not until two days ago when I boarded Flight 305 and you asked me to look into your eyes." Carlos was now pleading, "May we try it again? I want to see more of this fantastic movie."

Abby, "No better time than right now. Let me get comfortable and focused on the matter." She pulled a patio chair over to where Carlos had been sitting, sank into it and looked straight down at the terra cotta tile patio. Then she snapped her head up and looked straight ahead into Carlos' eyes, but it was not an entrancing stare as in hypnotizing someone. It was an engaging stare like two train cars coupling together into a locked position. And locked they became, as Carlos fell into her eyes and then sank into them like quicksand. And the harder he squirmed, the deeper he went.

Abby became very calm and content as she felt Carlos enter her through her eyes. The calming effect was overpowering Carlos' fidgetiness. Abby's demeanor became contagious like a horse whisperer taming a wild stallion. If this had been Pedro instead of Carlos, she probably would have become wet instantly between her legs. As it was, she instinctively felt motherly toward Carlos and had an urge to cuddle him. For Abby, she could not see the visuals Pedro and Carlos saw, but she could experience real sensation and vibration from an energy transference, sort of like cables used to jump-start a battery.

(Author's note: Psychologists call it a "simultaneous occurrence," and isn't this what dreams are all about? Wet dreams are fueled by energy transference when the dreamer actually experiences orgasm during sleep- either incubus or succubus- unlike dreams about having an automobile accident and waking without cuts and bruises. Yet one may self-inflict body spasms, thereby causing stiff necks or cramping while thrashing for the brake during sleep. And what about stigmata, she thought. So it is entering that realm of an energy field one experiences in the head, conjured up from a dream that remains unexplainable and metaphysical. And only when it is sensual does one receive pleasure from it. We hear of people who dream of something and then it happens in a waking state. True or false? It does not matter. Some people are gifted in different directions than others. To manifest a dream? Let's pray they are sensual ones and hurt no one, unless someone is practicing black magic and evil persuasions for a congregation to perform a foul act.)

These thoughts passed quickly through Abby's mind while Carlos was deeply enveloped in her eyes and saw himself as that same infant he had seen on the plane. He reached for her breasts and Abby, realizing Carlos was not Carlos, but her son, Artemus, undid her bra and allowed him to suckle on her left breast. He suckled like a child requiring the nourishment of mother's milk, yet knows not what he is doing. He bit a little too hard, and Abby flinched, pulling him away, returning him to his seat without a stir. He was right back into his stupor once again, but she realized it was fading, and Carlos was coming out of it. Abby did up her bra as Carlos took a great sigh and leaned back deeper into his chair. She prompted this, and Carlos only acted upon what he saw in her eyes. Abby wanted to hear his side of the story without influence or suggestion.

Carlos, "You were definitely my mother, no doubt about it. You were breast-feeding me. I could see us. You had on a peasant dress that looked like a burlap sack draped from your shoulders, but your left arm was out to allow for suckling on your left breast. I must have been two months old, and you were very young and beautiful. You loved me so much. I could sense it because of your grip on me and the way you looked into my eyes with love. You seemed so happy. Once I heard you speak during the feeding. You called to Argos, my father, to come hold your hand and watch his son feeding. He did. He was real close to me. I believe he stroked my forehead like stroking a god. It was so real, so vivid."

Abby, "It was real because it did happen 2100 years ago. I actually felt you nursing on my breast, and I felt the love I had for you. I would do anything to protect you from harm. You were my baby, my one and only. I wish I could see what you see, but I can't. I can only feel and experience what you are going through. How do you feel right now?"

Carlos, "Tired and hungry. Will we always be able to do this at any time we choose?"

Abby, "Only if I allow it. Remember, I am the transmitter and receiver, so I must be willing to let you go there through my eyes. Meaning, I must invite you in."

Carlos, "Well, whatever. I do not want to hurt anyone or go against the grain, so to speak."

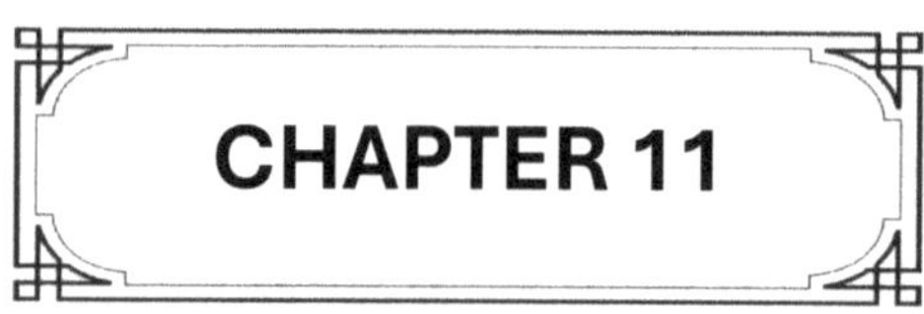

An hour passed during this contact transmission. Abby would never tell Carlos he was actually suckling from her breast. She left Carlos in the kitchen to fend for himself, as he was famished. Abby wanted to stroll the property and explore a little bit. She came upon a place in the jungle, about a mile from Pedro's home, where she fantasized that perhaps Pedro and Lolita would stroll for romantic interludes. It was just a little clearing about 20 feet in diameter right in the middle of dense foliage before the thick jungle began. It was knee-high grass with white blossoms floating about in the thin air. She collapsed to her knees and then flat onto her back to rest and stare straight up into the blue, cloudless sky. She was wiped out from Carlos' expedition and quickly fell asleep.

She could do this just about anywhere, fall quickly into alpha state, and then into napping state if she went far enough. Sometimes she could program her mind to hold the alpha state for five minutes, snap out of it, and be completely awake and revitalized. This time she was too relaxed and let herself go wherever the mind wanted to travel. She dreamed about this morning and the wetness she felt when Pedro stood in the archway to the kitchen. She knew that Pedro had made her that way. Maybe he was thinking sexual thoughts of her, or maybe he entered her through her eyes like he did in Salem when she had her wet dream.

Now her dream quickly shifted, and Argos entered her body through her eyes. She felt an erotic energy field around her in her dream. She felt a fire all over her skin-but no flames. She was an inferno. No flames. Her finger, unbeknownst to her, was stirring the flameless fire right on her wet button. Nothing could put this fire out. She certainly did not want that. She was dreaming of Argos inside her, passionately making love to her, while she masturbated in her sleep. It was unreal, just like the nameless fire—but it was so real. She could feel him inside her. Her finger became his penis. and her dream was exploding in glorious color. Multiple orgasms ensued as her erect finger did the job of a penis. Argos was on top of her moving and gyrating to assist her in her dream. She was experiencing an incubus. Blades of grass began to tickle her anus as she slithered in her nest. She was having a conscious thought as the dream abruptly ended. She was slightly startled as she realized, in her waking. chat a blade of grass was up her ass. She opened her eyes and Pedro was naked beside her. She blinked and he was gone. Now fully awake. she realized it was an apparition. Time became her lover as she lay there in thought. entwined in her dream of ancient lovers. Reality. what a concept. Pinnacles and crevices, peaks and canyons. clouds forming genitals, river highs and valley lows, all touched her soul with emotion so sensual that it made her horny just to breathe. Carlos was having his tortilla, cheese and salsa in the garden with a beer he had found in the refrigerator. Abby was in ecstasy lying in the meadow. The sky was forming clouds, and she felt rain was impending sometime this afternoon according to the way the weather patterns were this time of year in Central America. It could have poured on her right then and there, and she would have been content and happy. But she also wanted to get back to the house to see what Carlos was up to. As Abby was walking back from her erotic little nap in the sensual bed of grass, she wondered if other people did the same thing just to reach orgasm. -Yes." was the answer she said out loud to herself, the jungle and all of its inhabitants. She felt safe and secure. confident and at cast:. Along with her musings came a pondering that perhaps this was where sexual frustration came from if people dont masturbate and why people in general get so uptight with themselves, at the workplace or at home with the family, or are just plain frustrated for no apparent reason except. perhaps, they just do not masturbate enough. She concluded with an educated guess that everyone has at least cried it once. Who has failed at masturbation? She thought: My God, please don't admit it. Lie to me. So, having succeeded first time at the stroke, who would give it up—and why? "Go for the gusto" should be the universal motto, along with, "Don't worry about me. I can handle the light loads by myself."

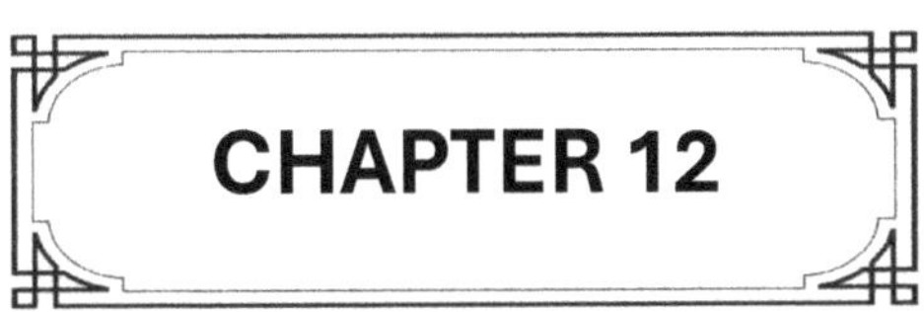

CHAPTER 12

Abby saw Carlos in the distance on the porch in a chair with a table pulled up in front of hint. He looked handsome and virile. "Well, well, well, aren't we cozy and at home with ourselves?"

Carlos, with a mouthful of sandwich, said, —My home is your home,' Pedro said, so I helped myself and, believe me, the favor shall be returned, if and when I ever get established."

Abby, You know. we should talk about this, but I don't want to seem like your mother. Can we talk as friends. nor channelers or mediums or mother and son- -or saviors?"

Carlos, "Yes, of course. I want to be your friend and get to know you better. Let's save the mother-son relationship for the movie and try to start fresh as newcomers in this day and age. current, in the here and now--although I will never forget how you saved me from disaster. Now, here I am in a foreign country with nothing in my pockets, nowhere to go, no future plans, no real education or vocational training. How long can I mooch off my new friends—you included?"

Abby, "Maybe we can both work for our keep. Pedro told me he might be able to use me around the clinic—and maybe you. too, for that matter. My God, we are capable, willing people who will work for room and board. I just feel there is a lot more for me here than just manual labor. I don't know Pedro and LOIII3 that well outside of the clinic and what they did for me after the accident. But I do know they are sincere. genuine and gracious people. I feel like I want to give something back to them. And yet I know there is something else for me here in the form of higher knowledge or maybe even higher consciousness."

Carlos, "Well, I will certainly work for room and board for 3 while. but I would like to be paid so I can save something for my future. I just don't know yet. It's too soon. I mean, we just got here. I should theoretically be in Cuba. Don't get me wrong. Thank God I am not. But I have nothing here. In Cuba I would have had distant relatives and Castro. What is your background. Abby? Do you have a formal degree from some university?"

Abby, "Yes, B.U.—ah, Boston University. That's where Stephan and I first met. I've got a degree in environmental studies. That's why Stephan and I decided to come to Central America, to study the environment, the people, get to know another part of the world first-hand, experience other cultures. We also wanted this trip to be fun and recreational, too, so I wasn't on some sort of mission to actually do an empirical study on my observations. We just wanted to travel and meet people. And look what happened. Stephan is dead, and I'm alive having widened my horizons without him. Stephan will always be in my hip pocket. I carry his spirit with me. In fact, it's my theory that while I lay unconscious in the jeep, as Stephan was dying, making his last exhalation. I inhaled his last exhale and that's how I'll carry his spirit with me forever."

She continued, "Way back when, in the sixties, I was quite indulgent with meditation. I tried to absorb everything the gurus were instructing me to do during meditation. And I admit, I was going nowhere with it. I wanted to be enlightened, so I kept offering them more money. 'How much do you want? Can't you just whisper something in my ear so I can become enlightened? What's the secret? You are in America now. We want the shortcut, the abbreviated course. How much does it cost?' And their response to my bastardized insistence was, 'Stay with your breath ... always go with the out breath ... sit with your breath.' Stupid me, it took me 15 years to finally realize what they were talking about, although I'm far from enlightened. I remain a dry sponge looking to be moistened by eye droppers of other people's knowledge. Yet the breath is everything. What's the first thing you do when you are born? You inhale. And what's the last thing you do to die? You exhale. And in between that first inhalation and that last exhalation. we are breathing. You can't willfully expire yourself by holding your breath unless you are underwater or being asphyxiated. The guru maintains you are forced to take your next inhalation, which is why they say go with your 'out' breath because it may be your last and you want to be conscious of it so you can send your spirit on its way to oblivion and enlightenment. And that's why native indigenous people all around the world feel it sacred to witness a dying person's last exhalation. That's what I did with Stephan," Abby concluded. Carlos, "Where did you come up with that?"

Abby, "LSD talked to me one day during meditation, and that's what I came up with. It's a belief. It's a theory. It's up for conjecture. Everything is based on something. It all starts with an idea, like beef stew or Hungarian goulash or tossed salad. I just tossed my thoughts around one afternoon while sitting in the lotus position wondering why I was doing this, and I suddenly came back to my breath. I took a ride on the vapors and came up with a religion-my religion. Meditation is not what you think. Next question?"

Carlos, a little baffled, "Well, that's a mouthful. Care to expound? You've got my attention."

Abby, "Here's another rumination from meditation laced with psychedelic lightning: For every new thing, there is a beginning, a birthing. Nothing new about this. Where there is a birthing-be it a village to a town growing into a city, a voyage, an expedition, a poem or a newborn baby-there is growth and expansion, as in the universe and all its galaxies. The trick is to learn how to accept and adapt throughout the growing pains, holding nothing back. so it won't get dammed up, clogged, stagnant or become extinct. Today we start anew, fresh, nothing left over from the past except what we choose to call the 'building blocks.'""

Carlos, "Very interesting. But where can I get a job?"

Abby, "You'll see. Only time will tell. When the time is right, BINGO, a job will be presented to you. Now, I'm not suggesting you sit around and vegetate waiting for someone to hand you something on a gold platter. No, it doesn't work like that, much to some people's dismay. You've got to go out and get it, but you have got to be right within yourself as to what you want. You've got to be true to your heart and within reason, so to speak, although sometimes unreasonable requests are granted. This is called taking a chance-casting all fate to the wind. And sometimes, it's okay. It seems the more desperate you are, the more destitute you become. Then there is a crossover no one can define or determine the whereabouts of this crossover, but suddenly you either perish, go to a parish or a temple, or you suddenly have a change in tide and things begin to go your way. One thing is certain: There must be a change of events in your path. Those with normal, everyday routines do not come upon such waves unless there is a chance presented to them. And most people are too afraid to answer the door. When 'fear' knocks at your door, if you don't answer it, it remains at bay, sometimes rearing up and charging, other times lying dormant. If you answer, what crosses through the doorway is courage, and then things change for you. No judgment as to 'good" or 'bad.' just prepare for a change in energy waves. So, you want a job? Let's go get you one."

Carlos, "No, wait a minute. Hold your horses. Let me finish my sandwich. And besides, I'm a little tired."

"Okay," said Abby with a slightly erotic tone in her voice.

She did find Carlos quite attractive and recalled how she wanted to kiss him upon their first meeting on Flight 305 just to let him know she'd be willing, but also that he was attractive to many women. He needed to know this from Abby, but she wasn't willing to discuss it. Instead, she chose to show him.

She easily sashayed behind Carlos and gently placed her hands on his shoulders. He stopped what he was doing and dropped his chin to his chest and began to groan. Magic was in the air. Abby turned her movie projector off in her mind. She wanted to passionately make stealthy love to him. She wanted to eat him up. but she did not want him to fall in love with her. She felt she could prevent this by taking charge-allow him to do as he pleased with her sexually, but stop him from advancing into evolutionary love. Be charming, but cold. Turn it on, turn it off. Love can be a faucet if you let it run, and when you are tired of it, turn it off before it runs dry. She felt a little awkward at first, wondering what he might think, but with this kind of magic running rampant in the air, there was only one direction and that was flat on your back. Yet she wanted to savor this and draw it out. This also reassured her command of the ship during rocky weather, because she knew this boat was going to rock and sway and perhaps capsize in this glorious orgasmic sea. So she whispered in Carlos' ear, "Relax and let it go. Let whatever happens happen and go with the flow. Does this feel good, my love?"

Carlos was indeed in an erotic trance and could only moan his agreement with his body. But he did utter, "Do as you wish."

Abby, "Well, I wish to please you with no aftertaste, no regrets, and I don't want to make stipulations about 'this' or 'that. Let's just unfold on the patio and let me rub you."

With that, Abby leaned over and nibbled his neck as she turned him in her arms from the chair onto his back, gently laying him on the flagstone. Then she quickly removed the cushion from the chaise, laid it beside his body and rolled him onto it, face up. She pulled his T-shirt off as if he were a snake shedding its skin. She kissed his lips and parted them with her tongue, tickling his tonsils. It was all over for Carlos. He was hers. He hardly did anything except to numbly participate. She worked her way down his belly, licking and lapping the sweat and juices. It was her favorite cocktail, but she wanted cream on the top, so she paused at his bellybutton and unzipped his pants. His moans became her mantra as she released his penis from its corral. Before she did anything else, she looked at this beautiful piece of his anatomy, so shiny and wet. It was long, thick and throbbing as if it had a personality and mind of its own. Carlos lay nearly still, moaning. In a second, Abby slipped out of her blouse and skirt. It was a tai-chi moment that looked like it was being done in slow motion, yet took just one beautiful flowing motion, and Abby was naked with Carlos.

As she was going down on him, Carlos came to life and swiveled Abby, pivoting her at the hips and landing her crotch on his face, splitting her legs at the same time. They both had each other in their glorious positions. It was Happy Hour and cocktails were being served. Abby had the straw, and Carlos had the chalice. Abby was coming and coming and coming, the chalice overflowing.

Carlos was having his sacrament, his channel that mediated ecstasy. and Abby was duplicating it from a woman's point of view. Yet Carlos did not unload in her mouth. He was stuck in a dream of whirling energy going into a sexual vortex and enjoying it. It was a peaceful, pleasurable hex, something he knew he couldn't get out of, short of a manly release, and he wanted to continue forever. He wanted to bring Abby to blissful orgasm and she him at the same time. Their synchronized breathing created a pattern driven by sensual instincts which should assure their divine wishes. So once again, they disengaged, broke the sacrament, reengaged and had another sacrament. This time Abby mounted Carlos, and her vagina began to eat his penis in a religious convocation. Oh, never before had the cosmos opened so wide, and nothing but stars after stars after stars began to flow with illumination and cosmic explosions that made the aurora borealis look like a child's spinning wheel being held out the window of a moving car. This was her fourth- no, fifth orgasm, and Carlos showed no sign of his one and only eruption into her yielding completion... done... caput... over... ending in, "This is it." So he stayed. He had staying power. Suddenly, with the next pelvic thrust perfectly matched with Abby's, he felt the near, no-return sensation of coming, so he instantly paused. No movement. Abby screamed, "MORE... my God, don't stop. GO!GO!GO! Come in me NOW!" But his pause only lasted a second, which was an eternity in a nymph's world. and then he moved his pelvis with Abby's and they gyrated rapidly together as she came, her sixth orgasm to his one, and he was walking on water, skipping stones in the sky, the clouds as his metaphor. He released his semen in her flooded chalice as the moans and groans sent them into an erotic frenzy. It was a minute past seven, and Happy Hour was over. Now the only thing remaining was their breathing. There was nothing else existing on this earth except them lying naked together on Pedro and Lolita's patio. Oh, and, of course, Stephan in Abby's back pocket lying next to her, and he couldn't be happier.

Abby stayed flattened out on top of Carlos, exhausted and sweating. Their breathing was dwindling from a raging moan to deep breathing, to a more normal pattern which could only follow intercourse. Carlos' throbbing penis shrank and withdrew from Abby's chalice into the shell of his body, mimicking a scared turtle. She rolled off him and he instinctively cradled her in his arms. She felt a chill from the flagstone. The sun was shining. It never did rain that afternoon. Ten seconds later she was standing looking down at Carlos' naked limp body. He said. "What's wrong?" Abby replied, as she was pulling on her skirt-she did not wear panties- "The chill of the flagstone sent me back to reality. Aren't we supposed to be looking for a job for you? I kind of remember where Pedro's clinic is, but maybe we should call him first."

Carlos exclaimed, "Jesus, what about the past 30 minutes you and I just spent together, Abby? Doesn't it mean anything to you?" Abby, "Yes, it was an event... a happening... a very pleasurable experience. I don't know if it could ever happen again. Maybe, maybe not. For me it was penned up sexual frustration that had to be freed, released. You were the carrier, the vehicle. i felt this urge the first time I laid eyes on you when you sat down beside me on the plane."

Carlos. "Yeah, it was great for me, too. But where to from here?" Abby, "Here is here, there is there, now is now, then was then in the past. Could we possibly view this as a realistic movie that we actually did watch and participate in, but the reel came to an end and we must now walk out of the theater, just like the movie ends after one of our contact transmissions? I blink and the movie ends. I don't mean for this to be so cut and dried, lacking emotion. I'm just asking for you to participate as a character in a real-life movie, but don't get emotionally involved leading into a love commitment. Yes, I agree, emotions are naturally involved, but it doesn't have to necessarily be the prelude to love. I just don't want to be attached to the commitment Christians or Jews or other people feel when they take marital vows. Those are only words made up by theologians and religious leaders. Laws are meant to be broken, just like vows and peace treaties, but sex and emotion are natural instincts every living create follows. And I obey these drives, these feelings, these urges without conditions. I had a commitment to Stephan, and he had one to me. But we are only human. If you want to keep something a secret, tell no one. That's why he and I both agreed not to have a traditional religious ceremony of any denomination because we wanted our relationship to be open and unconditional. It's like going to the top of a mountain and meditating. You create your own space if you own yourself."

Carlos, "I'm not asking you to marry me, for crissakes. We just made love. I just don't know if I can practice this pseudo-platonic love that you desire."

Abby. "We didn't make love. Stephan and I made love. We had sex. So all I'm asking is that you view this as sex and sex only. and let's keep our friendship as a priority and not create a loveship. Hey, I like that: friendship versus loveship. Two completely different emotions, yet it takes one to lead to the other. And if one is lost, both are lost. I don't want to lose our friendship, do you?"

Carlos, "No, of course not."

Abby. "Then let's stay friends and sail on this ship without taking the wind out of our friendship."

Carlos, "I don't think it's that simple."

Abby. "Does the chemistry of intercourse have to involve commitment and loveship? We aren't whores without feelings. It's natural to seek a mate and have sex, and variety is the spice of life. Lord knows, some people play the field their entire lives and never get married. We had sex one time. Let's just play it by ear. I'm not about to move into your bedroom, and I don't want you moving into mine. I have no regrets. I simply practice, practice,

practice my life beat with a few attachments and hope I don't hurt anyone along the way."

Somewhere during their conversation and philosophical discussion on friendship and loveship, Carlos was getting dressed alongside Abby. Once, Abby slipped putting on her shoe and grabbed Carlos' arm for stability. He instinctively reached for her while she was off balance and felt like a real man doing this for his loved one. He called it security; she called it stability.

Carlos said, "I feel and sense a strong connection to you. Abby. I don't know if it's true love or infatuation."

Abby, "Let's try infatuation for now, just to avoid the exact love commitment I was just talking about, and let's remain friends. In other words, let's practice friendship and steer clear of loveship. Agreed?"

Carlos, "Yeah, you couldn't have put it more clearly, not wanting to jeopardize a friendship by allowing love to slip in the back door."

Abby, "Beautiful. You understand. Now let's call Pedro and see if he can show us around the clinic."

Carlos, "Okay, lead the way."

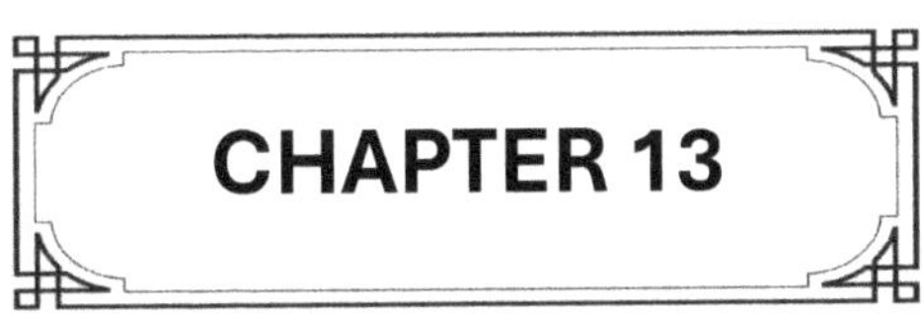

Lolita answered the phone and said, "Come on over. Pedro's work schedule is slow right now. We just had one person come in to have his arm put in a cast and sling after a fall." Lolita then gave Abby directions, and she and Carlos hopped in her rent-a-car and started the 12-mile drive to the clinic. However, she took one wrong turn, so it took them a half mile out of their way.

They pulled into the dirt parking lot and saw Lolita and Pedro in the reception room window. Both waved, and Pedro made a move to come outside and greet them. As Pedro approached, Carlos and Abby both got out of the car, and Abby caught Pedro staring in her eyes. At that instant, Abby wondered if she was a nymphomaniac because she felt a tickle in her crotch and her labia getting slightly moist. She could have taken him right then and there in the dirt, or in the back seat of her car, or in the storage space where they had once kept Stephan's corpse. But she didn't. The visual contact transmission lasted as long as it took Pedro to look away and greet Carlos. Yet, she wondered: Did he feel it, too?

Pedro said, "Greetings, and welcome to our place of healing. Did you two manage well on your own this morning?"

Abby. "Sure did. Walked the property... got to know the surroundings... and made a little lunch, of sorts."

Carlos appreciated her side-bar comment, chuckled, and said with a choke, "You and Lolita have a beautiful place. What a set- up. I envy you two."

Pedro, "Thank you, Carlos. It would be a pleasure to show you around and even explore the possibility of you working here alongside us. I had mentioned to Abby when she was recovering from her accident last month that there would be work for her, too, should she decide to come back to Callebocca."

Abby, "That's true, and that's why I'm here. Carlos and I were just discussing employment after our little interlude at lunch. I'm excited to meet your parents and check out your orchards and manufacturing of Fruit Flows."

Carlos, "What's that?"

Pedro said proudly, "A delicious fruit drink my parents created years ago and have been bottling ever since. All my brothers and sisters participate in the production, sales and worldwide distribution of it. We have about a thousand acres of varietal fruit trees and, believe me, they take constant care and attention. I know there would be definite labor work for both of you there, should you choose."

Abby, "You know, I am more intrigued with the spiritual and medicinal aspects of Guatemala I've heard so much about. Didn't you mention it once when I was rehabbing about the 'people of knowledge' on your farm?"

Pedro, "I am quite sure I didn't, but there may have been some indication of it when I was briefly talking about the workers in the orchards."

Abby. "Carlos and I have had contact transmissions as well, Pedro, and you sort of hit on it last night when we arrived. You sensed a certain kinship, or at least a connection or affinity to Carlos. I believe Argos was his father when you and I were ancient lovers and I was Felicia. That would make Carlos Artemus from another life. Weird, isn't it?"

Pedro. "That's an understatement. Fact remains, we are who we are in this life and nothing can change that."

Abby. "Absolutely right. But the phenomenon is one that can only be explored with the understanding that there's no real proof and nothing can be done with it anyway. So we explore and perhaps grow from the contact transmissions as they occur. Are you afraid or unwilling to participate, knowing what you know now?"

Carlos and Pedro both simultaneously nodded affirmatively that they were, in fact, willing and wanting.

"So let's proceed," Pedro said.

Carlos agreed. "All right.

I'll give it a go again."

Abby said, "Not now, and not in front of the clinic. I think it would be better if we don't involve Lolita just yet."

"You're absolutely right, Abby. Thanks for bringing that to my attention. Some other place, some other time," Pedro said with a sigh of relief.

Abby. "Pedro, Carlos and I want to drive around a bit. Any suggestions on where to go or what to see?"

Pedro, "Callebocca is 40 kilometers due south on this paved road which will take you to downtown market areas and unique shops where local artists sell their wares and there are a few cafes and drinking holes."

Carlos and Abby together, "That sounds great." Abby, while walking away toward their car called to Pedro, "We'll see you back at the house later on."

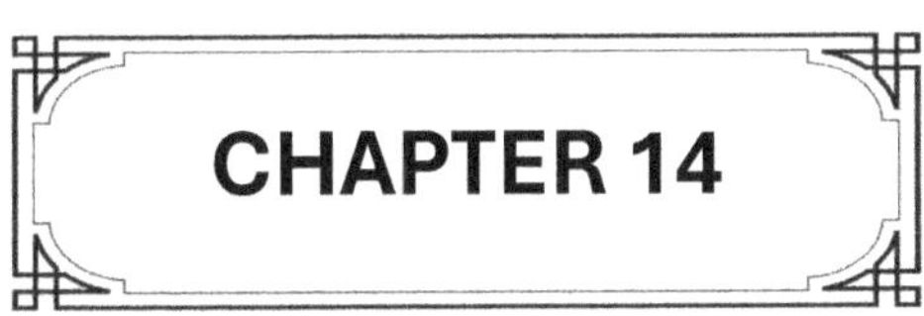

CHAPTER 14

bby hopped in the driver's seat, Carlos in the passenger seat. Carlos brought it up first. He wanted to revisit their lovemaking session on the patio and the conversation that followed. "Abby. you said you don't want to share a bedroom and get emotionally involved with me in a lover's kind of way; you simply want to practice your life steps to your life's beat. I agree. So the beat goes on, like the song says. I suppose I'm game to being a player as opposed to being a spectator."

Abby, "That's what I want to hear. Now, do you suppose we could find a brujo in Callebocca, or do we have to go into the jungle? I want to find some arcane fellow who might be willing to share some knowledge with us."

Carlos, "I don't know. What does a brujo look like?"

Abby, "I guess it's not so much a look, but more like a stare, or even more of a feeling; a sense of wanting to stay around this person because you sense something of wonderment."

Carlos, "Have you ever met one before?"

Abby, "Yeah, in Arizona once on Hopi land. He was a full- blooded Native American Hopi and he made me feel like the entire universe was in my gut. He turned me on spiritually, got my engines running and set me loose, shouting, "If one burns up, don't worry. I installed more. Some you gotta kick-start and some you gotta prime, but they'll get you to where you wanna go.""

Carlos, "Gosh, that's a trip and a half."

Abby, "Yeah, blew my mind. I guess that's what got me here, there, and everywhere on those engines he installed."

Carlos, "Little empty pockets full of wisdom."

Abby, "What did you just say? Where did you hear that?" Carlos, "I don't know, somewhere in my past. Why?"

Abby. "Well, you just had a contact transmission without looking into my eyes. You see, Argos used to say that around our hut from time to time when he spoke to Artemus. And now for you to blurt it out as if you heard it before without going into the movie is remarkable. You brought it forward to the present from when you were Artemus."

Carlos, "Let me look into your eyes right now. Pull over."

Abby, with the quickest of responses and reflex, pulled the car over almost into the jungle edge and stopped it dead. She was extremely excited for some reason, yet knew that she should not have this temperament when she allowed Carlos to look into her eyes and travel into the movie. So she got out of the car and started walking briskly into the jungle. Carlos followed. She found a clearing after about a good 15-minute focused stride, determined to clear her mind.

It was a lovely setting similar to the one behind Pedro and Lolita's house, with tall grass, a few large boulders and the jungle's edge 50 feet from the clearing. It was an arena, an amphitheater, a stage. What better place to perform an act in life's beat of rhythmic chorus a chorus of a heartfelt contact transmission. Nature's harmonic symphony whispers. "Let the show begin."

Abby settled herself on a rock and motioned Carlos to join her. The rock was certainly big enough for the two of them. They only had to take one step on the side of the rock to project them three feet up to the somewhat level rocky top. When the time was right-and only when the time was right-Abby allowed Carlos to swim into her eyes. The movie reel was loaded and the projector running. Carlos sank into a trance. No traveling or spiraling into a vortex like being hypnotized. When a contact transmission occurs, it is instant. One is zapped into their past destination in a millionth of a fraction of a second. And that's how quickly you come back, too, with no lingering feeling or side effects. Carlos became Artemus, looking into Abby's eyes. He saw a little boy crawling on all fours, pausing and looking up at his mother, Felicia, and his father, Argos. His father bent all the way down to Artemus and picked him up. His robe and wrap- around, which we know as a diaper, were wet.

Argos handed Artemus to Felicia, wrinkling his nose. She began to change him and Argos leaned over to hand her a fresh wrap-around and whispered in her ear, "Here is a fresh wrap-around with little empty pockets full of wisdom. Be sure to fill them up and spill them over."

Felicia, "Oh, Argos, you are the kindest, most loving human being I know. You illuminate the way for others to see."

Just then. Abby heard something in the periphery and flinched, then blinked. Carlos snapped out of it, exclaiming, "WOW, there I was as Artemus, and I heard a man-my father. Argos-say those exact words I did earlier, 'little empty pockets full of wisdom, to that beautiful woman, my mother, Felicia. This is outstanding. What will a brujo tell us?"

Abby, "I don't know, but perhaps we are about to find out. I think someone is nearby, watching us."

They slowly peered into the thick forest of banana, palm and bamboo trees looking for a sign. Two native men came out staring at Abby and Carlos with such a glare that it felt like they were looking right through them. Abby and Carlos felt no fear. In fact, Abby took a long sigh of relief as they approached, thinking she had found what she was looking for without searching. Yet she suddenly wondered: How are we going to communicate with these natives? Abby reached into her backpack and pulled out some Wrigley's Spearmint gum. The two men got within five feet of them at the base of the large flattened rock so that they were eye- to-eye with Abby and Carlos. Carlos did nothing except stay motionless, although perhaps cracked a smile. Abby said. "Hi," and offered both of them a stick of gum. They grunted and took the gum. Abby took a stick, peeled the wrapping, and slipped the gum into her mouth. The natives followed suit- "monkey see. monkey do." They immediately got the taste of sweet spearmint on their tongues and exclaimed, "WOW," or so it sounded. They both vigorously chewed as if something was stuck to the roof of their mouths and then swallowed. Carlos and Abby both laughed out loud. Then the natives started laughing. They fell to the grass, rolling from side to side laughing in stitches, holding their sides. Abby and Carlos laughed even harder.

When they stopped laughing and got control of themselves. the natives motioned for Abby and Carlos to follow them into the jungle.

"Uh-oh," Carlos whispered.

Abby said, "No, there is nothing to fear. Let's go with them. I think they want us to meet someone."

They walked for about 25 minutes into the thick jungle. They were on a path which led them to a place where there was a little fire pit and some smoke rising from the coals. There were stumps for stools placed in a circle around the pit about 10 feet back from the fire. The two motioned for everyone to sit. Abby was still chewing her gum. She wanted to show them what it looked like but decided that wasn't a good idea when she realized how they might react looking into her choppers.

Within about two minutes, another two natives came strolling into camp as if nothing strange was happening. They also sat on the stumps. Soon, one of the newcomers pulled out a pipe and filled it with grass. He placed it to his lips. pulled a stick from the fire and ignited the bowl and began puffing. He offered it to the person next to him who also puffed on the pipe. It got to Carlos, and he took it, repeating as he had observed, then served it to Abby. She took a big hit and choked. Everyone laughed hysterically, then one man spoke. "Too much. Too big puff. Next time, smaller."

Abby, with watering eyes and gasping for fresh air, said. "You speak English?"

"Yes, pretty good," the native said. "You have come to ask something?" Abby, "Well, yeah, sort of. We are actually looking for someone." The native, "Who?"

Abby, "I don't know his name. We are looking for someone who knows medicine and has secret knowledge."

The native, "You mean a brujo?" one?"

Abby, with great exclamation and relief, "YES. Do you know

The native, "What would you ask him?"

Abby, "I just want to learn his ways."

She looked over at Carlos, who looked real groggy, and said, "Do you feel all right?"

Carlos mumbled something, then said, "Man, I am really fucked up. I'm stoned out of my gourd."

Abby. "Yeah, I feel very strange, too."

She then looked at the English-speaking native and said, "I think we'd better go."

The native said, "Okay. It was a pleasure, but don't go asking for people to teach you their ways. Let it unfold if they are willing. but never ask. They might think you are trying to take something from them. So, off with you."

Abby and Carlos stood from their stools, wobbly-kneed, stretched their arms to the sky and walked away after thanking them.

It took them a long time to get back to the car. Once in, Abby looked at Carlos and sighed with a stoned expression. Then she started to chuckle. Carlos chimed in, and soon they were laughing. driving down the road, not knowing what had just happened to them and not questioning.

Moments passed, wheels revolved, corners were turned. Carlos looked over at Abby and said, "Was that a brujo?"

Abby said, "I don't think so, but I think they know where there is one." Carlos, "So do tell, what would you ask of a brujo?"

Abby. "I don't know. According to that guy, I shouldn't ask for anything. I know they are capable of telling you the future and offering you guidance and direction based on energy waves emitted by you. They can also confirm the past according to those same energy waves. It all depends on what they pick up from your energy and where they go with it-or are taken. And so like a contact transmission when you look into my eyes and see a movie, we have to be on the same wavelength or connection to the past. A brujo should have the power to pick up on that wavelength and ride it to and fro without a past fellowship. It's all based on energy and body language. The same way you sense fear or happiness. The same way you get goosebumps. It's all based on energy, what you do with it, and how you project it."

Carlos, "Where do you find one?"

Abby, "Not where, but how do you find one? I don't think you can actually find one in a phone book, like looking for a doctor or a specialist or a teacher. This involves guttural, intuitive sense engaging the most natural of animalistic instincts in a human sense. Meaning, if you give up the desire to find something or someone, it usually comes knocking at your door, or you literally bump into a brujo and flatten him on his ass. So instead of looking for one, let's just go to Callebocca shopping."

Carlos, "Good idea."

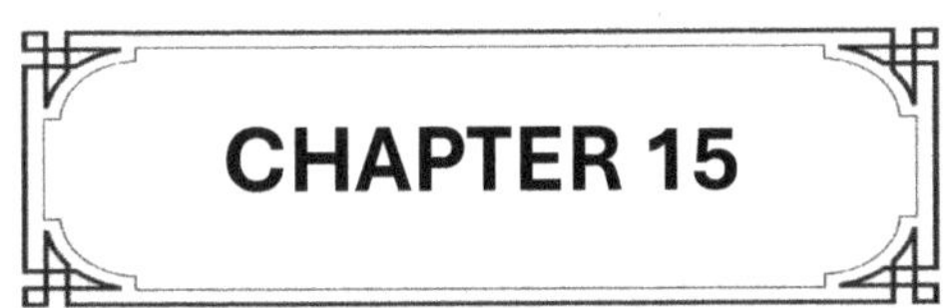

They rounded a bend and the outskirts of a little village with clearings lay before them, meadows and huts scattered here and there, dogs barking, little kids running, cars coming and going. They proceeded down the road into a much more dense population of houses and stores. "This must be the downtown market area Pedro mentioned," Abby said to Carlos. They were still very high.

Carlos said, "Looks like it to me, unless you took a wrong turn and we're in some other town."

Abby parked in the first convenient parking space on the street and got out. Carlos followed, and they started walking. It was an open-air market full of vendors peddling fruit, produce, jewelry and garments.

Abby said, "I guess Callebocca is a tourist town that doesn't have any first-class accommodations, and yet tourists who discover it like to buy the colorful clothes the locals weave."

They found a little cafe and decided to sit and have some coffee. Their buzz started to wear off as the caffeine kicked in. A dirty little boy approached them and asked them for money. He was shooed away by Carlos, who said, "Vamos!" They had a lovely afternoon and thought how quickly the time had passed. "

We should get back to the house and meet Pedro and Lolita," Abby suggested, although in no particular rush. Carlos, "Let's go. The car is just down the street." While walking to their car, they spotted the same four natives who got them stoned. Abby and Carlos saw them simultaneously. but said nothing. The English-speaking native was wearing a wide brim, tattered panama hat and smoking a cigar that looked like it was hand-rolled. It was a simultaneous occurrence, energy waves uniting in harmony-tuning forks in the key of C.

As they passed, they got a whiff of the cigar and knew it was tobacco. The hombre nodded at Abby and Carlos, saying, "Wain- nis-tee-is. Still looking? Remember, don't ask."

Abby smiled and walked past him, then turned, approached him and said, "Then how am I to find what I'm looking for?" The native said, "I already know. No need to ask. Just wait now."

Abby "Oh, I get it. This is a game." The native, "Not at all. Just wait, you'll see. I am here to help you, not hurt you."

Abby and Carlos got into their car, turned around, waved, and drove out of town, back to Pedro and Lolita's.

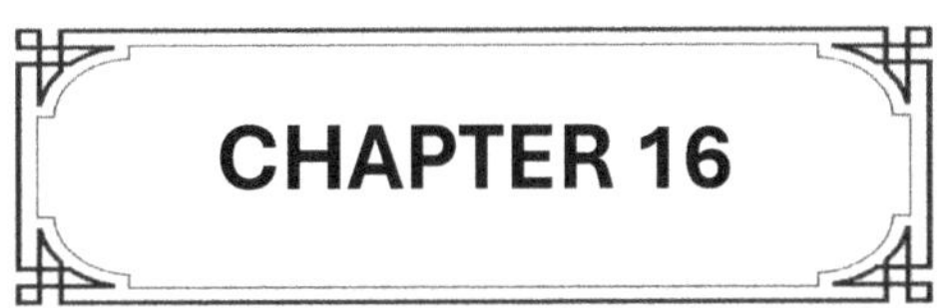

CHAPTER 16

They arrived home an hour later and helped themselves to a cool drink, adjourning to the patio.

Just then, Pedro pulled into the gravel driveway, cut the engine and came in through the kitchen door looking straight out onto the patio where Carlos and Abby were drinking and resting.

Pedro shouted, "Hello, anyone here?"

Abby responded with glee, "Out here, Pedro, on the patio."

Pedro, "Oh, I see, there you are. The setting sun was blinding my view. Stay right there. I'm coming out."

Pedro slid the big screen door open, dragged a patio chair over to Carlos and Abby and set it right in front of Abby.

Pedro, "Let me look into your eyes right now, please, Abby."

Abby, "Oh, boy. I'm up for this."

Abby looked down at the flagstone, took a deep breath and with a long, slow exhalation, lifted her head and allowed Pedro to enter her eyes. It was instant, as always. Pedro slipped into a contact transmission and was transported back to their village outside of Rome and was inside his thatch-roofed hut with his wife, Felicia. She was calling to Argos, "Argos, take me to the well. We need water. Little Artemus is thirsty."

For the first time, they communicated during a contact transmission. Pedro was so deeply engrossed that Abby could see his lips moving to respond to Felicia's request. "Yes, I will get the buckets and we shall walk together with Artemus."

Time passed according to the way they kept time back then which was how many oars Argos could make in a day and the growth of little Artemus. So from that two-mile trudge to replenish their water supply to the time it took Argos to finish four oars for the fishermen, approximately two days, the plague wafted down their dirt road from Rome like a deadly fog. Argos was not destined long for this world. Felicia and Artemus would be left husbandless and fatherless only to carry on with their lives alone, together in grief deep grief and bewilderment. Of course, Artemus did not register this emotion as such. He was left with a spiritual void of wonderment. "Where is my father," not knowing that Argos left him with empty pockets full of wisdom that would someday reappear in another form. Carlos was to be the gifted bearer of this wisdom.

So Pedro was deep into Abby's eyes. He was living the life of Argos while watching the movie. Abby could sense his trance, but didn't know where he was going or what was transpiring at the time. In the movie, Argos had returned from the well and transferred the two 5-gallon wooden buckets of water into a much larger potbelly vessel with a skinny neck and a pour-spout mouth. Felicia and Artemus were right behind Argos as they entered their hut. The walk seemed to have really taken the energy out of Argos. He was short of breath and perspiring more than usual for such a non- exerting task. He sat down and looked at Felicia. "I feel not myself, Felicia. I think something is wrong with my head and stomach."

Within minutes of Argos lying down on the dirt floor, the chills began. Felicia lay Artemus in his wooden box of a crib and tended to Argos. Argos began to shake and quiver. His forehead was sweating profusely. He looked at Felicia, now cradling him, and let out a sigh. "Oh, my wife, I am going to lose my stomach. There's a gurgling like the ocean in it, and my mouth is strange with liquid." He erupted a spew of vomit that splattered Felicia's burlap covering, and, not able to get up, rolled to the side, spewing more digested fish and vegetables onto the dirt floor.

Felicia gently laid him down and ran to the vessel, spilling water as she tipped it to douse a rag. He didn't think he had much more in him to bring up, but he did. Hours later, he was weak and dry-heaving. The sunlight was dimming and night was near. Felicia continued her vigil for days on end, tending to her failing husband and what appeared to be her healthy and vivacious son. Argos was tremendously dehydrated, and now that the diarrhea had replaced the vomiting, it seemed that delusions were setting in, as well as hallucinations. Yet he had his moments of awareness and consciousness.

More sunrises and sunsets passed. Felicia, when she stole at moment from tending to both her loved ones, would step outside her hut and search the horizon for a familiar face. All she saw was hysteria amongst the local townspeople. People were shuffling up and down the dirt roads toting carts stacked with dead bodies.

She shouted, "What's going on? Can someone help us, please?"

One passerby, empty-handed, stopped and answered her desperate question. "Poor woman, there is a strange happening here and the streets are filled with wretched, dying people. The village squire has been calling out for people to beware. You must stay inside and tend to your dying. When someone dies, you must do away with the body immediately. That's what all of these fellow men are doing, those who are able. Stay healthy and pray you do not get overcome with such dreadedness."

The man quickly scurried off shouting to others, "Beware, stay inside and bring out your dead."

Felicia and Artemus never succumbed to the deadly plague, but Argos was lifeless within the turn of one more light and dark. He spoke at times of prophecy and looniness, about empty pockets full of wisdom, meeting Felicia some other time, some other place.

Argos spoke in a whisper. "Take care of our son. Love is the universe. I shall be washed up upon a distant shore in some other form and we shall find one another, Felicia, entwine and become one. But you must believe. Tell me you believe."

Felicia said, "Yes, my husband, I shall do all of those things you ask with obedience, love and devotion, because I believe you."

Pedro twitched in his porch chair with sweat dripping from his nose. This was his return ticket back to Callbocca and his reentry into the present setting with Abby and Carlos. He appeared to be slightly stunned as he shook his head, wiped his forehead, ran his fingers through his hair with both hands, and exclaimed, "WOW!"

Abby asked. "Where did you just go, and what happened while you were there?"

Pedro snapped out of it quickly and realized he was not in a hungover stupor as one might suspect.

"Well," he began, "I was for sure Argos this time and lived through my death as evidenced by my presence here and now as Pedro. Do you believe me? I don't understand what goes on here by observing this movie every time I peer into your yes, Abby, but this has got to be medical history."

Abby. "I don't think so. It has just never before been documented with such profound effect. Don't you think Jesus Christ's disciples had similar thoughts and beliefs as Jesus? He was just the one that proselytized it best because he was an orator and won his audiences over with articulation. He was, in essence, zapped with a vision-the best politician of them all. He heard voices speak to him about creation and the origin of man coming from God himself. So don't you think the phenomenon of contact transmission has been happening since the beginning of time, too?"

"Well, I guess I can't say, or at least justify it with proof. So as far as I am concerned, the Wright brothers were the first to achieve flight, and I, the first to space travel through someone else's eyes as an incarnate," Pedro said with confidence.

Carlos said, "Whatever... I'm next to fly into your eyes and see my movie as I was way back then. Are you ready. Abby?" Abby, "Please, not yet. I want to hear exact details of Pedro's viewing.

Pedro, "Okay. As soon as I fell into the contact transmission, I was transported to the village outside of Rome and into our hut. You were there, Abby, as Felicia, my wife, and I know now that Carlos was there as our son, Artemus. I know this because part of my dying conversation with Felicia mentioned 'empty pockets full of wisdom, and I heard Carlos say that phrase earlier, so he has to be Artemus. Anyway, I died of the bubonic plague. I know this due to the bubo I observed on Argos. His-my-armpits and inner thighs and groin area were like red hot balloons, so sensitive and swollen, ready to burst. Yet I felt the love I shared with my wife, Felicia, up to the last moment, and then I expired, was wheeled away on a cart and taken to the sunken pyre outside of the village."

Pedro continued, "The smell was horrific. Death defines love. Felicia was left with an emptiness in her heart, but knew Artemus would fill it soon with his childlike innocence and love. She was left with life and knew that Argos' death defined love for the rest of her life. She could only hope and pray that his prophecy would come to fruition at some later time and that with her passing, she, too, would swim ashore on some distant land in a strange new future and they would find one another, intermingle their energy and entwine as one. DNA, the strand of life binding death, binding life."

Pedro was finished, and this time he looked exhausted, having just revisited his experience and explaining it to Abby and Carlos.

In the beginning, when their contact transmissions were first discovered, both Pedro and Carlos thought this was very cool to look into someone's eyes and watch a movie starring the three of them. They had no idea explaining it could unfold such beneficial attributes in their lives today pertaining to personalities and reasons for their actions and yet be so draining in the process.

Carlos looked at Abby who was studying Pedro. The air was clear and refreshing. No one really questioned Pedro's contact transmission, yet Carlos wanted a go at it, and he knew Abby just wasn't ready for it. So Carlos stood and went into the house to retrieve a beer.

"May I get anyone anything," he asked over his shoulder. walking from the porch and sliding the glass door open.

Pedro said, "Yes. Get me a cerveza if you would, please. "Me, too," said Abby. And Carlos walked inside.

Pedro asked Abby how her leg felt now that the cast had been off for a day. "Not bad." said Abby. "I even took a stroll around the grounds, and Carlos and I walked around a bit in Callebocca. My leg is a little tired now, but not really achy."

"That's a good sign. I do not think there will be any need to hold back with your comment as such, but may I look at it now and manipulate it a little." Pedro asked while reaching for her exposed leg.

"Not at all," was Abby's response, pulling up her skirt even more so that he might have plenty to look at and feel, should he choose.

The invitation was like letting the barn door open to allow the horses to meander out into open pasture because you felt they needed some freedom, but wanted it to look like an innocent oversight. Oops, now how did those darn horses get out of the corral?

Pedro reached delicately for her leg, propped it up on his right thigh, and proceeded to feel up and down the leg. When satisfied, he bent her leg at the knee and put her foot on the patio floor and placed both his hands behind her right knee and began to gently tug, pulling the upper calf closest to the knee articulation toward him to determine any looseness in the joint, tendon or ligament. There was no extreme slippage, so he stopped, but kept his hands behind her knees while conversing with her, making sure to look over her shoulder to avoid looking into her eyes and falling, once again, into a trance. Also, he was watching for Carlos because he didn't want to get caught in an awkward moment. He felt slightly sly with his intentions.

Abby said, "You are such a concerned, caring doctor. The townspeople are very privileged to have you and Lolita here with your clinic open almost seven days a week, 365 days a year."

Pedro, "Oh, they would somehow manage without us, if we chose some other place. But this is home for both of us, and we are so fortunate to be close to both our families and help out where and when we can."

Abby. "There, you see? When you aren't helping the townspeople with their medical woes, you're looking to help the families at their businesses. By the way, how is Fruit Flows doing, and the orchards?"

Pedro, "Just fine, from what my mother tells me. Lolita's parents live quite a distance from here and manage on their own without much input or help from us. So they tend to communicate only during holidays and when they want to visit. We have basically informed the families that we have guests staying with us for an extended time and that if they want to visit, it might take advance notice of a week or two. You and Carlos are welcome to stay indefinitely. Lolita and I have discussed it and agree wholeheartedly."

Abby responded, "Well, that is so nice, Pedro. Carlos and I are footloose and fancy free, but I can sense Carlos is going to need a job real soon or drift away into his own space. He is a big boy, and after that flight from Miami and the aborted hijacking plan, he's feeling his oats and seems ready for anything."

Pedro was still holding onto Abby's leg when the sliding door glided open. Carlos, "Beers as ordered. Who gets what?"

Abby, "I believe I get a beer."

Pedro, "Me, too. That leaves Carlos. Carlos, what did you want?"

"Cerveza for me, okay," Carlos said comically.

Pedro gently let go of Abby's leg, and she sighed with pleasure and disappointment. She was beginning to get that certain tingle between her legs that sent a message to her body requesting the juices to flow, but then a roadblock went up and passports were demanded, so the juice flows came to an abrupt halt.

Pedro, "Carlos, do you want to work on my parents' farm with the rest of my family picking fruit and making juice?"

Carlos, "Wow, what an offer! How far is it from here?"

Pedro, "About a two-and-a-half-hour drive on these roads."

Carlos. "What's it pay!"

Pedro. "Good pay, lots of benefits, time off, paid vacations. bonuses, plus room and board in very nice dormitory-style accommodations. You will feel like part of the family and blend in in the exact same fashion. That's why our friends and family stay with us for the long haul. People just want to stay, raise their own families, should they choose, or be a part of the whole. We help all of our pregnant women with medical expenses and delivery. That's where I come in. At least once a month, I go to the farm for general medical purposes. We basically respect all people's rights and privacy but are open to any discussion, should anyone come to one of us for advice."

Carlos, "It sounds worth checking out. When can we visit?"

Pedro, "I'll call my mother and father today and first see if they can use an extra body, then ask when is a good time to pay a visit. Abby, of course you are more than welcome to explore with us and stay on the farm. I think you'll love the experience and exposure."

Abby. "That sounds like a good opportunity for you, Carlos. I'm ready and willing anytime."

Carlos, "Please place that call, Pedro. I'm ready, too."

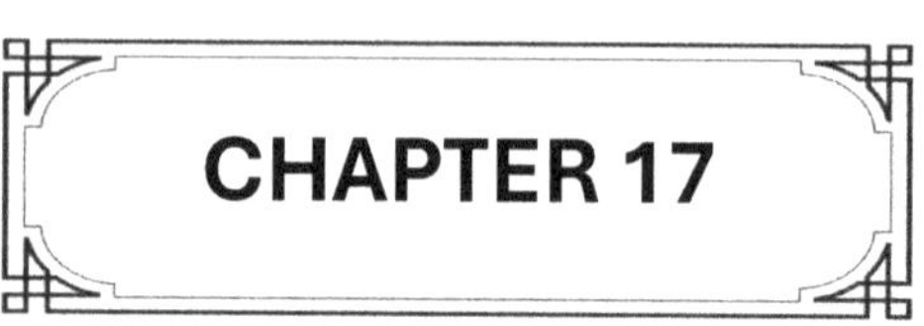

CHAPTER 17

Abby and Carlos remained on the porch while Pedro called the farm. They sipped on their beers and relaxed a little, mulling it over in their minds.

Pedro returned in 15 minutes with thumbs up. "We're on. Mother says to come straight away. They just lost a young man who needed to pursue a different road. There's a bed waiting for you and lots of picking to do. Mother did ask if you knew how to cook meals for large numbers of people. She said they need help in the kitchen preparing employee meals for their 25 or so workers and their families."

Carlos, "Yes, but I am versatile and willing."

Pedro, "She said it would be okay if you didn't desire that so much. You can definitely be useful anyway and will be needed in the orchards."

Abby. "When do we go?"

"Either tonight when Lolita gets home, or early tomorrow morning, as long as she says nothing serious happened in the clinic today that requires my attention tomorrow," Pedro answered.

Lolita came home two hours later and found them all on the patio drinking beer. She grabbed one from the refrigerator and walked onto the terrazzo. "Well, I'm glad to see everyone enjoying themselves. Abby, how is your leg feeling?"

Abby, "Great. It's healing nicely thanks to all of your attention and healing powers. I believe your clinic serves such a philanthropic purpose. We need more of these types of places in America-and across the globe, for that matter."

Lolita, "Well, thanks for that. We are glad you found us, but sad for the reason, and especially for your loss of Stephan.

As far as the world's need for this kind of place and attitude and devotion, that's called utopia and can only be acquired in one's own mind. I believe it does exist, but only when you find people like Pedro who are willing to give."

Carlos, "Right on. I'm just glad to be here and not in Cuba. Thank you all for your presents of love, unconditional boundless love, and empty pockets full of wisdom."

Pedro, "You are so kind."

Abby, "I believe it is more than that. I believe it's our past that gets us to the here and now. And I'm talking the past as far back as one can go."

Lolita, "Sounds like reincarnation to me."

Abby. "Kind of. It's my own deep-rooted approach to lifetime explanations. And explanations are about all anyone can come up with, no matter what the mind contrives. It's in the eyes that takes you back. And even then, we call that perception. It's all in the eyes of the beholder."

Pedro and Carlos both kept quiet. It was Abby's performance. The stage was set, curtain up. But it didn't go any further than Lolita nodding with an "Mmhmm"-type acknowledgement and then letting it trickle into thin air. It was just one of those comments that one hears, registers, then either walks away from or engages in discussion, controversy, debate, argument for the sake of convincing that goes nowhere, ending in confusion. You either approve or disapprove. Lolita had her own opinion, heard Abby's, and didn't want to voice what she thought. Lolita was a polite and courteous person and would never say anything to offend anyone's feelings. It was a very comfortable exit to Abby's conversation.

Lolita, "Pedro, have you thought about-or started dinner?"

"Not yet. We were discussing jobs. Carlos wants to check out the farm, so I called Mother and she invited us to visit pronto. Are you guys hungry?"

Carlos, "I'd rather put it in gear and go as soon as possible."

Abby, "Me, too. Maybe we can pack a snack?"

Lolita, facetiously, with a chuckle, "So you're off on an exploration leaving me behind to take care of the clinic?"

Pedro, "Yes. You don't mind, do you, my dear?"

Lolita. "Nah. I was just kidding. I think it's a great idea. You'll love the farm, both of you. Carlos, I think you'll be happy there."

"Then it's settled. Nothing serious happened today that needs my attention at the clinic?" Pedro asked Lolita.

Lolita smiled and said, "Simple, easy patients. Treat and release. Nothing pending. Go have fun. Say hi to the family."

"Then we'll be off within the hour," Pedro exclaimed.

He suggested for Carlos and Abby to gather their belongings. Carlos to focus on every possession he came with, and Abby just her essentials for an overnight stay.

Lolita offered to put together some nibbles for the drive.

Within an hour, they were on the road and driving south toward Honduras. They would reach the Salvarezes' orchard farm within two hours, driving 75 and 100 kilometers, and would be about 50 kilometers north of the Honduras border.

CHAPTER 18

The three of them talked in the car during the drive. Carlos was excited about the venture and the prospect of living and working on the fruit farm. Abby was excited about the natives she and Carlos had met in the jungle and then on the street in Callebocca. She sensed there was more union to come. She fathomed, perhaps that one Indian is a brujo. Perhaps that's what he meant when he said, "I already know you." Dreams that don't really happen, and dreams that do. Dreams are made up. And what of the waking world? Is this, too, made up another dream? Is life really happening as a dream or as real life? Which is which? Abby wasn't really confused, yet she did think them and therefore deserved the merit of time a few seconds anyway. Her thought-bubble burst, and she was back in the car cruising to the Salvarez farm. Carlos and Pedro were talking about the passing jungle terrain and its inhabitants.

They approached the entrance to the farm as noted by an arched entryway of steel and angle-iron forming a gate with the Fruit Flows logo, colorful formed fruits made of steel, oozing metallic juice dripping down the gate. From there the drive was pebble stone and led them to

Pedro's family home at the end of about a half-mile of this curvy road. No dust was stirring as Abby glanced back over her shoulder at the automatically closing gate. She turned forward and saw nothing but fruit trees to her left and right. Some workers were scattered about the rows tending to the trees and pruning them where necessary.

As they drove to the last gentle curve in the road, Pedro's childhood home was standing there as if a monument. Abby and Carlos gasped simultaneously, exclaiming. "WOW!" It was a one- story ranch-style house made of authentic adobe brick from the local mason. The porch was huge and sprawled all around the circumference of the house. Large round timbers made the struts for the uprights holding the roof of a porch, which seemed to beckon them to lounge on it and relax with a fruit drink. There was wooden twig furniture everywhere on the porch, which looked to be 20 feet deep, a well-shaded area year round. About 100 yards to the left of the house were different buildings, one for fruit production handling and another for the bottling plant. Workers were mingling about both buildings, but when they recognized who was driving in, they all began to hasten toward the Jeep. Then the double front doors to the house opened and Margarette came running out with open arms as big as God's, shouting. "Pedro, my boy." Pedro was out of the car and in her arms like Jesus welcoming the shepherds. All the workers gathered around and bid Pedro warm welcome as Abby and Carlos stepped out of the Jeep, too. Introductions were made to Margarette first, and then to the rest of the crew with a sweeping motion from Pedro's outstretched arm, as he said, "These are the rest of my friends." Some of them said "Welcome" in broken but understandable English.

Juan came sauntering out of the house with a smile on his face as wide as the Grand Canyon. "Pedro, my son, welcome, and to your friends, too. Come in."

All the hubbub quieted down, and the workers went back to their designated buildings. Family members and friends walked arm-in-arm into the house. Abby linked to Pedro. On the other side of Pedro, Carlos linked to Margarette, with Juan on Margarette's other arm.

The inside of the house was grand, in a shibumi way, not oriental by any means, but "simplicity with elegance" would be the correct way to describe their beautiful decor: not overdone and pretentious, but top-notch all the way. Large candles were seen in the little alcove-like cutouts mounted in the adobe walls. It was mid-afternoon by the time they had arrived, and no candles were lit. Rest assured, they would all be lit come dusk.

Servers began preparations for a superb dinner in the large dining room. Their hand-carved wooden table could seat a king and queen and their court. Fruit was plentiful in wooden bowls placed up and down the length of the table. No cloth, just the beautiful surface of the wood and all of the accompanying wooden throne-like chairs surrounding the entire table.

They all adjourned to the kitchen, from where life pulsates. The Salvarezes thoroughly enjoyed dining because it held the essence of nourishment which they loved to share with their family and friends. Once a month, they held a company barbecue, and all the workers and their families were invited to partake in the festivities. They built a special picnic area out back and an outdoor kitchen and grill with a fire pit for this reason. Bales of hay served as seating. along with benches and wagons.

Margarette participated in the cooking along with her kitchen help. Like Pedro and Lolita's house, the Salvarez kitchen was a place to socialize. Everyone gathered and pulled up a chair. Juan poured wine for those who wanted it. Further introductions were made, and the conversation became more personal as Abby and Carlos told their individual stories of their pasts. Certain specifics were obviously left out and so, their experiences were portrayed in general, good and bad, happy and sad.

It was then brought up that Abby and Carlos were looking for work. Margarette said, "Pedro, as we discussed on the telephone, we will take any friend of yours in for room and board in exchange for work. The more skilled, the better the pay. And as I recall, you mentioned that Carlos has some talents in the kitchen cooking for large numbers of people. We do need someone now to replace Ricardo who recently retired and moved back to his home in Guatemala City. Ricardo cooked breakfast, lunch and dinner for the whole crew in the community staffing center by the workers' housing huts."

The Salvarezes employed between 45 and 100 farm hands throughout the year. The numbers varied according to the season, the production of harvest, and the bottling of juices. The Salvarezes also provided housing units for the workers and their families. who participated in one way or another according to their age. Babies were given total freedom to be babies, and mothers were expected to raise their children until an age where they could manage in the orchards with mother, father, brothers and sisters. close at hand. Everyone served as built-in nursery care for the newborns. No one was neglected or made to feel unwanted.

Margarette loved the children and would invite them into the main house quite often to play and help in the kitchen. She also maintained office headquarters in the house to manage the operations of their employees, production and sales. Juan supervised the hands-on work in the orchards, as well as testing for disease in the fruit trees and plants. He had his own science lab and workshop in a separate building.

Carlos wanted to be part of this working family. He knew he could prepare employee meals with tender loving care for such large groups. He also fantasized about working in the orchards periodically for a change of scene. He sipped from his goblet and asked. "Where are the bunkhouses? May I see one?"

"Of course," Pedro said. "Follow me-Abby, you may come along as well or stay with Mama and Papa and chat a little."

"I'll stay in the kitchen," she replied, looking into Pedro's eyes and becoming excited.

"Pedro said. "Suit yourself."

Abby said, "Well, now, wait a minute. Is this where I might be staying tonight? Perhaps I should come just to see where I'm sleeping."

"Oh, no, my dear. You will stay in the house with the family. Pedro will show you your room after dinner," Margarette chimed in most hospitably and with pride.

"Well, then, I'll stay here. You two go see the bunkhouse and maybe some of the fields."

CHAPTER 19

arlos liked everything he saw in the bunkhouse-but this was not like any bunkhouse he had ever seen. This was like a quaint and roomy lodge that you might find in Nepal or Kathmandu for the weary traveler or hiker. They walked into a large gathering room with sofa, chairs and tables spread all around. Then, off to the south end of this auditorium-style room, there was a very wide wooden staircase that went up to a balcony where some rooms were located. This particular building could house 30 people. A family, depending on how many children, had larger family-style rooms with separate bedrooms. There were three buildings exactly like this one for the employees. Everyone ate in the community building where the commercial kitchen was located.

No one cooked in the private rooms, yet anyone, at any time, could come over to the community kitchen and prepare something to eat. If Carlos accepted the cooking position, he'd be placed in the closest convenient available studio space in the community building. No one stole anything from anyone while working for the Salvarezes basically in the same regard that villagers didn't steal from the medical clinic back in Callebocca.

It would deprive all the rest of the people of a very valuable commodity. The community of workers valued these two establishments as if they were their own. Both served substantial and amazing needs: one, food, work, pay, benefits; the other, medical treatment, and both, a healthy lifestyle with a purpose. Socialism at its essence.

A couple of the children came running up to Pedro for hugs and kisses. They recognized him as the doctor who had more than likely brought them into this world. Most babies were born on the farm, and Pedro and Lolita delivered them, as well as treated their mother during pregnancy. The children also knew that Pedro brought medicine if someone was sick.

After viewing one of the bunkhouses and the community building, Pedro and Carlos were heading back to the main house when Pedro's brothers and sisters came running out of the orchards to tackle him all at once. It was now the end of the workday, and word had travelled quickly throughout the orchards that Pedro was here with friends. After the heartfelt greetings, Pedro introduced Carlos to Miguel, Florencia, Roberto and Juanita. Something strange happened between Juanita and Carlos upon meeting. Their eyes connected and Juanita fell into his gaze. She blinked twice and snapped out of it, but she knew she had suddenly shifted gears. Carlos sensed it, too, but this now seemed "old hat" to him. Still, he made a mental note of this.

Everyone walked back to the main house arm-in-arm, chattering and laughing all the way. Carlos listened intently, feeling the sensual connection with Juanita.

When they walked into the house, they could smell the many varied aromas coming from the kitchen: meat, beans, salsa, and blenders mixing up margaritas.

Abby was sitting there with her legs curled up under her on the wicker loveseat farthest from the action around the stove where everyone was cooking. She jumped to her feet when she saw the entourage of people entering the kitchen.

Pedro did all of the formal introductions of his brothers and sisters. Abby greeted all of them openly, but felt a little overwhelmed. Pedro sensed this and came to her aid, comforting her by putting his arm around her, pulling her in to his chest. She practically melted on the spot as the juice dripped from her chalice.

Carlos saw this, but thought nothing of it, as he fell into Abby's eyes from five feet away, and she soulfully became his mother, Felicia. Abby actually directed this contact transmission from afar to divert any suspicious attention away from Pedro's affection toward her. Abby was in charge, and she did not want Carlos to inflict any of his maleness onto her turf.

Carlos, meanwhile, thinking nothing of what had just transpired, concentrated his attention on Juanita. He was focused on her eyes and loved what he saw. She wasn't paying any real attention to him at that moment, but she felt the tingles and pheromones. She approached him and asked him if he wanted anything to drink. He said, "I'd love a cerveza."

She said, "Coming right up.

When she returned, she had a beer in each hand, offered one to Carlos, then toasted him, clanking bottles, asking if he wanted to join her on the porch. They strolled out together, everyone noticing, but no one caring. It was social hour and a time to mingle with the guests and get to know them.

Abby moved closer to the kitchen activity and started up a conversation with Margarette. It was basic chit-chat about food, herbs and what it means to everyone's health. Then Margarette asked if Abby had an interest in the farm as far as work was concerned.

Abby thought for a moment, then answered with diplomacy and directness. "My real interest is in Pedro's medical clinic, his background. But most importantly, I have a strong affinity for exploring the possibility of studying with a brujo."

"Well," Margarette exclaimed, "Lord knows, we have enough 'people with knowledge' working right here on the farm. But do not approach them and ask them to give up their knowledge. They must first offer to share it with you. Do not ever go in quest of such a thing, and especially don't ask them to give it up."

"Exactly why is that, Margarette?" Abby asked politely.

"Because they feel it is theirs to offer and, if asked, perhaps do not want you to know. Therefore, they feel you may be taking more from them--not in stealing, but in terms of the time it took them to acquire their knowledge handed down to them from their elders. You don't just snap your fingers and expect to get something from someone that it took years to learn. They will sense who to pass. their knowledge on to-and when. So, you see, it is not like your universities where you pay to learn from the teachers. Here, you pay nothing bur time, and only if you are chosen. Still interested?"

Abby, "Yes, of course."

"Then let me take you around the farm and introduce you to a variety of workers. Some of them are brujos, and some aren't. You will not know the difference, but they will know. They will see it in your eyes. And if you ask for something, they will not give it. So it would be best if you practice 'not wanting. Give in. Give in to time. Let time elapse and simply wait. Then-maybe you will begin to see things unfold, change, and perhaps one of them will connect with your energy-sort of like your 'cosmic fashion,' what you wear, and how you wear it. Their perception is out of this world."

Margarette had been telling this to Abby as she was stirring the rice and beans. Things were starting to smell really good in the kitchen, and the love vibes were heating up as well, stirring the fermenting pheromones.

Pedro was sitting on a barstool the whole time his Mama and Abby were talking. He told Abby that he grew up with brujos on the farm. Every time someone took ill or needed medicine, they were always there and knew just what herb to use and where to find it. Seldom would they resort to modern medicine and doctors. But if they had to, they collaborated on things like witch hazel and hydrogen peroxide to treat an open wound.

Margarette asked one of her cooks to watch the beans and rice and essentially take over the dinner preparations while she, Abby and Pedro walked through the orchards.

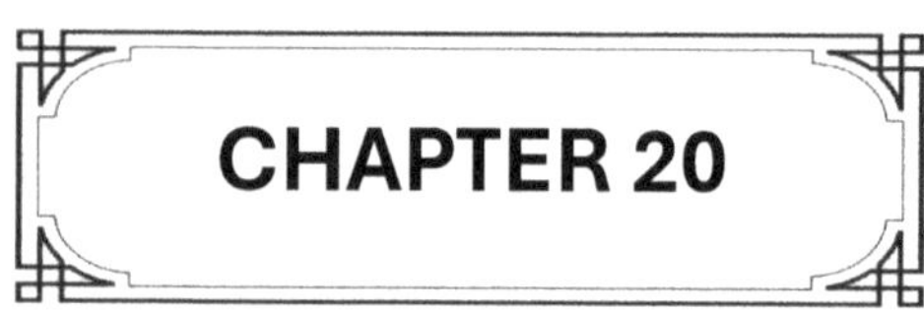

CHAPTER 20

The three grabbed their drinks after refilling each glass from the margarita pitcher. They went out the front entry onto the porch where Carlos and Juanita were sitting having beers and romanticizing in each other's eyes. This was obvious to all who passed by them because Carlos and Juanita didn't blink an eye to acknowledge anyone.

Margarette, Pedro and Abby strolled across the grounds, entered an orchard and disappeared among the fruit trees. They walked about a quarter of a mile before seeing a picker. Most of the workers were out of the trees and on their way back to their homes after the day's work.

Margarette spoke in Spanish to a worker whose name was Fernando. She was asking where most of the people were gathering tonight for the community fire. Fernando thought his family would go behind the third bunkhouse called the Ponderosa.

Margarette then addressed Abby and suggested that perhaps after dinner they could go to the fire to chat and listen. She went on to explain that every night, somewhere behind one of the housing projects, a few-

or many-would gather, build a fire and begin to swap stories, create tales, spin yarns, embellish truisms, and boast lies as truths. "Medicine for the mind" the "people with knowledge" called this, and a brujo was most often present at these fireside gatherings.

Margarette explained that you would not be able to identify a brujo-or a bruja-except through their laughter. You could ride their spirit and feel the blessing of being in their presence. You would certainly know by the goosebumps running on your arms, legs, torso, back and neck, which could stay for minutes that would seem like hours. Brujos were funny that way. Sometimes goosebumps could come and go unrecognized, just like the brujo himself. That had happened to Abby and Carlos in the jungle the day that they met the four natives and chewed the Wrigley's spearmint gum with them. Their skin crawled like a boa constrictor shedding its skin, but Abby and Carlos did not recognize the goosebumps-probably because they were too stoned. Yet, the one with the ragged Panama hat, smoking a cigar, laughed at Abby when they met in the market in Callebocca. He laughed a laugh that tickled Abby, and she remembered how pleasant and funny the sound was. She did not know she had met a brujo, soon to be her teacher.

The three walked back to the house. Carlos and Juanita had not broken their trance, and the flirting became contagious. Pedro held onto Abby's arm as he helped her up the two steps onto the porch and into the house.

Margarette resumed her role of orchestrating dinner by asking the cooks to start the grill and put the meat on it. Others began to set the large banquet table for 15 people. Colorful placemats were set at each position around the wood plank table. Wine and water glasses were placed at each setting with beautiful gallon water jugs positioned up and down the 20-foot table. Peppermills stood beside bowls of raw sea salt for the pinching, to sprinkle on the steaks, refried beans and rice.

Dinner was 20 minutes away, and the smells were making everyone horny for a culinary orgasm.

Carlos and Juanita sauntered into the kitchen with romance in their eyes. Abby looked at them and felt tremendous joy and relief as she thought Carlos had found a place, a mission, a goal achieved. Better than Cuba, Abby mused.

An unusual sound erupted in the air and filled the kitchen with a reverberation that automatically ushered everyone to their seat. "Dinner is served," the melodic gong seemed to chime in a deep, deep tone.

The steaks sat sizzling on everyone's metal platter, and huge pots smoldered with the tantalizing aromas of beans and rice. Ten bottles of red wine were placed in between the water jugs and condiments on the table.

Once dinner was served, the servants did not stand around or offer servings to individuals. Their job was finished. Diners were left to help themselves and pass the food around to each other.

Talk was as plentiful as wine. The spirits flowed that evening. Carlos, Juanita, Pedro, Abby, Margarette, Juan, Roberto, Florencia, Nigel, Rosita, Pancho, Paco, Miguel, Nelly and Franco were fully engaged in the romance of dining and conversation. The Salvarezes were in love with living and shared their joy to all with enthusiasm, especially those who gathered around their loving table of nourishment. If you could bottle this, you would have the private reserve of Fruit Flows, and it would be priceless.

As dinner progressed, the evening chatter became even more lively and loud. No one conversation dominated the table. Everyone was speaking about something to their dinner partners, but no one was speaking of anything of importance. Business was never discussed at the Salvarez dinner table. Never. It was strictly taboo. Business talk was left for after dinner, if one must, while smoking cigars on the porch and sipping brandy. The day was open for business discussions and meetings, not the night. Dinner was a communion of family, not a stage setting for indigestion from discussing business problems.

(Author's note: One should not delve into hyperbole, nor dwell in absurdity. Save serious discussions for more austere business meetings. Be jovial, be silly and laugh a lot at dinner or social gatherings.)

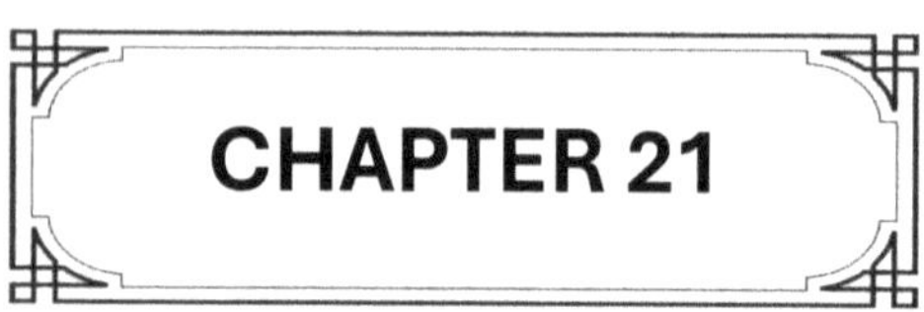

CHAPTER 21

Laughter was the perfect ingredient for the alchemy of digestion, and so was a stroll around the property under a starlit night. And by all means, coming upon a community fire was medicine for the spirit as well as the belly.

Pedro and Abby were sitting beside one another closest to Juan who sat at the head of the table. Juan was asking Pedro about Lolita and how he wished she could be there with them that night. Pedro expressed the same sentiments.

Abby then braved a question to Juan about his science lab. Juan replied, "In brief, I will show it to you tomorrow and discuss my research then. For now, I want to know more about you. Not necessarily 'what' you are, but 'who' you are. And I do not want to barrage you with questions. I want you to open up and offer pieces of yourself like a sacrament. We have time. Not all in one night."

Abby, "Well, that's a relief. Sometimes I don't know whether to start with the present and go backwards, or start at birth and come forward."

Juan, "There, you see, already a sign, a message about your thought patterns and organizational skills. It is obvious you care. You think before you speak, and when you speak, you have something substantial to say. But it's your eyes, Abby, that enchant me. They are so beautiful and deep. I imagine someone like Carlos could fall into them and not be able to get out."

Pedro, "That's funny you should mention that, father. There is quite a good story that follows that line about how Abby and Carlos met."

Abby, "Shhh. Pedro. Do you think I should offer that story now?"

Pedro "Of course. It's no real secret or private affair. My father would be very interested. But for now, let's adjourn to the porch and then perhaps find a community fire."

Once on the porch, Abby related her story, in detail. Juan was sincerely enthralled and allowed Abby's words to flow like ocean waves. When she was finished describing Stephan rolling the Jeep and her recovery at Pedro and Lolita's clinic, Abby took a deep breath and let out an exhale that marked the end of the story.

Juan said, "Aren't you leaving something out? Didn't you forget to mention something? What about your return to Callebocca? You came back here for something, didn't you? Certainly not to revisit the site where you lost your husband, and obviously not to build a house and retire. I sense you are in quest of something beyond your reach, yet you are reaching because you want that thing. You desire something you don't have. I overheard you talking with my wife about brujos and seeking knowledge from them. This is not a warning; it is advice only. Give up. Stop looking- and, by all means, do not ask of someone to give up what is in their mind that took them many lifetimes to acquire. You must earn before you spend."

Abby, "Wow! So many people have given me the same advise, but not in those words. 'You must earn before you spend.' You are right about why I came back to Callebocca. I felt there was more for me here than in Salem, North Carolina. And, yes, I do want something. But you tell me not to go looking for it. The native from the jungle told me the same thing at the market in Callebocca two days ago."

Juan, "I know."

Abby, "Wait a minute. You know? How do you know this?"

Juan, "Because I know what brujos know, I just don't practice it or claim to be one. To claim to be a brujo is to say you know magic, and that is to say you can fly into the sun like a phoenix. 1 cannot do this, but I know some who can, and you will not meet them until you give up. Oh, you may be introduced to them, but they will not let you in- yet. In fact, you have already met one and you didn't even know it because you didn't feel the goosebumps. You did hear him laugh, though, because that's what they do when they are teasing you. They love playing with you. You are like a child's toy to them, and when they outgrow you, they change right before your eyes, laughing all the while. So, you see, your eyes must feel the laughter and your skin must see the goosebumps. Goosebumps appear when in the presence of fear or the sensation of pleasure."

Pedro, "You mustn't take my father too seriously. He means you no harm. But you must hear what he's saying to you."

Juan, "I am saying you should be careful and have respect. Ancient tales come at a price, and that price is usually time and patience, that is all. You lost your soulmate here, and you've come back because you answered a calling. This is good. You have feelings and intuition. But as you will find, there are other soulmates. That's right. More than one. You'll see if you remain open to receiving them. But first you must give up. And I mean give up- relinquish go into yourself and exit through the other side. That's giving up."

Abby, "Whoa! Are you sure you're not a brujo, Juan? You sure seem like one."

Juan, "I cannot be a clown because I fall short of flying into the sun. And so far, I haven't made you laugh. I am a fraction too serious, and I know one cannot be serious at all to make people laugh. Everyone has a calling, and life teaches us what that is. Mine is here at the farm, experimenting with synergy and harmony in relation to the orchards and Fruit Flows. If insects invade my fruit trees, I respond to them by introducing a new bird, bees, or a new aroma. That's where my knowledge is focused. Yet I have experienced goosebumps and uncontrollable laughter when Jesús does his dance around the fire. Let us go to the Ponderosa building and see if the people are gathering."

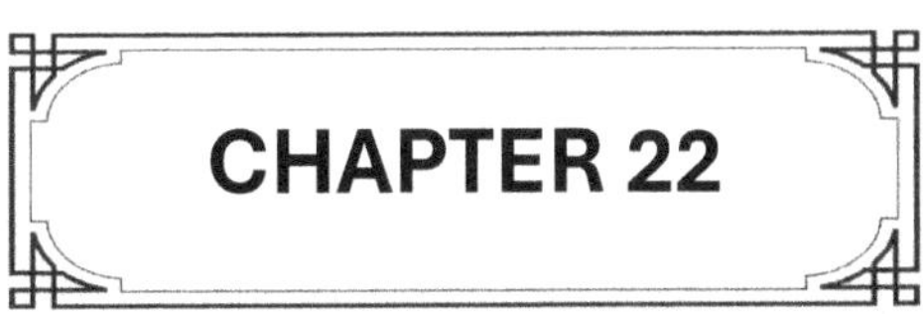

Juan, Pedro and Abby announced to the others on the porch where they were going. Carlos, Juanita, Roberto and Margarette were the only ones who followed. They heard calls from those remaining on the porch that they would join them later.

The seven together strolled across the dirt courtyard, past two large buildings and the research lab, and turned the corner at the Ponderosa.

It was dark, but many burning embers of cigarettes were seen as they approached the flames of the roaring fire.

Abby immediately focused on one of the pickers standing on the far end of the fire pit intently looking into the fire-and through it. From 20 yards away, Abby could see the flames flickering in his eyes. He was completely hypnotized by the dancing flames. Abby then saw his ragged Panama hat and recognized the fellow as not only the man who had spoken English to them in the jungle, but also the man they had seen again at the market in Callebocca. She was startled and this time recognized the goosebumps that instantly made an appearance over her entire body like a stigmata. She gasped and nudged Carlos to look. By this time. Juan and Pedro were chatting with a few fellows gathered at the fire's edge.

Abby then tugged at Pedro to get his attention. It worked, and Pedro put his arm around Abby and whispered, "Have you come ashore and found the cord?"

Abby, "Pedro, you are my ancient lover washed ashore yourself, and now we must tie the cord. But first, who is that man across from us staring into the fire?"

Pedro, "His name is Jesús, and if we are in the right realm tonight, we will witness him dance with the spirit of the fire."

Abby, "I know him-rather, we met in Callebocca. I told him I was looking for something-someone-and he told me not to ask, that he already knew."

Pedro, "Well, then, he does. Watch."

Jesús was barefoot. He had on a pair of jeans and a long- sleeved white peasant shirt, but it was filthy, like a khaki color, and not tucked into his pants. He moved like a black panther stalking a gazelle as he stepped into the fire, walking across the burning logs and charcoal embers. Everyone began to clap and hoot and holler.

Abby felt the goosebumps shivering down her spine, on her legs, and exiting out her toes. Then they reversed direction and left through the crown of her head. It was one of the most amazing sensations she had ever experienced, short of orgasm.

Jesús traveled the 8-foot diameter of the fire pit like it was the crater of an erupting volcano. He came out next to a group of pickers and then began to circle the pit, staggering and dragging both feet side by side, digging a trough, making an outline of the fire in the sand. He circled the fire many times, never taking his hypnotic, entrancing stare from the fire. It was as if he was having a staring contest with each dancing flame. Abby was watching the world's greatest ballet. Everyone continued to clap and chant, spurring Jesús on. He began to throw his arms into the air, thrashing at nothing or so Abby thought. He was actually gathering energy to move matter. Everyone stepped back. Jesús then began to strut like a rooster gathering his hens in the coop. It seemed so strange, looking at all the spectators beginning to laugh, even Carlos and Abby.

Jesús was now pecking at women's rumps to get their attention. The people began to scatter quickly as the women cackled and laughed. The men were holding their bellies in an uncontrollable cacophony of laughter.

Jesús was suddenly at Abby's feet, pecking her legs and nudging her crotch with his nose, then up to her belly and between her breasts, into her face, shouting. "Ugga-bugga," and shooting his arms in the air, spreading his fingers, outlining Abby's aura like it was an atmospheric garment and he was draping her in a spiritual tunic. The laughter was heard around the world.

Jesús was the funniest man on earth. But he stopped his shenanigans as quickly as he had begun them and stood face-to- face, nose-to-nose with Abby and stuck his tongue out revealing to her a stick of gum he had been chewing. More goosebumps for Abby. Ice cold shivers that made her insides warm.

He said to her, "Welcome back. I know where you've been, and you're not ready yet." Abby, "How do you know?" Jesús responded, "You ask too many questions. You must begin by listening." Abby, "Listening to what?" Jesús "There, you see? Another question. While you are listening, you must begin to see as well."

Abby, "What am I looking at?"

Jesús, "A most baffling question. I do not know. Why don't you tell me and that is not a question, it is a statement."

Abby, "Is this a battle of wits or something?"

Jesús, "Go away from me. You are not funny. Come back after you 'fix the leak' so you may capture some humor. You are dripping your guts all over my bare feet."

Pedro, Juan and Carlos observed this whole dialogue, and on Jesús last note to Abby, Juan cracked up laughing so hard he thought he was going to split his pants.

Juan said, "Oh, my god. Stop this or I'm going to pee myself. Go fix the leak." Jesús looked at Juan and said, "Well, I am glad to witness your sense of humor. Will you please teach your beautiful guest to stop looking and start laughing? She is leaking her spirit all over my feet."

Juan, "Yes, of course. She does need to lighten up a bit, don't you think?"

Abby. "This isn't funny."

Jesús, "There, that's very funny. You didn't preface that with a question."

Abby, losing control, said angrily, "Why don't you just go screw yourself? Don't you have anything better to do than ridicule an innocent bystander?"

Jesús, "Well, I'd love to screw myself. That would be a very funny act. And then I wouldn't need you."

Abby, "Oh, trust, me, you won't be screwin' me."

Jesús, "I already have. Did you enjoy the goosebumps?"

Juan, "Oh, Jesús, stop. I can't stop laughing. It hurts too much."

Pedro, "Yes, enough. Jesús, why don't you introduce yourself to Abby?"

Jesús, "Introductions have already been made, and now I am beginning to get to know this beautiful creature. We have shared gum together."

Abby, "I gave the gum to your friends and they swallowed it."

Jesús, "Yes, I know. They didn't like the Wrigley's spearmint. They prefer willow bark. It eases their pain. We traded gum by flapping our jaws."

Abby, "Yes, I guess we did, but you didn't have much to say."

Jesús, "Because I was allowing the jimson weed its turn to speak."

Abby, "I see."

Jesús, "It's about time."

Abby smiled, and Jesús said, "More. Give me more and perhaps I will give you something back."

Abby, "What do you mean?"

Jesús, "I am not mean. I am not even serious. Now, Juan, Juan is serious."

Abby laughed and said, "I don't know him that well yet."

Jesús, "That's funny."

Juan, "You guys get me going. You allow me to change and take leave of the serious side of me."

Jesús, "This is good and healthy for the soul. A lot of laughter will raise the spirits and make them dance in heaven's aisles. Miles and miles of aisles with angels lying on their sides laughing. When they stop, the storm is over and the sky becomes cloudless. That's when God has his big blue eyes on us."

Pedro, "What a funny metaphor, Jesús."

Jesús. "That's what it's for, laughter."

Abby thought it was quite profound that Jesús should show his gum to her. It was as if he was making a statement to her-and he was. He was saying, "I already know why you are here, but you are trying too hard, so I am just going to give you little signs and see what you do with them." Abby got the message. She figured out the first sign without asking a question. She got goosebumps because she was experiencing a sensation of pleasure. It tickled her own insides, and her heart was cooking.

Carlos approached Abby and whispered, "A penny for your thoughts. Where were you, trying to fill empty pockets full of wisdom?"

Abby, "Yes, I think so. Carlos, Jesús is a brujo."

Carlos, "You're kidding! Are you shittin' me?" Abby, "No. He is who I've been looking for, and now I don't want to lose him."

Jesús had turned his attention to Juan, Margarette, Pedro and Juanita. Roberto walked back to the main porch.

Abby, "So what do you think about this place, Carlos? Are you going to take the job and move here?" in?"

Carlos, "Absolutely. I'm home."

Abby, "I see you are hitting it off with Juanita."

Carlos, "She's nice and beautiful."

Abby. "She certainly is. Her skin is a lot like Pedro's."

Carlos, "What building do you think I should choose to live

Abby, "The one closest to the community kitchen."

Carlos, "Yeah, I guess that would make sense."

Pedro stepped over to Abby and Carlos. He entered their conversation with ease, like water flowing in a fountain. He spoke and his timing was perfect, sensing Carlos and Abby had reached a lull in their dialogue. "Well, what do you think of all of this? I know it is a lot for one night."

Carlos, "What do I do to commit to a job and be assigned my living quarters? Where do I sign?"

Pedro, "There's no signing anything. We do not have work contracts here. You simply perform. If we do not like your act, we'll try to change the stage. If you do not like the act, the stage is yours to take with you. You simply walk on this earth to attend. another performance."

Carlos, "Wow! I am so thankful!"

Pedro called for Juan and Margarette to come over and join them.

Jesús had already drifted over to another migration of energy.

Pedro told his mother and father of Carlos' intentions.

Juan said, "Welcome. You do know how to cook for 45 people or more, don't you?"

Carlos, "Yes, I've acquired experience along the way."

Margarette, "That's all it takes. You know we will hear from the others. The proof is in the pudding around here.

Why don't we put you up in the co-op building next to the kitchen."

Carlos, "Which one is that again?"

Margarette pointed to the building in the middle, next to the Ponderosa.

Carlos, "Looks like home to me."

"We'll show it to you tomorrow. Tonight you will stay in our house in the room next to Abby's," Margarette said.

The fire was crackling and spitting out sparks of hot embers.

Jesús was with another circle of friends when Pedro touched Abby's arm as she was gazing toward Jesús and said, "Shall we go tie the cord? I'd love to look into your eyes."

Abby, "Charming idea."

Pedro kept hold of her arm and walked her back to the main house. The others stayed by the dwindling fire.

Carlos found Juanita and started speaking with her.

Margarette and Juan were arm-in-arm, waltzing to a different drum, aglow in radiant love.

Pedro and Abby reached the porch. All the others who had remained on the porch were still there.

"We heard everyone's laughter all the way back here, and it made us laugh almost as hard." Pancho said.

Pedro, "Yeah. Well, you should have been there. Jesús cut loose and did his fire-spirit dance, strutting his stuff, pecking at the women. Father was on the ground in stitches."

Roberto and the rest of the people on the porch laughed.

Pedro, "I'm going to show Abby to her room and then come back out and join you."

Abby, "Well, maybe I want to stay and join in the fun."

Pedro, "Hey, great. Would you like a brandy or Kahlua, Abby?"

Abby, "Kahlua for me."

Pedro, "I'll be right back."

Pedro entered the house and came back two minutes later with two snifters in hand. They sat together with everyone else lined up on the porch, sitting on rails or in the twig furniture.

Nigel was puffing on a cigar and sitting on the top step leading down to the flagstone stepping stones. Pedro asked his friend for a toke of his half-smoked cigar. The mouth end was not soggy yet with Nigel's saliva. Pedro took a big puff and exhaled a cloud of smoke into the cloudless night. Abby watched it rise and dissipate in the heavens with the stars twinkling like a zillion diamonds-some as large as 200 carats.

Abby felt stoned, the way she'd felt when Jesús passed her the jimson weed. It was a contact high similar to a contact transmission. Abby lusted after Pedro, but, in fact, wanted Argos. She was excited to engage Pedro in her movie and regress in time-but not at this moment.

They sipped their drinks hoping to prolong their euphoria. The contract transmission could wait a little longer.

After Pedro exhaled his cigar smoke, he moved over to Abby's chaise and sat beside her. The cigar smoke he inhaled gave him a slight rush to the brain. He felt a little dizzy, but it passed quickly with his next couple of fresh breaths. Then he glanced into Abby's eyes and fell.

At the same time, Abby purposely blinked to prevent a transmission. Pedro found himself in and out in a split second. Abby didn't even have time to feel the titillation between her legs. Pedro was anxious for more and Abby knew it.

Abby, "Pedro, please tell me more about Jesús."

Pedro, "He is an enigma. Sometimes I think he is omni-present. He appears everywhere at the same time. He has taught us much, and I believe that because he is so humorous, he has taught me to take him with me wherever I go. Hence, I find him always in my thoughts. But I cannot teach you what he knows. This is not like Harvard or BU, where professors teach you what someone else taught them. Only Jesús can spread his knowledge--and only when he chooses."

Abby, "I find him so intriguing. I am drawn to him as I am to bamboo and oriental philosophy like Buddhism."

Pedro, "I can only advise you not to pester him or show admiration for what he is. He will catch you and then call it and throw you back like a rejected catfish on a fisherman's line. Once, when I was about 14, I was fascinated by his magic tricks. He would appear, then disappear in the orchards, right before my eyes or so I thought. He's quick. He knew what he was doing. He was enticing me because he saw into me and through me. One day he used a large mirror and set it up against an apricot tree, then stood back 20 feet. When I saw his reflection, he called to me to come to him. I went straight toward the mirror, confused by the reflection, and fell into a deep well. I didn't hurt myself, but I was scared senseless and couldn't get out. He stood at the rim of the well looking down at me, drenched, standing knee deep in muck, and laughed hysterically at me. He threw me a line and pulled me up to safety. He made me furious, and he simply said. 'Look at yourself,' and began laughing again. I looked at myself and laughed, too. He taught me to trust through practical application."

Abby. "Where's the trust in that lesson?"

Pedro, "I knew it was a mirror, but I didn't trust my instincts. I was enamored of his trickery and allowed him to perform it."

Abby, "I don't understand."

Pedro, "Of course not, because you question the obvious just as everyone does. He will show you the ropes, if and when he chooses, and teach you nothing. You must be prepared to expect the unexpected."

Abby, "I think I want to go to bed now. I know my way to my room. You don't have to show me."

Pedro, "All right. I will see you in the morning for coffee and huevos. Sweet dreams."

CHAPTER 23

With that, Abby floated back to her room, horny and wet. She decided to shower before bed. She stripped off her clothes, slipped into the robe hanging on a hook in her room, and walked down to the bathroom at the end of the hall. The bathroom was of gorgeous mosaic tile in a rainbow of colors. The shower stall was huge, with a bench in it and a copper watering can attached to the shower head, with a water spigot that, when filled, spilled over like a god pouring a never-ending bucket of rain. She adjusted the water temperature to be somewhere between tepid and hot. She could smell the freshly picked southern wood in a vase on the sink, and she began to think of her wet dream in Salem and the one in the clearing behind Pedro and Lolita's house. As she lathered herself and touched her body, she felt between her legs and dreamed of Argos making love to her. She was panting excitedly, standing under the watering can, using her finger as a penis. This was her favorite place to make a contract transmission when she was by herself. She had finally discovered how to do this through masturbation, and she had always thought masturbation was only for self-gratification.

Now she knew she could have a fantasy partner. So she entered herself and thought of Pedro standing there with her. She sat on the bench and spread her legs allowing her finger to work as Pedro's penis. She neared climax and wanted Pedro to please her. The thought of that stole her virginity once again as the fresh, new fantasy took her to orgasm. She had come a million times in one and did not want to let go. She whimpered and shivered as she withdrew her finger from her enchanted chalice.

"Ancient lovers entwine as one, and one becomes the other," she said out loud to the ghost of Argos and the silhouette of Pedro, who was standing as an apparition outside her shower curtain. She gasped and immediately pulled the curtain aside. He was gone, but Abby felt certain that Pedro had been there. He was not. From dream to reality.

She dried herself off, satisfied, and returned to her room, fell into her bed and entered her dream world once again.

CHAPTER 24

The fire was smoldering, nearly extinguished. Jesús and his audience disappeared to their own dwellings. Juan and Margarette had retired as well. That left Carlos and Juanita holding hands, sitting on a bale of hay. They were romantically connected. Carlos leaned closer to Juanita, bashfully wanting to kiss her, when Juanita took the initiative and deeply thrust her tongue down Carlos' throat. Carlos then laid her down on the straw and mounted her. Their bodies, not yet one, gyrated and pumped rhythmically against one another. His erection was poking her Levi'd crotch like a loaded .45 with its hammer cocked-but safely holstered. Juanita wanted to pull the trigger, so she aggressively reached down to Carlos' zipper and unleashed the weapon. He, in turn, followed suit and took down her Levi's, freeing one leg and leaving her panties and jeans on her left ankle. He finally was completely in her, and Juanita was moaning, swaying her hips like a pendulum sex toy. Carlos was shifting gears like Parnelli Jones in the Indy 500 reaching top speed in fifth gear, spinning his tires, burning rubber to the wheel rims and going nowhere except to erotic heaven.

Juanita, with her most sensuous voice, said, "NOW… give it to me."

Carlos delivered, spilling a trillion seeds into her corral of wonder. They held each other in a sexual pause, breathing together-lasting only minutes, but seemingly hours.

Juanita said, "You've added another brilliant star to the sky, and I've added a whole new constellation. I've just named it "The Brilliant Lights.""

Carlos, changing the subject for a moment, said, "You know, Juanita, I've accepted a job here, and I'm moving in tomorrow."

Juanita, "Well, I hope we can become great friends."

Carlos, "And lovers, too."

Juanita, "We'll have to see what the future holds. We've already gotten pretty close, you know."

Carlos, "Yes, for sure. And your parents are my boss."

Juanita, "So am I, and I'd hate to fire you."

"Whoa, slow down," he exclaimed as he withdrew his weapon and slipped it back into his jeans.

Juanita, "I just want to set the record straight. We all live here and work well together, so we must be communal in thought and actions looking after the prosperity and overall well-being of the farm and its inhabitants."

Carlos, "I agree."

Juanita reached down and patted his crotch, zipping Carlos' pants. Then she pulled her panties up and put her pants on and zipped herself up. The deed was done. They rose from the hay bale and looked up at the illuminating stars and mesmerizing constellation, now known as "The Brilliant Lights."

Their slate clean, they walked back to the house. Only Pedro was on the porch as Carlos and Juanita approached.

"Beautiful night," Pedro sighed.

"Never another one like it. Enjoy this one, my brother, for what it is," Juanita said, poking Carlos lovingly in the side.

Carlos, "Never another one like it-except maybe tomorrow night."

Pedro, "Bound to be different."

They all said goodnight and entered the house. Carlos went to the left, Pedro and his sister Juanita to the right.

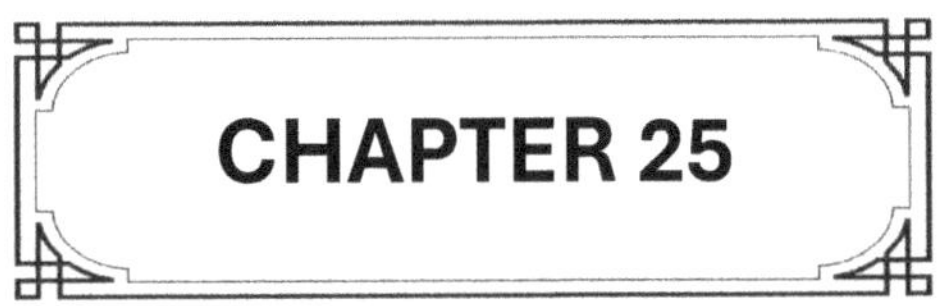

The next day dawned as the roosters crowed at the rising of the sun. Van Gogh once again must have painted the morning sky in the most brilliant colors of sunflowers and irises. Those who were up with the sun could pick a cloud, put it in a vase on the table and use it as if it were a flower arrangement.

While Abby showered again, Carlos knocked on the bathroom door. He had to pee real bad, so he cracked the door and asked if it was okay to come in. Abby heard his request and allowed him to enter. What's the difference, she thought to herself, we've already made love. I know what he's made of, and he certainly knows my pudding content.

Carlos sat on the john, a most peculiar mannerism for a man. Carlos didn't care. He preferred sitting while peeing simply because it was more comfortable and, besides, you could contain the spray within the bowl. Of course, he always stood at urinals in airports and soccer stadiums.

Abby purposefully took her time in the shower so that Carlos could finish his business and leave. She was thoroughly enjoying the artificial rainstorm once again splashing on her head and body. Finally, after Carlos had washed up, she heard him exit after shutting off the basin faucet.

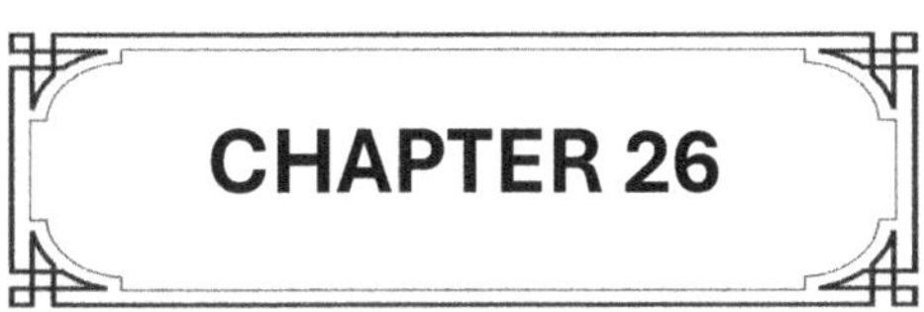

There was activity in the kitchen, and the aroma of Guatemalan coffee brewing in the enormous brass urn filled the house with its scent. Obviously, everyone drinks coffee all day long in Central America. Guatemala is one of the prime spots on earth for raising the brown bean that turns to gold upon harvesting. It was quite amazing that the Salvarezes didn't grow coffee beans on their farm, but then it would have been called a plantation. They preferred fruit trees and the title of "orchard farm." Their friends and closest neighbors had a coffee plantation. The Salvarez and the deVegas families swapped fruit for coffee.

By the time Abby was dressed, everyone was gathered in the kitchen sipping coffee and reminiscing about the night before, Jesús being the topic of conversation.

Carlos was at the counter cracking eggs into a large ceramic bowl and so began his employment on the Salvarez farm.

Pedro looked at Abby as she rounded the corner from the hallway into the grand kitchen. A contact transmission was instant as their eyes locked in on the target that they saw in each other's eyes. For a brief moment in time, Pedro became Argos kissing Abby as Felicia. It was their way of saying to each other, "Good morning, my love." Abby blew Pedro a kiss, and Pedro was brought back to the kitchen all the way from Rome and the year 17 BC. He said to himself: What a nice visit that was.

Abby said good morning to everyone and walked over to the brass urn where 10 perfectly thrown clay mugs were waiting to serve their purpose.

All objects have a function, and mugs are for coffee. Coffee is for drinking, and the mouth is for tasting, chewing, swallowing, speaking, blowing bubbles, smoking and kissing.

Everyone either helped themselves to breakfast or skipped it altogether and went out to the orchards. Carlos was informed about the buffet tradition. This morning, Juan and Margarette were going to orient Carlos to his new surroundings and duties. He was told that he would earn 2000 pesos a month, have two days of rest per week, and two weeks of vacation per year, full health benefits- as provided by Pedro-and meals. If he requested more time off, it was without pay, and arrangements had to be approved at least 30 days in advance through Juanita, unless it was a medical or family emergency. Also, he might be asked to pitch in around the farm when needed.

Juanita was acting as domestic supervisor and counselor. She helped those who had personal matters and took care of the general appearance and cleanliness of the family home.

Carlos accepted all obligations. He was shown to his furnished accommodations and allowed to get settled in. He moved his duffle bag from the house over to the co-op building. He loved his new digs. It was a basic bedroom, large enough for a bureau and wooden armchair, sink, mirror and toilet. Plumbing was modern and efficient on the farm, with absolutely no septic or drainage problems. This allowed them to have a toilet in each room. Shower stalls were poured concrete, very private, but in a communal setting. There were five stalls per building, with a large dry changing room in each stall. Showering was a celebration and ritual. Everyone either sang, whistled or laughed while showering. Respect of privacy was honored at all times. The shower room was considered the local public watering hole where people gathered, bathed, scrubbed their clothes and told stories. There was a washing machine with a ringer. Wer squeezed clothes were taken out back to air dry on the line.

Carlos felt he never had it better: freedom, a job with pay and benefits, room and board and someone he thought he might be in love with.

Now what was Abby going to do, he wondered.

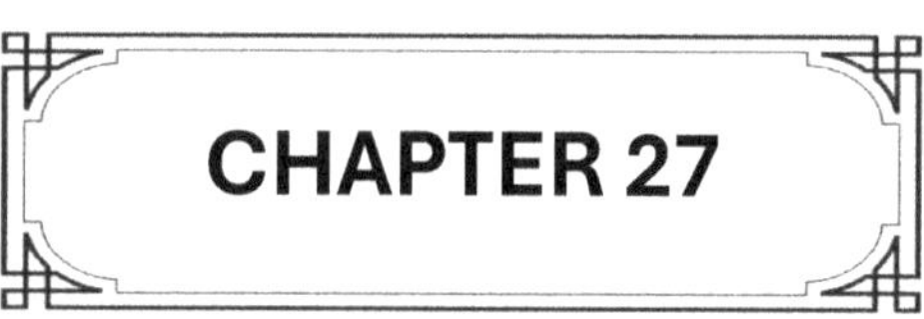

Abby had found her brujo, but he wasn't ready for her. She had more dues to pay, more time to pass, and experiences to gather. Most importantly, she had a leak to fix, but didn't know where to begin. By now, everyone was busy getting on with the day.

Pedro invited Abby to walk with him up and down the paths of the orchards. He wanted to see how the fruit trees were bearing "hi" and "bye" to all of the workers. and say

This was the time when the workers could ask him medical questions about this and that ailment plaguing them or their families.

One woman stopped Pedro and Abby and asked Pedro about her 14-year-old daughter, Penelope, who was having severe menstrual pain and excessive bleeding. Before he could answer, Jesús interjected from the top of an apricot tree, "She should take a potion of a combination of passion flower, wild yams, penny royal, golden seal and echinacea, grind them together with a mortar and pestle, bring it to a boil and drink it as a tea three times a day until her moon passes into the next phase of womanhood. I will go and gather these herbs and prepare the tea. Where is Penelope?"

The woman, "In her room in the Siesta building."

Jesús, "It shall be done immediately."

Pedro said, "Well, there you have it. You are in good hands."

"Gracias," Jesús said, "bueno."

Abby looked up into the tree where Jesús was, but couldn't see him. Suddenly, she realized he was behind her as he poked her gently in the back and said, "Gottcha, woman-who-asks-questions."

Abby, startled, spun around and asked, "How did you do that?"

Jesús, "There you are-here I am. Don't ask."

Abby, "There are no stupid questions, only stupid people who don't ask them."

Jesús, "But to truly understand the question in your mind is the answer. Therefore, you need not verbalize it, unless, of course, you are in danger."

Abby, "That's really stupid and no way to learn anything."

Jesús, "Ah, a statement without a question. You should feel better now."

Abby, "Yes, I do. How'd you know?"

Jesús, "I didn't. You just told me because you answered your own question, and that's exactly what I want you to practice doing. Don't ask me what to do. You already know. Don't ask me where to go. You already know. Ask me what this herb does, and I'll tell you to eat it and report back to me in a day. If you don't want to eat it, it must be a poison-twin, an impersonator, or a remedy you're not ready for."

Pedro, "Abby, he's offering you a sign. Can you read it?"

Abby, "What do you mean?"

Jesús, "Certain lessons require no explanation, only execution."

Abby, "All right. I read you loud and clear."

Pedro and Jesús couldn't stop laughing, and soon Abby and the woman were laughing, too.

Jesús, "Ah, at least you got the joke. Life is pretty funny, isn't it?"

Pedro and Abby walked back to the house to prepare for their departure, shaking their heads at their encounter with Jesús.

Jesús exited the orchard, too, and headed the other way to an open meadow. It was obvious he was going herb hunting. Herbs called to Jesús. You don't just go to the same herb patch and pick I yams as if they were parsley. This was a spiritual calling one must be attuned to. And it was most definitely not a religious conversation some zealot might have with a god conjured up in his own mind. Plants are real and tangible. Sometimes they beg to be picked for specific healings, not because they know what's ailing you, but because you passed by them. For example, perhaps you were in pain, brushed up against the needles of a thistle and instantly felt relief in your joints. For every herb, there is a modern drug. For every disease there is relief in medicine. Take too much of anything, and you can ultimately die, so you should be aware when on an herb gathering.

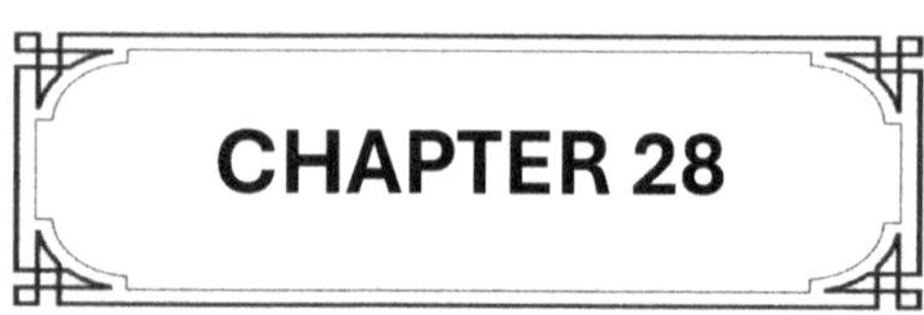

CHAPTER 28

Pedro and Abby stepped up onto the porch and entered the adobe abode.

Pedro told Margarette they were preparing to drive back to Callebocca, and he and his mother embraced. Margarette expressed pleasure at meeting Abby and said how she looked forward to Carlos' performance on their farm.

Abby bid adieu with gracious thanks and told Margarette how happy she was to have met her and the rest of Pedro's family.

Pedro then asked his mother where his father was, and she said, "Where else but in his lab."

Pedro, "Thanks, Madre. We'll see him on the way out and say good-bye to him."

Pedro and Abby headed to their separate rooms to gather their belongings.

Once Abby and Pedro had packed the Jeep, they walked across the driveway to Juan's lab. Juan gave Abby the grand tour, and she was in awe of his scientific equipment. Juan took his work quite seriously for an amateur, as evidenced by his volumes of texts. His focus was bees, flowers and insects, all pertinent to the continued fruition of their healthy orchards. He had done a superior job in dealing with the problems that had arisen from disease and infiltration of pesky insects invading their fruit blossoms, and had managed to protect the fruit itself. Suffice it to say, Juan's fruit trees were a thriving success for the family and all of its employees.

Abby and Pedro left the lab, waving good-bye to Juan.

As they drove away from the farm down the long and winding pebble road and approached the entrance gate to the farm--or exit gate, depending on which direction you were going--Jesús was perched on a rail eating something.

Pedro said, "Abby, look at that raven sitting there eating a mouse."

Abby couldn't believe her eyes. She blinked and realized Jesús was in her eyes, but the raven was in her view. She laughed and said, "That Jesús. I see what you mean about him being everywhere at once."

Pedro, "Did you just see him?"

Abby. "No, he just saw me. He cut right through me with his razor-sharp vision."

Pedro, "Wow."

Abby, "Pedro, will through the gate?" you stop the Jeep when you have passed.

Pedro, "Yes, of course. I'd love to go back in time."

Abby, "You knew."

Pedro, "Of course, because I didn't get to do it last night."

Pedro pulled over as soon as he could after leaving the farm property.

Abby got out of the Jeep and walked a short distance to a clearing. The sun was penetrating. Abby waved for Pedro to join her.

When she was ready, she took Pedro's face in her hands and lovingly turned it so that he faced her eye-to-eye. He went under quickly and deeply.

As Argos, he envisioned a time before the plague struck their village and before Artemus was born. It was, in fact, the conception of Artemus. Argos and Felicia were entwined as one. His one seed fertilized her one egg and conceived a DNA code that became Artemus, to be transported for centuries into the future and reunite once again as Carlos.

Pedro, as Argos, could see clearly the evidence of this as he actually went deeper into the plot of this movie in Abby's eyes. He saw Argos' parents' egg and seed uniting, fertilizing and conceiving him 25 years prior when they were in Greece. Then, in a flash, without blinking or stirring up a commotion that might bring him back to reality, he was projected 2000 years to his very own parents, Juan and Margarette, making love and conceiving him, Pedro. The DNA was planted that made up Pedro's entire being. He was so confused in this contact transmission that Abby became concerned because his breathing had become very labored. Jesús appeared before Abby's eyes. Pedro collapsed, prone in Abby's lap.

Abby said, "Jesús, what are you doing here?"

Jesús said, "I'm not here, you are."

Abby sensed danger just then, and shouted-with goosebumps "Help!"

From across the field, Jesús came running to the clearing near the Jeep. Abby took Pedro's pulse and felt nothing. She was afraid that Pedro was having a heart attack.

Jesús rolled Pedro over, lifted his eyelids, snapped his fingers in Pedro's face, then quickly took off Pedro's shoes and slapped the arches of his feet, then punched them like punching someone in the stomach, and finally pinched the joints of Pedro's big toe. Pedro instantly took a deep breath and groaned. He lay on his back smiling, eyes wide open. His heart was beating rapidly and felt like the pounding of war drums in his chest.

Abby said, "Pedro, you've had a heart attack."

Jesús interjected, "No, he didn't. His heart was attacking nothing, which is why he came back, because he wasn't welcome where he was headed. I saw where he was going. He's not ready for the next world."

Pedro, still smiling, said, "You two are a welcome sight."

Abby. "This is so freaky. What happened during your contact transmission?"

Pedro, "I saw it all. I witnessed my parents conceiving me, first as Argos, then as Pedro. I observed seed fertilizing egg, and then experienced my personality through my DNA code of, not only who, but what I was to become-an oar-maker for one-uniting with you, sharing our love, entwining as one. I saw my seed fertilize your egg when we were Argos and Felicia conceiving Artemus. I even saw the rest of his life, what he became, and his DNA decomposing at his death, becoming vapor and entering the DNA code that was to become Carlos. We were all made from other people. This is why the world today is so messed up and headed for self-destruction, annihilation, unless we come to grips about our origins and destinations. As a mass of humanity, we can all make a difference."

Jesús, "But we must begin with ourselves."

Pedro, "And I must return to my clinic and Lolita."

Abby, "And me-what about me?"

Jesús, "Oh, you poor lost soul. Look at the world's population and all of the lost souls, confused and up to no good, practicing evil ways. Each lost soul has the potential of being found. They are not lost. All they have to do is look inside themselves and then look outward at the world differently. If something doesn't work, change it. Move over a few feet. Change your position. Take a different stance and make a difference for the better. Pedro came back for the people as one medical soul who chooses to make a difference. I am not worldly. I have not traveled to foreign places. I do not read newspapers or watch TV. But neither am I an ostrich, sticking my head in the sand. I meditate, I am intuitive, and I love. Yet I do not know what meditation is-nor an ostrich, for that matter. I am simply a product of my environment. And we have just witnessed Pedro shifting gears, coming and going from one plane to another. Now I think he had an experience that made his mission clear."

Abby, "Hallelujah, Jesús. Where did that come from?"

Jesús, "From that raven sitting on the fence." Abby, "Man, you are too much for me." Jesús, "No I'm not. I'm not enough for you. You require too much. You need a jolt of something-or someone-other than me. You need a shift into altered states. You need to become that fence post to serve the raven as a resting place. Now you have purpose. 'Fix the leak.'"

Abby, "You know, Jesús, you just gave me something worth thinking about. If Pedro found the answer to the secret of life and shared it with us, then we need to spread it around like manure to fertilize the earth. We came from other people. Our parents are gods. Every parent is a god because they have created a being independent from others, yet dependent on their own DNA code which, in fact, came from someone else. We are all equals, every living creature on this earth. And if you believe in reincarnation, then being an animal in this life-without reason to think and deduce could perhaps account for evolution from the sea, losing the fins and gills, growing tails and lungs, wings and appendages. So can animals think for themselves because perhaps they used to be human and now simply cannot express themselves by spoken language? Or can they? Haven't the botanists and zoologists decided that every living organism has communication skills by using sounds, instincts and smell?"

Pedro, "Slow down. Let me take time to set a stable rhythm here."

Abby, "Oh, yes. How are you feeling?"

Pedro, "Better now, thanks to you two."

Jesús, "Timing is everything."

Abby, "You got that right. The wind blows and time ticks. and the sand drips through the hourglass, one grain at a time."

Jesús, "Time is the answer. It all depends on how you use it. It's not worth the time for me to spend philosophizing on where we came from when Penelope is calling for relief."

Abby, as though lost in time, said, "Everything you show me, Jesús, is a sign."

She looked over her shoulder, and Jesús was gone. Pedro began to sit up. Abby reached behind him to support his back. Now he was sitting upright on his own, holding Abby closely. She felt the warmth of his body and the normal rhythm of his heartbeat.

Ancient lovers entwined as one, and one became the other. Some other place, some other time. Perhaps they would again unite and entwine as one.

But first, each must swim their ocean and pray to be washed ashore and find their cord. After all, we all came from someone else. What makes who you are is not an original thought. The only thing original about you is what has been borrowed from the aborigines. We are all aberrations destined for doom on a reckless collision course unless we abolish all religion and become in tune with one focus, one goal, one mission: to be self-preserving. It may sound simple but impossible to achieve. It is never too late, but I don't see any one god taking steps on the right course.

Pedro broke their embrace and said, "Shall we carry on?"

Abby, "Of course. Why not?" She laughed and said, "We've got nothing keeping us here. Since we don't have to bury you, let's move on. Should we ask Jesús if he wants to join us?"

Pedro, "Ask him yourself. He's sitting in the back seat."

Abby quickly turned and saw Jesús sitting alone in the Jeep, laughing and pointing out the window at them.

Abby stood up and went running to greet him. There was no one there. She turned and shouted at Pedro, "He's gone."

Pedro, walking her way, "No, he's not. He's there because you wanted him there, and when I told you he was in the back seat. your mind pur him there."

Abby, "I think I've had too many head games played on me."

Pedro, "Signs for the learning. I grew up with Jesús, and certain inspirations eventually rub off on you. People are created from other people. Life is contagious, should you choose to spread your seed. Lolita and I decided not to have children because we both feel our lives are complete this time around and chose not to spread our seed so we could focus on us and what we have chosen to do with our lives."

Abby, "So you're saying that according to the inspiration and state of mind of the individual, we all have the potential to transcend?"

Pedro, "Yeah, sort of. You have to be devoted to a certain way of things to be able to accomplish a direction, the right course. Stumbling blocks and dilemmas in life will make us want to shift tracks and possibly derail. Focus and devotion are the keys."

Abby, "All right. Let me work with that one for a while and let it sink in."

Pedro, "If you want that jolt Jesús was talking about, we'll come back here someday and I'll ask Jesús to prepare a vision sweat for you."

Abby, "What's that?"

Pedro, "You'll see. Nothing more for now. Will you please drive? I need to rest."

"Yes, of course," Abby said, as she slid into the driver's seat of the Jeep.

Pedro reached into the back seat and retrieved two cold bottles of water from the cooler. He handed one to Abby and then gave her directions, signs to follow to get them to Callebocca. Road markings were vague, and there was not much warning before the turns they had to make. The roads were rutty, always appearing to be under construction, but there never seemed to be anyone working on them. Road crews in Guatemala were practically nonexistent, and the crews there were usually assigned to road work in the cities, and Callebocca did not qualify.

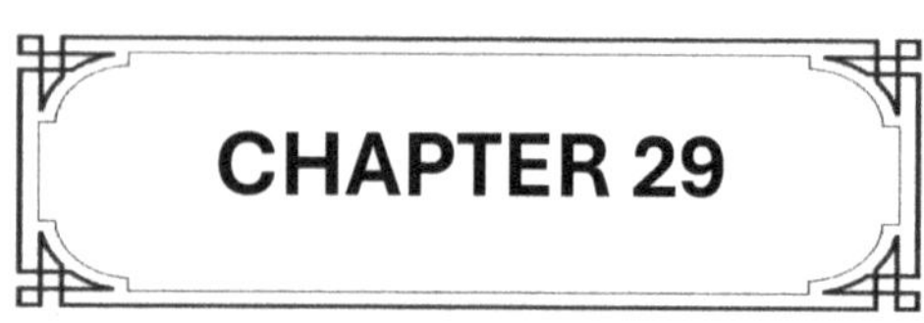

The drive was rather uneventful for Abby. Pedro slept the whole 2-1/2 hours. The only redeeming value for Abby was the scenery: green and brown jungle, open meadows and pastures with no livestock, tall groves of giant bamboo, banana groves. Locals walked on the fringes of either the forest or the road.

Abby's bladder was ready to burst, or at least she felt ready to overflow, so she finally pulled over to relieve herself in a thicket near the road. Pedro awoke and had to do the same thing.

When they got back in the Jeep, Pedro exclaimed what a restful nap he had had. Then he informed Abby that they were just 20 minutes from home.

He then asked Abby to take the next left-hand turn coming up shortly. She did, and then asked where they were going.

Pedro, "Your savior lives here. My good friend, Fidel, who drove you, unconscious, to my clinic after your accident."

Abby, "Well, this ought to be interesting."

Pedro, "I think you'll like Fidel. I've known him my entire life. He's a thinker and an explorer of animism. He has written books on his findings and thoughts from the experiences he has absorbed from other people's ways. He's taken their influences and inspirations and constructed foundations and pillars in his mind to erect pyramids of new thoughts."

Abby. "Wow! You have such a way with words."

Pedro, "Just an expression of wind-bad air looking for a way out. My words travel on CO2, an exhaustion of gas. Our vehicles pass gas in the form of carbon monoxide. We pass gas out our ass, but it's not lethal... except for the smell."

That comment brought Abby to tears of laughter.

It was a long, winding driveway to Fidel's, like the one approaching the Salvarez farm. And sure enough, at the bend up ahead, they saw a large timber entry announcing the name of Fidel's establishment. It read "Phantom Fantasy," and it was made of welded steel that hung suspended under a horizontal timber, resting on two vertical timbers spanning 30 feet or so.

Before them stood a rustic dwelling made of bamboo with a thatched roof. It looked sturdy enough, but it also looked like something from the "Three Little Pigs" fairy tale which, more than likely, neither Pedro nor Fidel would know about.

Abby asked, "Do you think he's home? Should I honk the horn?"

Pedro, "No, dear god! Never blow the horn unless something is wrong. There are more peaceful, polite ways to get someone's attention. If he is home, he's either meditating, reading, cooking. drinking, working in the garden or doing all of those things at once or he's traveling to some exotic place. Just park over there to the side by his Land Rover. That's the vehicle he transported you in."

Abby, "Well, well, well. Nice."

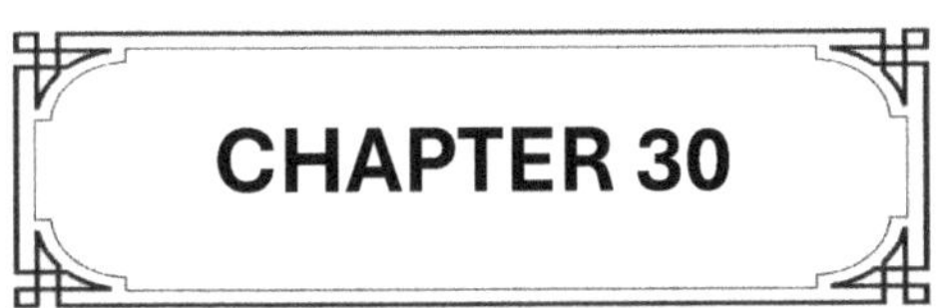

CHAPTER 30

Fidel pushed open the screen door, walked onto the porch, and showed his gorgeous white teeth with a beaming smile.

"Pedro, my friend, come in and bring your beautiful friend."

Pedro got out of the car and approached Fidel, who stepped down the four steps from the porch. Abby, too, was exiting, but slower. She wanted to observe the men greeting each other. She saw four arms and hands stretched high into the air, and then around Pedro's and Fidel's backs. They held their embrace until Abby slowly stepped closer to them. They broke the friendship lock, and Fidel said, "I remember you. Pedro helped me carry you from my back seat into his clinic. I guess you didn't die-or did, and my good friend put his whammy medicine on you and brought you back."

Pedro, "Fidel, this is Abby. And, no, she did not die. She was in a coma and suffered a broken leg. She came out of the coma in five days, and I took the cast off last week."

Fidel, "That must have been some crash. I never saw the wreckage, and, of course, I wouldn't read about it because there is no newspaper here. Word travels by mouth and tales ger twisted. Sometimes up in smoke-literally."

Abby, "Well, I guess I owe you my life, Fidel. It's nice to meet another of my saviors." Fidel, "Your life as wife or servant? I'm looking for both. All in one would be ideal."

Fidel held nothing back. There was nothing to hide. He was bold, forward, aggressive, gregarious, charming and immediately likable, with a sparkling charisma. But most of all, Abby thought, he was drop-dead Latin-American gorgeous, with short coal black hair, slightly disheveled, and the blackest of black eyes. He stood 6 feet tall and weighed a lean 200 pounds, but looked to be built like Charles Atlas.

Abby was instantly in love. Her thoughts ran to Stephan for a brief moment, whom she'd felt was her one and only soulmate, and then recalled what Juan had suggested, that a person could have more than one soulmate. Abby reached in her back pocket and subconsciously felt for Stephan. She was reassured of his spirit and remembered reaching for Stephan while making love to Carlos and then explaining to him how she had captured Stephan's last exhale and put the vapors in her back pocket. This seemed to make everything Abby did all right, not a betrayal. She was allowed to love again.

Abby didn't answer the question Fidel had posed with words. She focused her eyes at him and answered with a contact transmission.

Fidel, "You have quite the piercers there, Abby."

Abby, "What are 'piercers'?"

Fidel. "The gateway to floods of beauty."

Pedro, "Your eyes, Abby, you know, those eyes you carry around in your head."

Fidel, "Yes. Even my feet see where they are going."

Abby, "Well, that's quite the concept."

Fidel, "There are certain cultures which speak with their eyes, and all poets write of 'piercers' being the 'doors of perception.'"

Abby, "Did you know that's how The Doors got their name? Jim Morrison admired William Blake and read that in one of the passages he wrote while tripping on LSD and thought that would make a great name for his band, The Doors."

Fidel, "I love The Doors. I saw them once in L.A. at the Whiskey A Go-Go when I attended U.C.L.A. in 1966.

Abby, "You went to U.C.L.A and Pedro went to Harvard. I'm surrounded by a bunch of educated hippies."

Pedro, "So... time passes and the belly of the hourglass is filling with sand. Now there's less on top and more on the bottom. Seems as though the pinch in the funnel is allowing more than one grain of sand to pass at a time as we get older."

Fidel, "Great metaphor, Pedro. Hey, let's go inside and cool off and get drunk!"

Abby, "You have air conditioning?"

Fidel, "No, I have fans and yucca nectar."

Pedro, "Oh, no. Did you brew another batch of that hallucinogen?"

Fidel, "Always. I try never to run out. But if you are afraid of seeing yourself, don't swallow. Just rinse it around and spit it out. That way, you'll only frighten yourself a little."

Abby, "Very funny. What is this stuff?"

Fidel, "It's what the mountain men in the Ozarks might call 'white lightning' or in Appalachia, 'moonshine'. In Guatemala, it's called 'jungle rot'. It's potent and packs a wallop. I have beer if you'd like."

Abby, "That might be more refreshing for now."

Pedro, "Yeah, and for me, too, Fidel."

Fidel, "I shall return."

When they went into Fidel's house, Abby saw that it was no hovel the way it appeared from the outside. Things change when you penetrate the membrane and get past the cover. His living room was huge and the walls were floor length windows overlooking rolling meadows and the jungle off in the distance. The furniture was bamboo and wicker with thick fluffy down cushions. The abstract geometric-design area rugs adorned the floor space in the foyer and living area. To the west side of the living room was a large open kitchen with a connecting dining area and a nook for sitting casually and having breakfast or lunch. The ceiling was 12 feet high, with open rafters made from 80-foot giant black bamboo at least six inches in diameter.

Abby, standing in the middle of the living room with Pedro, watched this gorgeous hunk of a man go to the refrigerator and walk back with three bottles of beer in his hand.

Abby, "Quite the place you have here, Fidel. I have this tremendous affinity for bamboo, and it appears you do, too."

Fidel, handing a bottle to Abby, then Pedro. "Oh, yes. And I shopped for those beauties to make this fort of mine."

Abby, "Oh, where? China, Japan?

Fidel, "Nope. I found most of it locally. I even helped cut some of it down."

Pedro, "So what's your latest project,

Fidel?" Fidel, "Does Abby know much of what I do?"

Pedro, "I gave her an abbreviated version as we were coming up the driveway."

Fidel, "Well, Abby, I like going to places where there are no motor vehicles or very few. That's one of my criteria. Then I get to know the natives of these rare, sparcely-located villages and hopefully get invited to live with them for a month-or two, or three. I become one of them. We commune with animism. I take nothing out but memories. No people, no wampum, no heads, no souvenirs, just memories that I take home with me. Then I write about my adventures and get them published. Most of the time. National Geographic will buy my stories for top dollar. I do all of the photography in the last week I'm there, so those images are all that are removed, along with the memories. There was a magazine called The Laughing Man which bought many of my stories. At any rate, Pedro, right now I'm trying to get into the Yanamma people in the Amazon, or the Yaquis in northern Mexico. I like the 'psycho-tropics' in both places. It's not like I apply to visit these places and gain admittance, Abby. I meditate on a place, sometimes for months in advance, to set the spiritual stage which allows the chief, shaman or medicine man to receive my messages. Sort of like a first-timer who begins to work out rigorously so he can hike the Grand Canyon a year before he is scheduled to go there. Then, when I feel the time is right, I simply appear at the geographic location and allow myself to be discovered and hopefully escorted into the village. I present myself as a single leaf posing no threat to the rest of the tree, and that way I blend right in. And I always carry empty pockets full of wisdom-no weapons or threatening objects."

Abby, "Where did you hear that phrase you just spoke, 'empty pockets full of wisdom"?"

Fidel. "Oh, that's something I always heard my father say. He was an archeologist and read it on a tombstone as an epitaph, or in some script he always talked about from ancient times. I forget now. I believe there was this journal-or perhaps a manuscript- from pre-Christ that was found in Rome and donated to some Guatemalan museum. The guy who found it was on a dig with my father. There's nothing really that significant about it except some phrases that sort of stick in your gut. When the museum was destroyed by an earthquake in the '40s, my father was asked to come help salvage what he could from the rubble. They gave him that journal as a gift, although it was in such disrepair that it was barely legible. The only thing you could make out was that phrase, 'empty pockets full of wisdom', and the brief episode of an encounter with what appeared to be a family dying from the plague. It was written in Greek."

Pedro, "Oh, my God! Do you still have those Fidel? What did your father do with them?"

Fidel, "They were burned in a fire. I've told you everything practically verbatim. My father used to read us those few passages when my sister and I were young. The parchment it was written on was like delicate fabric. My father kept the few pages in individually hermetically sealed acrylic wrappings, and he was the only person allowed to touch the three or four pages. A real shame they got lost in the fire. But I do remember certain other passages about the man dying of high fever, dehydration and delirium because he talked about losing his stomach-and meeting his wife on some foreign shore.

It was obviously documented by her after his passing because it was written about a woman tending to her dying husband and infant son who she had to raise alone. She seemed to be quoting him about reincarnation and that the two were destined to reunite and entwine, but she had to trust and believe this would someday happen. I believe my father took liberties and embellished a bit, because he rambled on longer than it would take to read four pages. 'Empty pockets full of wisdom' was my most favorite line, though."

Abby, "Oh, Pedro, can you believe this?"

Fidel, "What's up? Why is this significant to you two? Tell me!"

Pedro, "We know that line, too. I said it to Abby when she was recovering in my clinic. She said she knew where it came from. Then this friend of hers, Abby's traveling companion, Carlos, said it to me, and..."

Abby, "Tell him about the movie in my eyes."

Pedro told Fidel the entire saga from beginning to end, including 'ancient lovers entwine as one, and one becomes the other, and about being washed ashore only to find the cord and plug their past lives into the present.

Pedro continued, "Abby refers to this movie in her eyes as contact transmissions. Fidel, you won't believe this, but I am that man who died of the plague in Rome. I was known then as Argos. Abby was my wife, Felicia, and her traveling friend, Carlos, was our son, known as Artemus."

Fidel, "And you can verify this from this movie you see playing in Abby's eyes?"

Pedro, "Yes."

Fidel, "Abby, may I try to see this movie?"

Abby, "Yes. Come, let's sit over here and I'll get myself ready."

The three went over to the large bamboo sofa and Abby and Fidel sat, as Pedro watched.

Abby looked down at the rug, turned quickly to face Fidel. and stared intensely into his eyes. He felt something, but it was beauty, not a movie. He saw extraordinary beauty in Abby's eyes which he had not acknowledged earlier when first meeting her. He continued to fall, but not into a designated movie set of ancient times. He was falling in love because Abby programmed her eyes for this.

Fidel blinked and turned away. It was over. Nothing happened--except something happened. A fire of passion was built, although no contact transmission occurred. It wasn't right. Perhaps it wasn't meant to be. Timing is everything, and the wind changes direction. Fidel's DNA code given to him at his conception from his godly parents did not travel from the same air currents and weather patterns as that of Argos, Felicia and Artemus. The rarity of this connection was literally beyond belief.

Pedro wanted a go at it so that Fidel might be able to witness the trance he'd fall into, but Abby did not cooperate because of Pedro's recent heart attack. Pedro had already forgotten about it and now knew Abby was correct and therefore respected her denying him a contact transmission.

"Some other time," Fidel offered.

"Yes, some other place," Abby added.

Fidel, "Oh! Those two phrases combined form one of the things my father quoted from those pages. 'Some other place, some other time. What an amazing coincidence."

Pedro, "Truly unbelievable. Ever since I looked into Abby's eyes and watched this movie featuring our past lives which we now experience as totally different people, I've been mesmerized, spellbound."

Fidel, "Do you know where all of this leads? What it indicates to me is perhaps an explanation of deja vu. And it certainly supports the theory of reincarnation or, even more, the existence of past lives."

Abby, "It could possibly make our current lives a little easier, perhaps, by realizing that we all come from our parents and that they came from their parents and it's what we call 'family trees," our ancestors. Realizing this as fact and then accepting this premise, people ought to be more civil toward one another since all of us are ultimately related."

Pedro, "Sounds like the incarnation of an old religion revamped for modern times."

Fidel, "Yeah, just another way to look at origins and evolution."

Abby, "It definitely calls for conjecture. So, the benefit we get from it is selfish in value. Pedro and Carlos have contact transmissions that revert them back to past lives that they can view in my eyes as a movie. So what?"

Pedro, "You've got a point, but as you said earlier, this may have greater humanitarian value than we think, if we can get it out to people."

Fidel, "Like how? Write books about it? Produce a movie? Start a cult?"

Abby, "Yeah. Those are good questions, too. But I don't have the drive, the desire, the ambition or the motivation to become a female Jesus Christ."

Pedro, "Maybe you already are. Isn't this what we're talking about, the existence of being? Didn't Jesus walk and preach because he was playing out a role he felt compelled to do because he was communicating with God, the Father, and the Holy Ghost?"

Fidel, "What about the 'primitives' who have no contact with the outside world or organized religion? What about their piercings, the 'eyes of perception? What about the 'people with knowledge, the brujos, shaman and medicine men?"

Pedro, "Well, it's possible they could be experiencing contact transmissions as well. It's just not recognized or documented as such. Yet, because Abby, Carlos and I have actually gone back in time, I, for one, feel like a different person. My world has changed. My perceptions are different. My attitudes are clearly more identifiable and therefore vulnerable to adjustment. It's all beginning to make sense to me now. I feel like I've had that jolt Jesús said you needed, Abby, that 'altered state' experience. You know the saying, 'You have to talk the talk and walk the walk? Well, I believe Jesús is the guy-a guy who walks his talk. He's never even seen TV before. He's never studied the Bible, and probably has never been to church, though he sort of knows there was a person at one time called Jesus Christ. Jesús supported the upbringing of me and my brothers and sisters with many beliefs, many gods for all occasions and for what ails you. So when the missionaries recently came to our country and attempted to shove Christianity down our throats like a sacrament, mother and father were polite and sent them on their way. They couldn't swallow this Christ wafer and follow the missionaries to church. Earth is church to my parents, and that's what they taught us," Pedro concluded.

Abby, "How old do you think Jesús is?"

Pedro, "As old as Christ. If he could produce a contact transmission on you, Abby, he'd probably show you a movie starring you as the Virgin Mary."

Abby, "There's a thought."

Pedro, "Well, you don't possibly think you're the only one who can do a contact transmission, do you?"

Abby, "No, of course not. Life is plagiarism. Quotes all came from someone else."

Fidel, "Exactly. And that's why I think the 'people with knowledge' have these supposed contact transmissions, as you call them. We also call them 'flashbacks.' I think TV and the news media have corrupted the morals of anyone who watches it, and it also desensitizes us and makes our intuitions and gut instincts dull and numb. This is why we cannot perceive individual thought."

Abby, "Can we perhaps change the subject and move on to more personal matters?"

All three took sips from their beers and gazed out Fidel's windows at the panoramic view of meadows and jungle, the bamboo within reach from the porch rail.

Pedro, "This is a good time to break and hold that thought because we've got to get going back home, Abby, unless, of course, Fidel wants to give you a ride home later if you would like to stay."

Fidel, "Why not? I'd love to get to know you better, Abby. I gave you a ride once before, but you were rather speechless."

Abby, "Well, sure. I'd be all right hanging out here for a while, maybe have some of that yucca nectar."

Fidel, "I've got some. Pedro, is your phone working?"

Pedro, "I don't know. It was two days ago when we left to go to the family's house."

Fidel, "We had a hell of a storm that night and some of my neighbors were out of power, but I wasn't here."

Pedro, "Oh, really? I'll call you to let you know when I get home."

Fidel, "Great. I'll walk you to your car."

Abby, "I'll come out and get my bag. Pedro, are you all right to drive now?"

Pedro, "Oh, sure, Abby. I wouldn't suggest it otherwise."

The three left the house and walked over to the Jeep. Pedro opened the back door and retrieved Abby's bag. Then he got in the driver's seat and said good-bye. Abby and Fidel were standing there waving, as Pedro left for home.

Then Fidel offered to show Abby the grounds.

Fidel, "I love walking around my property and working on it as ! go. It's a therapeutic meditation for me, kind of like tai-chi in motion in progress in sync."

Abby, "Have you been to China?"

Fidel, "Yes, I lived in Szechuan for three months and took tai- chi with a master there. Talk about intrinsic energy! This guy taught me so much."

Abby. "So lead the way. I'm all yours."

Fidel, "Oh, don't tempt me."

Abby, "At what, a tai-chi challenge?"

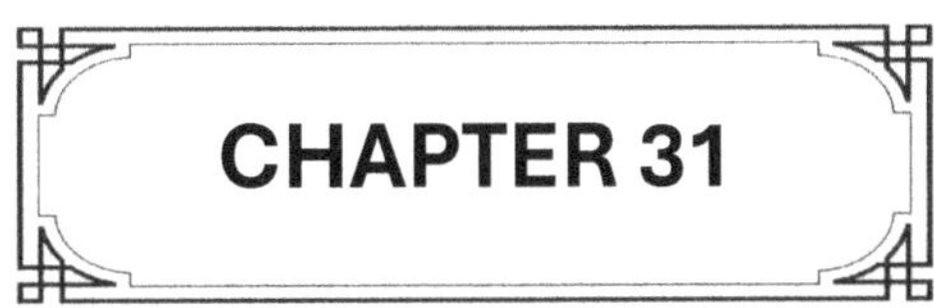

Fidel and Abby were off and roaming. Fidel had put much time and labor into the enchanting landscape surrounding his house. The path behind it led them to an area of neatly trimmed and groomed bamboo. At the far end of this was a zen rock garden with sculpted sand flowing like a river, with a gong hanging under a gazebo which looked like a pagoda.

Fidel invited Abby to sculpt in the garden. She added her own flair and moved two rocks. Fidel thanked her and said he liked to come out here once a day to change the position of the rocks and follow the Tao in doing so. Abby commented on how their philosophies, readings and habits paralleled one another. Then she walked under the gazebo, picked up the huge mallet, padded on one end, and banged the gong as if she was hitting a home run. The sound reverberated into infinity as both of them paused following the waves to the same endless destination. It was like emptying the mind of clutter, traveling on a sound wave a myriad of miles from the source. One wave to infinity, each time the gong was rung, and back again, always remaining in the present. It was a peaceful interlude Abby and Fidel shared together.

When the sound reached its destination, they were right back where they started, and the sound was somewhere out in space. They both exhaled with the same "ahh."

The path of mowed grass led them to a pond surrounded by tall cattails and saw grass. Water lilies were floating on the surface. The pond was only 30 feet across, but it offered another realm of tranquility. Bullfrogs were croaking as the sun was near setting. The sky was producing a pallet of colors found only in an artist's eyes to be captured on canvas.

Abby could feel the colors on her skin as goosebumps appeared. She knew she wasn't experiencing fear, so she must be in the presence of a pleasurable sensation.

Without a word, Fidel moved close behind Abby and wrapped his arms around her, dangling them across her breasts with his hands resting on her abdomen. She swayed, tugging at his elbows allowing her hands to glide down his forearms. He was pressed up against her. She placed her hands around his and moved them behind her, leading their way directly to his crotch. She spoke softly, "Listen to the sound of that gong kissing the sun good- night, and the sun making love with the horizon producing those orgasmic colors. It's no wonder the great painters saw something different, and the poets wrote to a different sound."

Reaching behind her, she circled Fidel's erection, then broke away, and pivoted to face him, raised herself up on her toes and kissed him with pent-up passion. The kiss lasted long enough for the sound of the gong to circle infinity and come back ringing in their ears. Fidel held on to Abby, and she held on to him.

She whispered in his ear, "Did you hear that? Perhaps we should go back to the house."

Fidel, "First, let's circle around the long way and complete the walk."

They rounded the corner through a grape trellis and came upon a beautiful black slate pool, 50 feet long, 6 feet wide and 4 feet deep. Abby slipped out of her clothes and dove into the water. It was dusk and her naked body slithered like an eel cutting the water without a ripple.

Fidel stripped and stood on the edge of the pool, marveling at her beautiful wet naked form. Abby rolled onto her back and floated motionless, studying Fidel's nakedness.

Fidel dove forward like Johnny Weismueller and brushed beneath Abby. He surfaced behind her, standing chest deep in the water and carried Abby, as he floated her loose and relaxed body to the far end of the pool where there was an underwater bench. He used it to prop himself up as he sat Abby up on the pool's edge. He then nibbled her earlobe, slurped on her neck, and slid down to her right nipple where he stopped and suckled. Then he used his tongue to slice her open right down the middle of her linea alba and paused at her belly button where he tongued her for an erotic moment. His left middle finger had been inside her since he had moved down past Abby's nipple. Abby slowly leaned back, elbows propping her up like a tripod so she could watch his head as he satisfied her. Abby gave way to a moan, the likes of which could raise a dead man from the grave. Fidel was a true Latin lover, and Abby had never felt like this before. He treated her like silk on velvet. Abby was in ecstasy-and Stephan was in her back pocket at the opposite end of the pool. Abby had no sense but the She gently pressed her hands on his head and cupped it between her legs. Then she lifted him up to her belly. She did a yoga move, like a sexual asana, and suddenly Fidel was on top of her kissing her lips and delivering some of her own juices to the back of her throat. He entered her gently, grinding his pelvis with hers. present.

Ancient lovers entwine as one, and one becomes the other.

Abby did a move that Fidel had never experienced before but that Abby had performed on Stephan. Her timing was perfect. She had already come many times during cunnilingus and she wanted Fidel to come during fellatio. She felt Fidel's energy reaching climax, and with a gentle pushing move, withdrew him from her and guided his penis up to her mouth as she slid down to meet him. He didn't lose a beat as he then delivered his own cocktail to the back of Abby's throat. She was stroking him at the base of his penis as she took his whole shaft into her mouth. She loved Happy Hour that way. Fidel was on all fours when he pulled out of Abby's mouth, rolled to the side of her and collapsed. She swallowed all but a thimbleful and kissed Fidel spilling that ounce of serum into his own mouth so that he could taste his own love juice. They shared a kiss and he swallowed.

Night had fallen and so did Fidel. He was limp a as Abby reached down and caressed him like a newborn mink. This was the best sex either of them had ever had, and they knew it without having to say a word. Abby had found another soulmate. Juan was right. You cannot go through life wearing blinders, thinking each person on earth has only one suitable mate. There are many, and the likelihood of finding just one is most probable, two is even easier if you lose one. If you thought that one was your designated soulmate and found out you were wrong, well, then, there was bound to be a second, third or fourth.

Fidel and Abby lay side by side in the dark, but their hearts, the darkest place of all, deep in the chest, shined like two brilliant lights that radiated illumination through their eyes at each other. They could see in the dark, guided brightly by love's lamp.

Abby stood and dove into the pool, drifting half the length underwater. Fidel quickly followed and was beside her before she surfaced. He gently nudged her as she stood in the water. Then he surfaced. They swam to the opposite end of the pool where they had left their clothes, climbed out and then air-dried before dressing.

Fidel invited Abby to dinner and to spend the night. She accepted on both counts.

When they returned to the house, Abby telephoned Pedro, as the phones were working, and told him her plan for the night, but more or less posed it as a question, not looking for permission, but more acceptance and approval. Pedro sounded thrilled for both of them because he never thought this would happen when he had left them standing together in the driveway two hours before. Hed just assumed he was doing the right thing because Abby seemed so enthralled with Fidel.

The dinner Fidel prepared was simple and delicious. The wine was like the blood of Christ as they both sipped the red sacrament.

After the leisurely dinner, Fidel invited Abby upstairs and led the way to his bedroom. They stripped and lay on top of the mattress of his king-sized bamboo bed.

Abby, "Fidel, have you ever been married?"

Fidel, "Nope, never found the right woman. And besides, I my freedom and independence too much to give them up."

Abby, "But you could keep all of that and share it if she were willing to share what she brought to the marriage table, couldn't you?"

Fidel, "Yes. But it has never jelled like that, so I wasn't about to jump into a relationship just for the thrill of falling without a safety net."

Abby, "Hmm, I see."

Fidel, "I have been with many women around the globe, and most of them just for the sex. I'd stay for a month or two, do tantra yoga with whomever was willing, and when the play was over, the curtain would fall and I'd come home. But I can assure you, never have I experienced the kind of lovemaking we did out there at the pool. Where'd you learn that?"

Abby, "Pure raw instinct and the drive of passion to please the man I'm with. I'm not promiscuous, but I love a good romp in the hay with the right man. I never cheated on Stephan, which means I never had an affair. But I was dating two other guys at the same time Stephan and I were dating. When I was at B.U., I had a number of lovers. I learned to satisfy them from a Swedish lover I chose when we were juniors. He was free-willed and taught me how to pleasure a man by allowing me to openly explore him. He was a handsome blonde, to say the least, and a good teacher. I was a meticulous scrutinizer and chose my lovers with zen-ful discretion. They all had to show that they had spirit."

As she was speaking softly to Fidel, she was stroking his manhood and, in between words, was licking his belly button. She mounted his totem, sticking it straight up into her and rode him like she was riding a Brahma bull in a rodeo-but in slow motion. Fidel reached back and grabbed onto two vertical bamboo poles that made up part of the headboard of his bed. He was the bull, but no one was being bucked off. Abby began to slide forward and backward, instead of moving up and down, and their juices provided lubrication. Her sensual female wiggle brought Fidel to screams of passion as he shouted, "I'm coming." And Abby laid it on him to glorious climax. She had been continually coming for many minutes. The romantic act done, she lay on his panting. sweaty chest and sighed, totally satisfied.

Abby had met her match, both in bed and out. So had Fidel. They did not need to talk about this confirmation yet. They didn't need to talk of the love they felt. Abby and Fidel knew intuitively that this sense of pleasure would leave them both with goosebumps like they'd never had before.

They fell asleep in each other's arms but didn't wake that way. Abby was spread-eagled, belly down, and Fidel was curled up in a fetal position facing Abby's backside.

It was well past dawn and the sun was just cresting the tops of the bamboo right outside his bedroom windows. They began to stir at the same time. Abby rolled toward Fidel, and Fidel slowly opened his eyes and was bestowed with her early morning beauty.

He rolled over close to Abby's face and whispered in her ear,

"Do you want to brush your teeth and shower with me?"

Abby, "I do every morning."

Fidel, "So you'll accept my proposal?"

Abby, "For life."

Fidel, "Because of life."

Abby, "Let's begin ours now."

Fidel, "Do you always talk in metaphors and riddles?"

Abby, "Only when the moment calls for it. I know you weren't asking me to marry you, but I also know you're looking. So the opportunity was just right for word play."

Fidel, "Well, let's get to it and savor the moment."

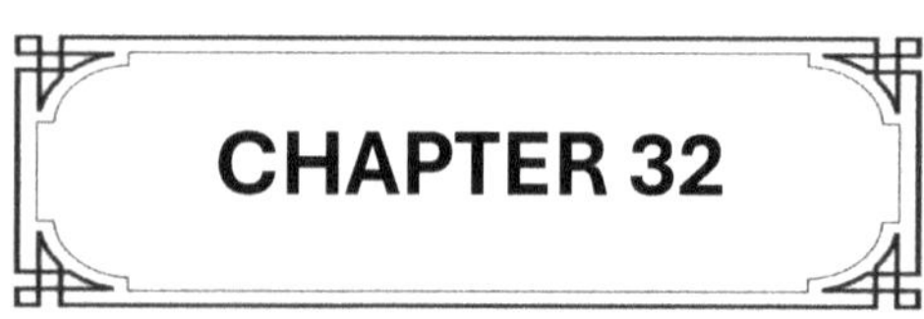

CHAPTER 32

Fidel rolled out of bed on his side, and Abby rose from hers.

Fidel's bathroom was huge, with mosaic tile everywhere, double sinks with brass fittings, a sliding glass door leading to a small observation platform overlooking the tops of the bamboo, and a wraparound shower stall that looked and felt like you were walking into the center of a conch shell. He called it his "Nautilus." The stall, too, was lined in mosaic tile, and the shower head was as round as one of van Gogh's sunflowers and released a spray that was both powerful and pelting. They brushed their teeth side by side at the sinks and then entered Nautilus.

Abby and Fidel stood under the sunflower and laughed and played with each other, lathering every inch of each other's body. Fidel embraced Abby and whispered in her ear, "I love every muscle in your body- especially mine! I'd like to have you for breakfast." And on that note, Fidel slowly licked his way down to Abby's fruit. She reached up to the shower head, spread her legs, and held on while Fidel finished his cocktail. She was delicious.

They didn't make love-they were in love. Fidel turned the sunflower waterfall off and led Abby out of the Nautilus. Coffee was in order.

After they dried off and dressed, Fidel went downstairs and prepared some fine-smelling Guatemalan coffee, their favorite.

Abby wandered around the living room, pulling books from shelves, reading the titles and pushing them back in place. She discovered three photo books by Fidel Hernandez and looked through them. They were stunning, beautiful photographs of people of the Far East, including some with animals and waterfalls from all around the world. One pictorial book was dedicated to manhole covers from nearly every city in the world. Each depicted an amazing design made of steel of a special weave, usually identifying the city's name. The book had won an award for creativity and uniqueness. It was titled, Manhole Covers of the World.

Abby asked Fidel what his last name was.

Fidel said, "Hernandez. You found them. Those three are my award-winning trophies. One bought me this land, one the house, and one the pool and 'Voyager,' my wonderful vehicle."

Abby, "Quite nice. You struck it rich as a shutterbug."

Fidel, "No, with my eye. It all depends on how you look at it when taking pictures or even taking a hike.

The beauty remains in the eye of the beholder. Nothing in nature is ugly." Abby put the picture books back and strolled over to the kitchen counter to get her first cup of coffee of the day. "

What would you like to do today,

Abby?" Fidel asked. "Hang out with me? Go to Pedro and Lolita's? Go sightseeing with me in my safari buggy?"

Abby, "What's the safari buggy?"

Fidel, "It's what I use for local transportation and special trips in Central and South America for photo shoots. It's the Voyager I mentioned."

Abby, "Let's see it."

Fidel, "Okay, in a while. Now it's time for coffee and a croissant on the deck."

Fidel carried a bamboo tray with two cups of coffee, two croissants, butter and jelly out onto the deck which stood about five feet off the ground. He set the tray down on a table and offered Abby a seat. They sat on wicker furniture while sipping coffee and tasting bites of the delicious croissants with boysenberry jelly.

The sun was beginning to sizzle, roasting their skin to a crisp brown, but not Kentucky Fried Chicken brown; more like the golden brown of a pancake from the Waffle House.

It was already hot-around 108 degrees with a 98% humidity by 11 a.m. Abby said she thought they should either get under some shade, indoors, or under some fans-or naked in the pool.

Fidel had another idea. He wanted to take Abby for a ride in Voyager. He loved naming his possessions like his h Phantom Fantasy, and the shower, Nautilus. So after co led Abby by the hand through the house, down the from the porch, across the dirt driveway and of lush, long, verdant grass. It felt so sensual on Abby's ankles. Her measured by her sexual barometer which covered every skin, inside and out, and it had become activated at birth. S this erotic sensation from her contact transmission with she knew she had it in her early teens during masturbation

(Author's note: I guess everyone has it-it just de what you do with it, how you perceive things, and the evolution of the maturity with time, like a grape ripening on a vine.)

Abby nurtured her visions, daydreams and wet dreams her wisdom, education and experiences of growing up. college, her sexual exploitations when she was single, refinement when she was married to Stephan. Stephan dead now for three months, but Abby still carried his spirit in her back pocket. She always would.

Fidel slid the huge barn door on its track to reveal Voz the rest of the barn. He kept a tractor-mower over on along with many hand tools which hung in their place wall. Voyager was a very special vehicle. Abby had never seen like it except maybe in videos of African safaris. The tires were massive and jacked the body of Voyager at least five fee ground. Solid steel rails were specially mounted below t as steps to assist in climbing up to the cab. There was a where three people could sit abreast and a pass-thru window so that one could access the open-air flatbed with high stee hold onto. In the center of the flatbed, there was a custom-made tripod for a camera that could swivel 360 degrees like an tank. On the back of the cab, on both sides of the p windows, were steel cabinets, the tops of which were for while standing. It was all so clear to Abby, the simplicity and efficiency of Fidel's vehicle, and helped explain why he was so successful at his trade, his passion, his love of exploring, writing, meeting natives and, of course, his photography.

Fidel explained that he had driven Voyager all over Mexico, Central America and South America. He said, "Hop in."

Abby, "This is quite the rig. Did you design it?"

Fidel, "Yep, and Ford built it in Korea."

Abby, "Figures. American-made, but not built. Built in a foreign country."

Fidel, "It is the way of the future. Pretty soon we will be one- with-all, no borders, no boundaries, bridges spanning the oceans, and one supreme dictator. I would have voted for Jim Morrison as our leader, and Dylan Thomas as the global social chairman."

Abby, "I didn't think they had elections in a dictatorship."

Fidel, "You're right. It's the winner of the war who appoints himself. It's also called 'utopia,' which means it will never happen."

Abby, "Yeah, whatever. I remain a conscientious objector, objecting to nothing and accepting my own conscience."

Fidel, "A good way to be. Shall we proceed and see if this of gal can propel us?"

Abby, "Onward. Mush!"

Fidel, "Maybe I'll take you to Alaska."

Abby, "In what, a photo book?"

Fidel, "I haven't visited Alaska yet, but I will."

Fidel cranked over the engine with a flick of the wrist and a turn of the key. It roared to 5,000 r.p.m.'s, then idled at 900, purring like a tiger. He dropped the automatic transmission into drive, and they began to roll out of the barn and down the driveway.

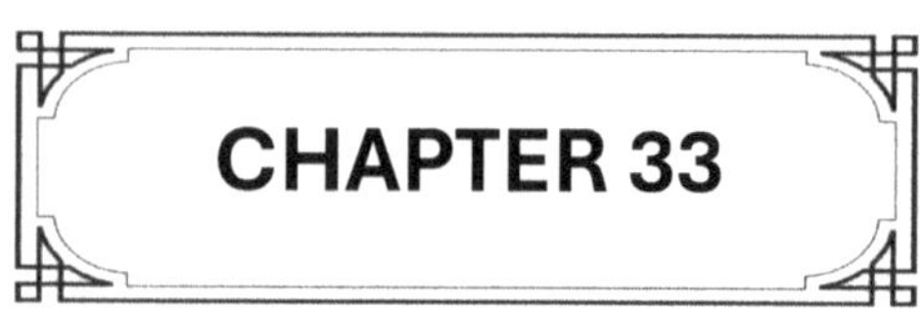

Within minutes, Fidel and Abby were cruising north on the paved main road. North was where Abby and Pedro had come from yesterday when they left the Salvarez farm. Abby felt as though she was going back there, but just when she was going to ask, Fidel turned around and was heading south.

Voyager was doing about 55 miles an hour when Abby recognized the driveway to Pedro and Lolita's house.

"I want to see my friends," Fidel said with passion, hitting the brakes.

"Fine with me," Abby said happily.

As Voyager came to rest, Pedro came walking out the kitchen door to greet them with open arms. Abby took the two steps down to the ground and hugged Pedro with love that he wore on his skin.

Fidel came around Voyager, and, too, hugged Pedro, slapping him on the back.

"Come in, my friends. Lolita is at the clinic," Pedro informed them.

He offered them drinks, but neither of them wanted one. They retired to the open courtyard.

Pedro asked, "Abby, may I go in?"

Abby said, "With Fidel here?"

Pedro, "Absolutely."

They arranged themselves in the appropriate positions.

As Fidel watched with interest, Abby closed her eyes, facing Pedro. When she opened them, her stare was entrancing, and Pedro was gone. Fidel studied both of them intently and tried to see and feel what Pedro was experiencing. Fidel felt nothing, so he comfortably sat back and simply observed.

This time, Pedro was gone for 15 minutes--an extended contact transmission. He was seen to smile, moan and groan. Finally, he twitched, as if he were having an epileptic seizure, and came out of the trance into the present, exclaiming, "Wow!"

He related, excitedly, "I became Argos and, Abby, you were Felicia. We were young and in love. Artemus wasn't even born yet. We were in our hovel in Rome. I had just come home from the open-air market by the sea where I had hand-carved oars for the big fishing boats. I had sold four that day and wanted to celebrate with you. We had some potent elixir in a jug, and I poured you some. Within minutes, we were feeling very happy and making love. As the movie reels played in your eyes, I became my own sperm and was, in fact, the individual swimmer who broke your membrane and penetrated your egg. Meaning, I saw how Artemus was conceived by watching the movie. Then I whispered something into Felicia's ear, and I heard what I said. I said, 'Uppa da nuva.' And then I said, 'I love inventing words and feelings. Some are invisible and some you cannot touch. Felicia, I pray you get big in the belly.' Then I heard Felicia say back to me, 'Your seed is in my belly. If I do not have my moon, we will have a baby.' We lay there naked, elated and daydreaming. It was such a marvelous feeling," Pedro said contentedly.

Fidel, "That was quite something to experience, but couldn't you just be making that up?"

Abby, "Not with me showing the movie."

Fidel, "But you can't verify any of Pedro's viewings, can you?"

Abby, "Only by our wavelengths that are on the same circuit. It can only be broached by explaining a deja vu which, in essence, can't be explained, like goosebumps brought on by fear or sensual pleasure opposites with the same physical results. It just is."

Fidel, "Then why can't I have a contact transmission looking into your eyes?"

Abby, "You just answered your own question, Fidel, about belief and the truth from Pedro's viewing. The reason you can't is because we're on different circuits. We have no past to connect us to the future. Pedro, Carlos and I are old souls reunited through a DNA exchange that occurred upon the deaths of Felicia, Argos and Artemus, and the conception of we three from our parents who breathed in the ancient exhalations of Argos, Felicia and Artemus' last breaths which have been traveling on the air currents and in the weather patterns waiting for those exact moments of orgasms during our parents' lovemaking."

Fidel, "Now, there's something for the medical books."

Pedro, "Well, I'm a doctor, and this certainly baffles me and my medical knowledge. All I can tell you is Carlos, Abby and ! have shared common past lives, and I do not mean reincarnation. We are who we are today, but looking into Abby's eyes is just like watching a movie starring us as other people in a past life. It's bizarre, isn't it? And what good does it do us now?"

Abby, "It's entertainment, like going to the theater, The Theater of All Possibilities."

Fidel, "How do I find a person to give me a contact transmission?"

Abby, "You don't-it's based on pure coincidence. Nothing can be predicted by looking into the future. There's no crystal ball, only energy waves of vapor, clouds and matter. And sometimes rarely when the currents are perfectly aligned, a breath is taken by two people and they become one. 'Ancient lovers entwined as one, and one becomes the other.' just like what you heard your father read to you from that ancient journal he was given. It's a shame it was lost in the fire, up in smoke. But would that offer something more believable than this?"

Fidel, "I guess it's all in the mind and how we perceive through our experiences."

Abby, "Exactly. And that's why I need to be around Jesús more. He knows by not knowing."

Pedro, "That's why we refer to them as 'the people with knowledge' on the farm."

Fidel, "Abby, you met Jesús at the Salvarez farm?"

Abby, "Yeah, a couple of days ago, and the day before that Carlos and I bumped into him in the jungle and then in Callebocca."

Fidel, "He gets around, doesn't he? A most interesting character."

Abby, "Yeah, a key character on this earthly theater of life's real play."

Fidel. "Pedro and I used to follow him around mesmerized. with his tricks and shenanigans. We'd lose him in the orchards, then realize he had doubled back somehow and was following us! He spooked us many times and gave us goosebumps of enlightenment with his laughter. He taught us one exercise I will never forget, to use our hands as our eyes and to see by feeling. He was referring to judging people by touch and using intuitive feelings."

Abby, "Let's go see him again."

Fidel, "No, you don't go looking for him. He'll disappear. You mustn't be in desire. It will backfire on you, and you may never see him again."

Abby. "Pedro's mother told me the same thing."

Fidel, "Then believe... and trust."

Abby, "All right. Sooner or later one of us must know who's been left behind, when you go your way and I go mine."

Fidel, "Bob Dylan has 'empty pockets full of wisdom.'"

Abby, "That's right. So you're a Dylan fan, too, as well as The Doors?"

Fidel, "Seen 'em all in L.A. in the mid-'60s when I was in college there."

Pedro, "I was so much older then. I'm younger than that now."

Abby, "You, too?" **

Pedro, "Yep. Influences paved the way in Cambridge and on hallowed Harvard pathways."

Abby, "Wow! I'm surrounded by open doors and windows."

Fidel, "Hey, should we all go for a ride?"

Pedro, "Would love to, but can't. Got my lovely wife at the clinic and must go to work. Work, remember that? My love of labor is like your bug for aperture openings."

Fidel, "All right, then. Abby, let's hit the road."

Abby, "You're on. But eventually I need to talk to Pedro and Lolita about some sort of work."

Fidel and Abby left the house. Pedro walked them out to the drive. He got into his car and went north. Fidel and Abby hopped into Voyager and headed south toward Callebocca.

Within 30 minutes, Fidel drove past the spot in the jungle where Abby had stopped to let Carlos into a contact transmission. She pointed it out to Fidel, and he mentioned the exact fire pit and sitting area as a common gathering place for Jesús and the "invisible people." He said, "The invisible people are the elusive ones who live and roam freely in the jungle. Some believe they don't exist because they've never seen them, only signs of their existence. Jesús grew up with them and returns to the small tribes when he senses the draw to be with them. They exchange energies, thereby acquiring each other's thoughts and knowledge. That's why they call them 'the people with knowledge.'"

And so Fidel passed by the place where Abby had stopped, and Abby peered into the jungle for a sign. She saw only bamboo and banana trees, but she dreamed of that time when she and Carlos smoked the jimson weed with Jesús and the invisible people.

Fidel asked Abby if anything peculiar happened, and she told him of Jesus' comments about asking someone for knowledge and how dangerous that might be.

Fidel concurred. "Don't go looking for it. The people with knowledge know what you want, but will only offer it when the time is right. If you ask for it, they think you are trying to steal something from their spirit."

Abby, "I guess I must respect that because I've already heard it more than once. In fact, Jesús told me to go and 'fix the leak.' What do you think he meant by that?"

Fidel, "Did he, by chance, suggest you ask too many questions?"

Abby, "Well, yes. But how else am I to learn?"

Fidel, "Listen, simply listen to the exchange of languages in the wind. Each creature communicates by means of sounds, vibrations and perceptions. Of all the places I have been and the cultures I have lived with, Americans ask the most ridiculous questions. They even write proverbs and children's books about curiosity and how it killed the cat. Curiosity kills everything when it turns to poison. Don't be curious for selfish reasons; be curious for the well-being of others. Learn through your mistakes. No animal ever asked a question. They stalk, they crawl, they fly, they swim, they burrow because of instinct. It's what the brujo lives by, and it's how the ancient martial art form of tai-chi was conceived by the observation of animals at play and in danger. Interpretation is the key to understanding, and when you don't understand the striking movement of a preying mantis attacking a grasshopper, mimic the interpretation and the answer will become clear to you."

Abby, "So wise. You remind me of Pedro's father."

Fidel, "Ah, yes. He is quite the man, and that was quite the compliment you just paid me. Do you know what Juan taught me the most about people? Be more kind to people; do better things for others now. He used to repeat that to Pedro and me over and over. And that's why he and Margarette have such a successful farm and also why their workers stay with them-sometimes for life-raising their kids there and eventually dying there. It is just because they are sincerely kind to others. And look at what Pedro has given back to his surrounding community. Kindness is contagious."

Abby paused and contemplated what he had said while Fidel drove through the outskirts of Callebocca.

He parked Voyager and led Abby by the hand down some back streets and alleys into a cantina full of boisterous characters, all telling stories-and not one question asked amongst them. Abby paid close attention to the conversations, although not intending to eavesdrop, and thus began her practice of "fixing the leak."

Fidel led Abby to the bar, and there sitting at a corner table next to the end of the bar was Jesús smoking a hand-rolled cigar with the same two guys Abby and Carlos had met in the jungle. "

He does get around, doesn't he?" Abby whispered in Fidel's ear, then stuck her tongue into it and licked deep to his eardrum, drooling on his anvil.

Fidel silently slipped his hand between Abby's legs and up into her crotch to serve as a thank you.

Fidel ordered two cervezas and two shots of Patron Tequila.

Suddenly, Jesús was sitting beside Abby laughing hysterically. He said, "Are you there? Did you get it?" Then quickly followed with. "Don't answer-it's really not a question. The leak is not fixed yet. You are still wet from the well. You will not be able to contain what I have to give you if you don't fix the leak."

Fidel, "Yo, Jesús, you're here!"

Jesús, "Si, here--there-and everywhere. Your friend here needs to learn some manners. She asks too many questions. She's got a mouth like a turtle."

Fidel, "I know, but she loves to swim."

Jesús, "Which accounts for her wetness, hence the leaks. Be like a pool and hold the wetness in. It is your internal lubricant. Use it only between your legs when you want to ride the bull."

Fidel and Jesús practically fell off their stools, drunk with laughter.

"She needs to hang out on a fence post to dry," Fidel interjected.

Abby went to slap Jesús violently, but he caught her hand aimed at his face, sobered, and looked into Abby's eyes and said, "! know who is in there. Now come out and play. I didn't mean to insult you. You took my joke too seriously because it hit home. Every living creature mates, so do not be ashamed or bashful. Play with Fidel and Carlos, too, for that matter. Play with me, if you choose. Just remember, I have a choice, too. Life is a game of finding a mate, then mating, and all along the way is playfulness. Do not take anything too seriously, except death. That's why I respect life so much because death is the beginning of another arena we know nothing about unless you can look into the past through someone else's eyes."

Abby, "Oh, my God! What did you just say? I mean, if I heard you right, how did you know that?"

Jesús, "My friend, you are not the only one with eyes. Look into mine."

Abby did, and she fell. She had a contact transmission and saw a movie playing in Jesús' eyes featuring Abby as a courtesan in Venice, Italy, 400 years ago. She was deep into a trance. She was easy and vulnerable. She watched-stared-with intensity as she saw herself seducing a nobleman, ravishingly eating at his manhood. She heard herself ask the prince what he wanted her to do, and then she saw the prince thrust her off from his privates, beating her, and then pulling his sword from his sheath. He yelled, "I have told you to stop asking such ridiculous questions. You know what to do, whore, but you will never get another chance," as he slit her throat and she collapsed in her own pool of blood.

Abby violently twitched and jerked herself out of the trance, blinking and gasping for air. She was instantly alert and in the present, shaking her head and looking at Jesús. Her hand was on her own throat.

Jesús, "Now you got it. You are there. Keep practicing. We will have another time, but not in my eyes. I just wanted you to know others have eyes of perception as well."

Abby, "I got it. You sent me back in time. I was someone else asking too many questions. I should stop and think it through before asking the ridiculously obvious."

Jesús, "That's right. Drink your tequila."

Fidel said, "Good lesson, yes? Jesús is always right on at showing people their stuff, like looking into a mirror."

Abby, "He certainly got my attention."

Jesús got up from his barstool and slapped Abby and Fidel on their backs and said adios with a wave. He left the cantina with his two friends. Abby and Fidel remained seated at the bar sipping their mind-altering nectars. They remained silent. Everyone else in the cantina was loud, with much laughter and joke-telling.

When they finished their drinks, they both felt the need to stretch and so left the cantina.

Fidel wrapped his arm around Abby's waist, and she did the same around his. They pushed through the saloon doors like John Wayne and Barbara Stanwick leaving the Lone Butte Saloon in Cerillos, New Mexico.

Now the day belonged to them.

Abby was quite taken aback by Jesús' comment about "all creatures mate. Don't be ashamed or bashful. Instead, be playful."

Did he mean infidelity runs rampant? Did he suggest I be promiscuous with anyone I wanted?

Fidel spoke as if he had been reading her mind. "Discretion is an art form, and that's what Jesús was referring to when he said all living creatures mate. But first there must be courting, then foreplay. But only after the selection of a mate is mutual is there an attraction. You just don't mate randomly."

Abby, "How did you know that's what I was thinking?"

Fidel, "How could I not? It was the most blatantly obvious statement Jesús made that could only lead to ridiculous questions. Why ask if you already know the answer?" Fidel theorized while they walked down the street toward where Voyager was parked.

Abby paused, stopping Fidel in his tracks and looked up into the sky. There on a rooftop was Jesús walking on the edge looking down at Abby and Fidel with his arms spread as if he was about to leap-or fly away.

She exclaimed, "Fidel, look, it's Jesús!"

Fidel looked up to where Abby was pointing and a huge raven swooped from the roof's edge downward directly toward them, then flapped its wide wings and took off straight up. "One of Jesús' masterful tricks, to be seen as a bird. Look up ahead of us. There he is on the corner with his friends. You placed him up there because you were looking into the sun and thinking of him. You wanted that raven to be Jesús so you turned it into his persona. Sort of like how we often see look-a-likes that remind us of someone," Fidel said, comforting Abby.

Abby laughed. Fidel laughed. And as they passed by Jesús, he simply tipped his ragged Panama hat and said, "Buenos dias... go fix the leak." They all laughed, and as Abby and Fidel walked away, Jesús' laughter drifted into the sky, and a breeze blew over Abby that felt like swooping, flapping wings of the raven they had just seen. Then there was nothing. The air was still.

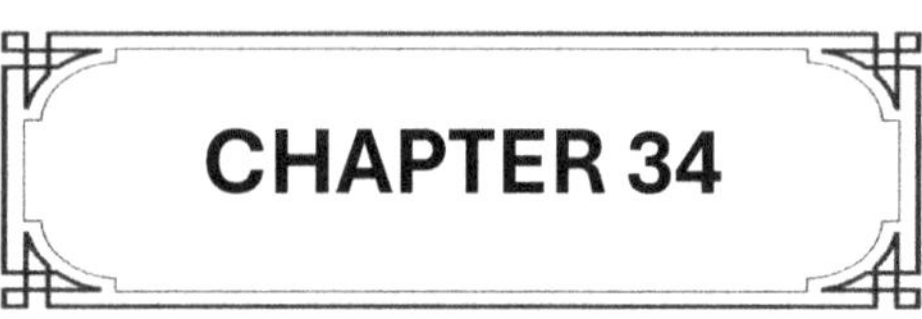

They boarded Voyager, left Callebocca and headed due east to the Caribbean where Fidel knew of a certain cove where they could swim.

They drove about 15 minutes to what was known as Escondido Cove. Fidel pulled off the main road and parked in some old tire tracks that went into the brush.

They walked together smelling the sea air like a fresh aphrodisiac.

"How do you know so much of what I am thinking, Fidel?" Abby asked innocently.

"Because I apprenticed with Jesús and Juan years ago. Jesús taught Pedro and me how to analyze the question in your mind before asking it, then how to answer it from within. If there is no answer, don't ask. If you don't know the answer, then know how to ask the question. When you ask someone what they do, do you want to know 'who they are or 'what' they are? It's like asking, 'How did you get here?' Don't ask--think it through. I was born, and I appeared here. The rest of who I am will be revealed in conversation if you take the time to get to know me and if I allow it. Truth is revealed like waves on an ocean, like mercury in a thermometer, like rain in clouds. Only if the clouds open will rain fall. We all have clouds inside our minds. It is through the eyes that rain falls--as in tears-- and that's how the salty oceans were formed."

Abby, "I've heard that before. Pedro told me that when I was crying in his arms at his clinic over the loss of my husband, Stephan. He said, 'Go ahead, let it out, cry over the loss of That's how the oceans were formed."

Fidel, "And Jesús taught us because someone taught him. All of life is plagiarism. You just hand the knowledge down to children and they grow wiser. So who started creation? A moot question, isn't it? One that really shouldn't be asked because from this type of thinking centuries ago came false answers which gave way to empires of religion, all based on conjecture, and that is no answer at all. Therefore, the question shouldn't have ever been asked and the idea of God would not have been invented."

Abby, "Fidel, let's soak in that tidal pool I see up ahead."

Fidel led Abby over the dune and onto the smooth, wet, slippery rock ledge that formed natural steps down into a deep tidal pool. It was peak high tide, the calm before the transition to low tide. They stripped off their clothes and carefully did tai-chi gracefully sliding into the water. Soft, mossy seaweed clung to the steps. At the bottom, they stood together embracing and kissing deeply. Fidel's penis was pressed between Abby's legs. The bottom of the pool was slippery, but they managed to keep their footing. Fidel turned Abby around and guided her over to lay on the top step with several inches of sea water at her back. He thought, Abby could charm the oyster right out of its shell. He mounted her and she groaned, taking all of him in, and they made waves of orgasms as the tide changed and the top step was drained of its lubricant.

They breathed deeply together, panting their steamy love breaths.

Abby knew Stephan was in the back pocket of her clothes left just a few feet from her sea of love.

Fidel withdrew and lay back into the tidal pool. Abby joined him and whispered in his ear, "That's how waves are made."

"From the sea came creation, and then came evolution. As long as we cry, the oceans will rise and fall," Fidel chanted.

They carefully exited the tidal pool. The full moon was rising and was gently tugging at the tide, pulling the water back like a comforter being kicked off a bed by two pairs of legs. They stood naked, air drying their bodies in the moonlight. Abby spread her arms wide and did a pirouette on the balls of her feet. Fidel bent over and pulled his pants up. Once they were dressed, they sat on the dune overlooking the sea. The last rays of sun glowed on their backs.

Fidel said, out loud, what he was seeing in the sunset. "People of greatness who have never been heard are those who are the people with knowledge, as well as the invisible people, and many, many more who have much to say and have never been heard. They live quietly, sometimes mute and sometimes loud, and they move silently, sometimes in tribes and sometimes alone."

Fidel and Abby walked on their path of love back to Voyager, illuminated now by the rising moon.

Once they were on their way, Abby let go a great sigh and said, "Fidel, you are one great Latin lover. The past couple of months have certainly made my head spin. You just happened to have saved my life by transporting me to Pedro's after the accident. It's now May, and it seems like life itself has so much to offer."

Fidel smiled, focused on driving at dusk and said, "Thank you. I guess I learned my lesson properly from Jesús, by putting my eyes in my hands and seeing by feeling. I love touching you that way, Abby.

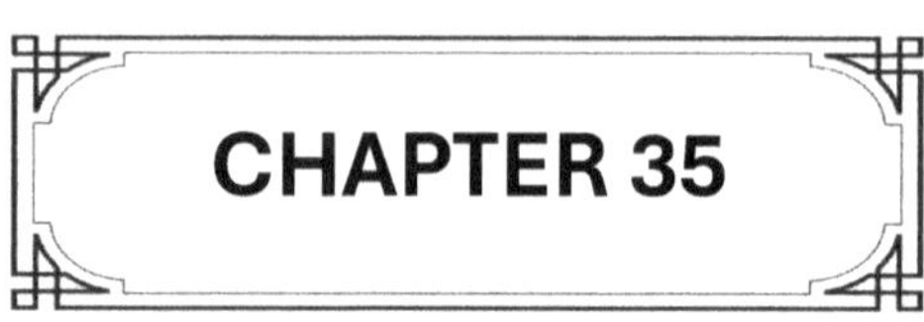

CHAPTER 35

Within an hour, Fidel and Abby were back at Phantom Fantasy, and Fidel parked Voyager back in her nest in the barn.

"I presume you didn't mind coming this far with me," Fidel said, with hope in his voice.

Abby, "I'd probably go the distance, wherever that may be."

Fidel and Abby slid the barn door closed and walked into the dark house. Fidel began to light large pillar-like candles that had been set in steel dishes on a large metal sculpture standing six feet tall, with 10 candle dishes strategically located around the grapevine stand. The illumination was breathtaking, seductive and brilliant.

He poured some red wine for Abby and himself while preparing some appetizers for them to snack on.

Abby walked onto the deck with her glass of wine. She began to cry ever so slightly, the tears trickling from her eyes. She was reflecting on Stephan when he was alive, just days before the accident. She wiped away the tears for Stephan and for a brief moment thought how her present life would not exist if their journey had continued with all four tires on the road, no rut, and no loss of control. She and Stephan, her first soulmate, would probably be back in Salem, North Carolina.

She turned and Fidel was there placing the tray of appetizers on the table where they'd had coffee and croissants that morning. Now they were having wine, cheese and crackers.

"Everything you think is pure and right, Abby. 'What if' is not to be considered or thought about. So let it go to drift with all of the other suspended thoughts in the sky. Colorful thoughts make rainbows refracted through the clouds, white light refracted through a prism to form colors because we think. That's how and why you see Jesús when he's not there. You think he is, so you place him there," Fidel explained to Abby. "Then why can't I place Stephan here now?" Abby asked challenging what Fidel had said.

"Because he is not in the physical world," Fidel countered gently. "But people see Jesus Christ, don't they?" Abby responded quickly.

"Or so they say. Here, take this, for example. I have a riddle for you. Imagine before you a 5-gallon glass water vessel, empty-no water, no cap and a narrow neck two inches in diameter, the kind of water jug you turn upside down into a dispenser with a water tap. Now, there's a live full-grown goose in that jug. How do you get that goose out without breaking the jug or killing the goose? Answer: The same way you put him in there, with words.

Make it disappear, then reappear. Here's another riddle. When is a door not a door? Answer: When it's ajar. And, yet another. When is a tire not a tire? Answer: When it's attire. These are the things you acquire when you hang out with Jesús and Juan."

The full moon was directly overhead now and it put forth such a glow that the two of them looked radiant to one another. They stood side by side, leaning on the deck rail while the bamboo stalks made a beautiful soft clanking sound in the gentle breeze. Someone was thinking.

"What am I going to do, Fidel? Where am I going to go?" Abby asked.

Fidel clapped his hands loudly, twice, and said, "Do this." Abby, "What do you mean?"

"Do as the people of New Guinea do. Go blank, without desire, and simply perform. You have opportunity and a will. Go act it out, or stay and perform on top of me. I have no commitments or anchors. You are free to do what you want. Let the answer of what you want to do come from within."

"I want to do everything. I want to work for Pedro. I want to apprentice with Jesús. I want to study people." Abby was thinking too fast.

Fidel, "You can only do one thing at a time. Too many irons in the fire will put the fire out."

Abby, "But what will people think of me back home?"

"Thoughts form clouds, and thoughts form rainbows. Turn your thoughts in and answer the question for yourself."

Abby, "I'll have to sleep on it."

"Careful, the thought may dissolve," Fidel said lightly. "Maybe it needs to be watered down," Abby responded. "Or acted upon full strength," Fidel pointed out. "Shall we retire to the bedroom?"

Abby, "Yes. Sleep will come quickly for me."

Fidel thought: Not too quickly, I hope.

Soon all the candles had been blown out. They walked upstairs to the place they had slept last night, The Passion Pit, as Fidel referred to his bedroom.

Fidel stood and stared at Abby undressing. She wriggled her hips, working her jeans down off her rump, then down her legs, then stepping out of them, leaving them on the floor-Stephan remaining in her back pocket. Her blouse was the only thing left, the bottom edge just above her pubic hair.

Fidel unzipped his fly. Abby crisscrossed her arms across her chest and peeled her blouse off, reaching, stretching for the ceiling.

Fidel dropped his trousers and adjusted his balls while his penis was aimed at Abby. He felt her silhouette could be framed and mounted as the most beautiful piece of living art he had ever seen. He approached her with delicate intentions as Abby draped her arms around his neck and pressed herself against him, kissing him with velvet lips. Fidel reached behind Abby and lifted her up from her ass onto his erection. One slight shift, a wiggle, and a little adjustment and Fidel entered her like a lug wrench going onto the lug nut of a tire-or shifting from second gear to third in a Porsche at 60 miles an hour. She let out a groan as Fidel held her in position supporting her entire gorgeous being on his erect penis. He was strong in many regards, but this was not going to last for long and was not the favorite position of either of them to achieve the greatest sexual satisfaction. Cruise control doesn't really work on such a bumpy, steep hill. The gear keeps popping out. So he lay Abby on top of the comforter and shifted into fourth. All wild animals screw like a bat-out-of-hell, but humans sometimes like to go slow, like butter melting in a pan. Fidel's thermometer was taking Abby's temperature, and their heat was slowly rising. For a brief instant, Abby thought of Jesús' comment about "fixing the leak" and being playful, staying wet by keeping the water in the pool. She was tickled as she thought that it was working. Fidel nibbled on Abby's earlobe and she squirmed with erotic pleasure. Eventually, the bat left hell and they went at it like the wild animals they were. Shouts and screams erupted from both as climaxes were reached. They simultaneously dropped the sex engine into neutral. There was no leak, except for Fidel dripping out of Abby as he withdrew and collapsed on his back beside her. Sleep was on the cusp as they drifted off together into sweet slumber.

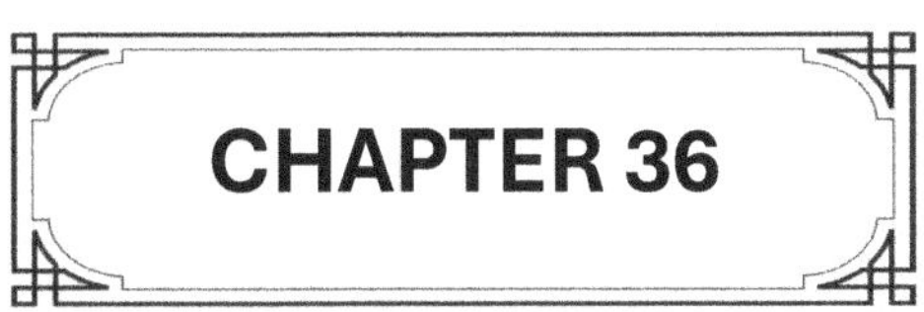

CHAPTER 36

bby and Fidel awoke to the sound of rain splattering on the deck. No words of love had been uttered yet between them.

Their eyes were on each other now as smiles were drawn on their faces. Abby stroked Fidel's face like an angel. Fidel rolled out of bed-Abby, too-and they strolled to the bathroom to brush their teeth, then into Nautilus for a shower. When they had bathed, Fidel shut the water off, but before they dried, he led Abby through the bedroom and out onto the deck to stand naked in the teeming downpour. It was incredibly sensual and invigorating, like the sunflower shower head in Nautilus. They both looked up into the sky, and Abby said. "God has a leak. He must be draining his pool."

Fidel, "Oh, God, wouldn't Jesús love to hear you say that!" Abby, "Yeah. And I bet he'd like to be here, too, to hear it live and in the flesh."

Fidel, "Oh, yeah. The women on the Salvarez farm call him Don Casanova."

Abby, "Hmm."

Fidel, "He is said to be the ultimate pleaser of women." Abby, "Sounds like a typical macho male to me."

Fidel, "Aren't you curious?"

Abby, "You told me curiosity kills everything."

Fidel, "It usually starts wars, too."

Abby, "Then perhaps I don't care."

Fidel, "It doesn't bother me one way or the other. Remember, we all have choices. You should have him and find out for yourself. Just don't tell anyone or brag about it like the rest of the women."

Abby, "Hmm."

Abby and Fidel stepped back into his bedroom and reentered Nautilus just to feel the warm water on their rain-chilled bodies. Then they dried off and got dressed.

Everything felt so natural and easy to Abby, as if she'd been doing this routine with Fidel for a long time. He had a way of making guests feel welcome in his home. But he didn't have many that often and certainly not such a prize as Abby.

Fidel led the way from the Passion Pit down to the culinary chambers where he ground the coffee beans and prepared the dripper.

Abby felt perfectly at home as she opened the refrigerator door looking for orange juice. She saw a big glass pitcher that had orange juice with pulp floating on the top.

The rain continued to fall, pattering on the deck, dripping from up above.

"May I pour you a glass of juice, Fidel?" Abby asked politely. "Yum. That would be lovely."

She could see the glassware from behind the glass cabinet doors above the countertop. Coffee cups were there, too. She reached up and grabbed two glasses, then two mugs.

They sat and savored the moment with the delicious, refreshing taste of fresh-squeezed OJ Fidel had made a couple of days before. The coffee brewing offered great aromas as did the wet, steamy rain.

Abby said, "Will you take me to Pedro and Lolita's sometime today? I must talk to them and find out how Carlos is doing on the farm and if there's work for me in their clinic."

Fidel, "Do you have any medical background?"

"No, I have a degree in environmental social science which is basically bringing a consciousness to inner-city populations about pollution and how to take care of it. It's so diverse with the different cultures within the ethnic neighborhoods and how they view their block on this planet. If they don't give a shit about their block, they sure don't give a damn about the planet. Many have never even seen an ocean, not to mention a river that wasn't polluted. I wouldn't sink into the Hudson River if I were pushed. It would be like floating in sewage."

"What do you think asked. you can offer Pedro and Lolita?" he Abby, "I could just be there as another body to help out and learn about medicine and disease. It would give them a little more time to themselves. They already have two helpers, so maybe I'd just volunteer and apprentice for a while if they could give me room and board."

Fidel, "What about working at his parents' farm?"

Abby. "That's an option, too. Then I could NOT pay attention to Jesús and NOT ask him to be my mentor."

Fidel, "Oh, God. He'd chew you up and spit you out if you even mentioned that to him. I am sure he'd think you were making a pass at him.'

Abby, "Oh, that's funny. I think I'd rather do something at the clinic."

Fidel, "Ready for some coffee? Hey, look outside, it's clearing up. God must have fixed the leak and is now thinking colorful thoughts because there's a rainbow shooting across the sky."

Abby. "He must be loving an angel. Do you think that's sacrilegious to say that?"

Fidel, "Do you know what 'sacrilegious' means? It's Latin and means to steal sacred things, not in the literal sense, but in the figurative sense. In this case, you'd better have a litany. You want God's forgiveness, don't you? You want your followers chanting 'we absolve you,' don't you?"

Abby, "I didn't steal a sacred verse. I made a dirty joke. You've got to have a sense of humor. Sometimes I say things that everyone else wonders about: making love to angels. I mean, really, is that a visualization or what? All parents are gods and they make love to procreate."

Fidel, "Well, I suppose it could conjure up images. If you could imagine God, you could imagine anything. Life, basically, is a spiritual event. Everything about it is sacred."

Abby, "It certainly ties a ribbon around organized religion and keeps God portrayed as this white man in a white cloud with a mane of white hair and a streaming white beard according to the Bible. Organized religions are for those with weak wings who cannot get their body off the ground to take flight."

Fidel, "And spirituality is the eagle's wing that can lift you into another realm."

Abby, "I don't know. I'm just glad you are not offended."

Fidel, "Not at all. I suggest we take Voyager for a ride-or Voyager take us for a ride-down to the Salvarez clinic of hospitality."

Abby. "I'm up for that."

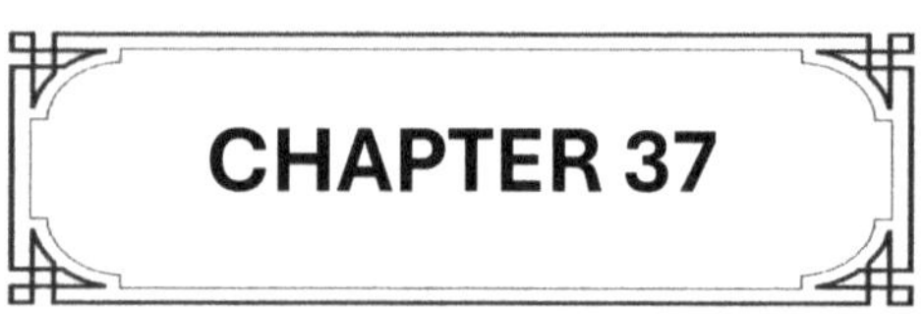

CHAPTER 37

Abby and Fidel finished their coffee and left everything on the table. The ground was soggy, soaking wet in places, leaving huge muddy puddles to walk around.

Fidel slid the barn door on its tracks, and there sat Voyager. They got into the vehicle and Fidel drove out of the barn and through some of the puddles in the driveway.

They took a left onto the main road and drove south. Steam was rising from the hot pavement.

Not even a half-hour later, they pulled into the clinic drive. A sign out front welcomed them. It read in Spanish and English, "A healing place for what ails you. We hope you leave in wellness."

Lolita greeted them at the front desk. She was happy to see them both.

"Fidel, it's been a while. Sorry I missed you two the other day. Abby, how are you doing, leg and all?" Lolita inquired. "You look like you are walking just fine."

Abby, "I'm great, Lolita. I was hoping to talk with you and Pedro about possible work you might have for me."

Lolita, "Oh, won't Pedro be happy to hear that! I am sure there is something for you to do around here and, besides, he promised." Pedro came down the hall from around the corner. He had on jeans, a T-shirt and a blue lab jacket, with a stethoscope around his neck.

"Hi, both of you," he welcomed them.

Fidel said. "Abby here is quite the woman."

"Isn't she, though." Pedro commented as he slipped into her eyes. Abby quickly looked away and the contact transmission had no chance to begin. She recognized that the sexual urge was no longer there. Her libido had been possessed by Fidel, and Pedro really didn't make her sexually hungry. Abby thought about this and decided that she must have been horny before, and now her sexual appetite had been satisfied. She also remembered telling Pedro, while under his care, that their past love lives would-or should have no effect on his current marital status. Basically she had inferred that she respected his devotion to Lolita and that whatever sexual attraction might occur between the two of them should not be acted upon except for discussions to confess to wet dreams or masturbation. Fantasy in action. She felt a tremendous sense of relief with her self-revelations. Yet she still reminisced about being Pedro's lover when he was Argos and she was Felicia. She would always have that movie playing, but only when she allowed for a contact transmission when Pedro gazed into her eyes. She had also come to the startling realization that she should perhaps show greater restraint in allowing the movie to be shown, because it could only lead to a dangerous theater of double trouble. The movie showing in Abby's eyes had had its heyday on the circuit of Pedro's and Carlos' movie-going. Maybe it was time to put the reels in the archives of Abby's mind. Perhaps, in time, there could be a remake or at least a review of the movie about "Ancient Lovers," but for now Abby felt it had served its purpose to get her through some tough times in this life and to learn a little something about past lives.

She had to tell Carlos the same thing.

The fact that these contact transmissions had reunited three people from an energy exchange of DNA vapors was living proof they had come from people, and all people are related.

"Be more kind to people, our relatives. Do better things for others now." That should be the universal creed for all to live by, Abby thought.

So is it back to fantasy or ahead in reality for Abby and her adopted brood? Reality is being here now. Fantasy is space traveling alone, or it's dreaming, conjuring, or having contact transmissions with brujos or those whose energy waves coincide. She could do of these, but the only one she seemed to be in control of was the contact transmission. She was, in fact, the producer, director and actor of her own movie when she permitted the reels to roll, if and when the observer was allowed to fall into her eyes. Yet she marveled at Jesús' own abilities in his eyes.

Was he mimicking Abby in mockery or was there truly a connection of energy waves that sent her back to another life where she was a courtesan, murdered for asking too many questions? The point was, what Abby experienced at that instant of falling into Jesús' eyes put her into a trance, and she revisited a place someone else had previously been and experienced a rush of goosebumps as if she was experiencing a deja vu.

(Author's note: We all have this ability, the capability of daydreaming or night-dreaming or seeing visions. Some people roll with it, some fall into it, and some deny it. Fear is a builder of courage if you answer the door. Otherwise, if you allow fear to run your life, there will be no growth, which can only yield stagnation, stillness or even death.)

Abby had no fear of anything. Stephan taught her that while rolling uncontrollably down that embankment meeting his demise. He had passed on into oblivion and now resided in spirit form in Abby's back pocket. Where did his DNA vapors go? Abby unconsciously breathed in his last exhalation, but she was not the sole possessor of it. She only got a breath during her next inhalation of Stephan's last exhalation. The spirit in the weather patterns always heed the potential to be breathed in by a special couple who were making love and trying to create a miracle, the miracle being a dead person's final exhalation being breathed in during climax, a male and female, having a creation of joyous pleasure when a seed impregnates an egg. Stephan cosmically told Abby not to be afraid of his passing, to accept it as a growth pattern for a richer, fuller life, because life goes on. It took one instant to pass this on to Abby, and in the next moment, Stephan was gone.

Abby had laid in a coma absorbing this message as she dreamed of a past life of hers that she was in and so made a movie of it.

Fidel and Pedro looked at Abby and clapped their hands simultaneously to bring her back. They had moved outside the clinic and were standing by their cars.

"Whoa, where did you just go, my special friend?" Fidel cried out. Pedro, "Yeah. You were out there. Care to share?"

Abby, "Let's just say I was reviewing an old movie I once saw. Now I'm back and ready to go to work."

Pedro, "Glad to hear it. Do you want to be here in the clinic or on my parents' farm?"

Abby, "I want to start here."

Pedro, "Sounds good to me. Lolita and I will put you up at the house, as promised, but you will always have the freedom to come and go as you please-no attachments, no commitments, no anchors. That goes for work and play, the most important message being choice, always your choice to be your own person. In other words, 'own yourself,' be responsible for your actions and hopefully realize the consequences. Enough said. I am not your father, nor your guardian. I am a friend and that means I am offering you unconditional love. I am also your spiritual twin, so to speak-if you please, your ancient lover. And I say this in front of Fidel because he is one of the people with knowledge. You didn't know that, did you, Abby?"

This took Abby by total surprise, and she gasped, "No, I didn't. He only said that Jesús and your father and even you taught him many lessons."

Pedro, "It's true, but he and I are one and the same. We grew up together. He helped out on the farm. His parents worked and lived nearby on a coffee plantation their whole lives. Jesús was a clown, a trickster, and we used to laugh so hard at his shenanigans. We didn't know he was teaching us something until later. Timing is everything, and knowing something about the ways of others is equally important. Jesús has never traveled outside the perimeters of his native jungle. How do you explain his wisdom and knowledge of others? The only explanation comes from within. He has had many past lives, and he brings the knowledge that he has acquired with him by way of 'trans-spiritual' airways. He was washed ashore and found the spiritual umbilical cord to plug into in this life. That's why he laughs so much and so hard-from the gut-because he feels life and death is only a joke. He has discovered the recipe to happiness, and he spreads it on the wind for others to breathe in. Your choice is what to do with your next breath. It's what Buddhism is based on, and brujo-ism as well. The people with knowledge call it the breathing choice.'"

Abby. "So you're a brujo, too, Pedro?

Pedro, "Oh, my God, no. I'm a doctor."

Pedro and Fidel were on the ground laughing so hard, rolling. holding their guts. Abby started laughing, too.

"I think the leak is being fixed here," Abby announced happily. "Everything for a reason, but don't take life too seriously. There are 'many here among us who feel that life is but a joke'..

Fidel, "But you and I have been through that, and this is not our fate. So let us not talk falsely now. The hour is getting late." Pedro, "Oh, Mr. Dylan. Perhaps we should turn Jesus on to this new prophet."

Fidel, "Wouldn't that be interesting?"

Abby, "I don't know. I like Jesús the way he is. Maybe we should turn Dylan on to Jesús."

Pedro, "Hey, that sounds like a movie script. Let's write the dialogue."

Fidel, "Could you imagine it? Jesús meets the Rabbi."

Abby, "That's it! That's what we'll call it, 'Jesús meets the Rabbi.'

Pedro, "I think we're on to something here. How do we get Dylan down here?"

Fidel, "Don't jump the gun. Let's write the script first." Abby, "All right. I've got a journalistic hand."

Pedro, "I've written a few papers, too, and, lord knows, Fidel has done some composition."

Fidel and Pedro got off the ground after their laughing fit and brushed themselves off.

Fidel, "First, let me clear something up here for Abby. Pedro and I are not brujos. We would never take claim to that, just as Jesús wouldn't. That's a label, and labels have ingredients. If you list all of the ingredients on the packaging, you have a title. If you have a title, that's all you can be. Brujos are everything. Pedro is a doctor. That's a title. That's all he can be because he chose that from the heart. I am a photographer, a traveler and explorer. We take what was given us from life's lessons and place them in our own personal vaults. People like Jesús have moistened us with eye droppers of knowledge, but he himself is not in the limelight. He refuses the spotlight of fame. So, you see, brujos have achieved contentment. They are pleased with life. They laugh at everything even death and pass it on. That's why death is a passing on."

Abby, "I gathered that from when I saw myself as Felicia. That's what Argos said to me when he lay in my arms dying of the plague." Pedro, "So you see, we have a connection here, a likeness, a bonding. Why don't Lolita and I come over to your place, Fidel- with Abby, of course—unless she wants to go with you now, and we'll discuss 'Jesús meets the Rabbi' over dinner and a swim." Fidel, "Marvelous idea. Abby, are you coming or staying?" Abby, "I'm coming-or am I just panting hard?"

Pedro, "Oh, that's funny."

Everyone got a chuckle from Abby's little double entendre. So plans for dinner were set and the time was agreed upon. Pedro walked back into the clinic to run this by Lolita. He showed a thumbs-up to Fidel and Abby who were standing by the Voyager. They acknowledged, hopped in the safari buggy and headed back to Phantom Fantasy.

Pedro explained everything that had just transpired, minus the contact transmission, and asked Lolita if she concurred with him about Abby joining their team.

Lolita exclaimed, "Pedro, I think that would be marvelous! I know you would tell me if something else was going on between you two. I trust you ultimately, and when the time is right-if there is a time-you will offer it up."

Pedro, "There is no time-meaning there is nothing going on between us other than past lives and dreams. I must ask for your understanding on this issue, my love. You are the one and only for me. Trust me, there is nothing going on between Abby and me other than this fantasy dream and a hint of reincarnation."

Lolita, "I can handle that, Pedro. Thank you for telling me. I don't have a jealous bone in my body. What is is, and as long as you don't fall out of love with me, that's all I care about. I hope you never love another more than you love me. Equal is okay, unconditionally."

Pedro, "Oh, Lolita, that's why we're together. I love you so much."

Lolita said, "You do not have to explain anything else. Just let it be. Time will tell who has fallen and who's been left behind."" Pedro, "When you go your way and I go mine'. Wow, Lolita, you remember that great Dylan line from when I brought his records back with me from America?"

Lolita, "Yes. I listen to him often on my headset at home."

Pedro, "Well, that's what we're going to discuss tonight at Fidel's. We've sort of spontaneously created this movie script happening between Jesús and Bob Dylan meeting on the spur of a moment and shooting the shit around a campfire at Mother and Father's, drinking jungle nectar."

Lolita, "And we're going to brainstorm this fantasy rendezvous?" Pedro, "Oh, yeah! You want to be a part of it?"

Lolita, "Of course. But what about the clinic? Have you forgotten Marga and her baby in Room #1?"

Pedro, "No-I mean, yes. I must go tend to her jungle-rot rash."

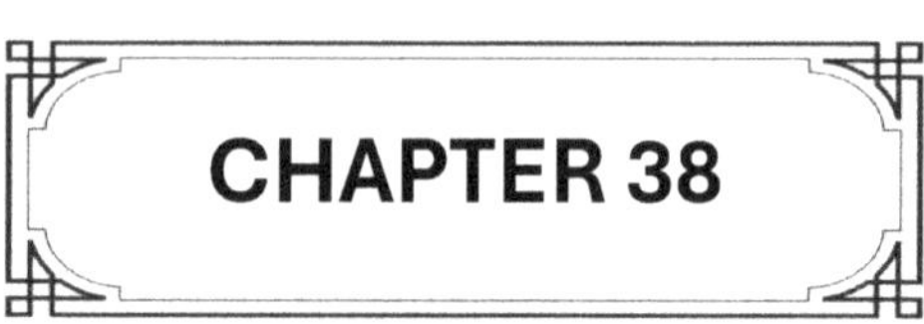

CHAPTER 38

The Voyager was pulling into Phantom Fantasy. Fidel parked in the barn. The puddles were drying up from the morning's love rain, but the ground was still damp. Abby loved the tickle of the grass between her toes. She took her sandals off to feel the slushy wet ground, gurgling with every step.

As Fidel and Abby entered the house, they found Jesús sitting on the back deck rail smoking a cigar. Abby pointed and laughed, shaking her head at Jesús. Fidel slid the glass door back and Jesús said. "Welcome."

Fidel said. "That's my line."

Jesús, "Oh, well, welcome to my world."

Abby. "Are you crazy or something?"

Jesús, "Oh, God, more questions that you already know the answer to."

Abby, "I'm sorry. Let me rephrase that. You're crazy."

Jesús, "Thank you, seniorita. 1 practice constantly."

Fidel, "Join us for dinner? Pedro and Lolita are joining us to discuss something."

Jesús, "Like me?"

Abby, "Yes, like you, but we're not ingesting you for dinner. We're discussing you as a possible movie character."

Jesús, "I won't be pictured on film, I'll tell you that right now. On earth's stage, yes, as a living play, but not on film." Abby, "Well, that's an idea."

Jesús, "At least it's not a question."

Fidel, "Let's get ready. They are coming in 3 hours." Fidel assigned chores. He had all the makings for a cookout.

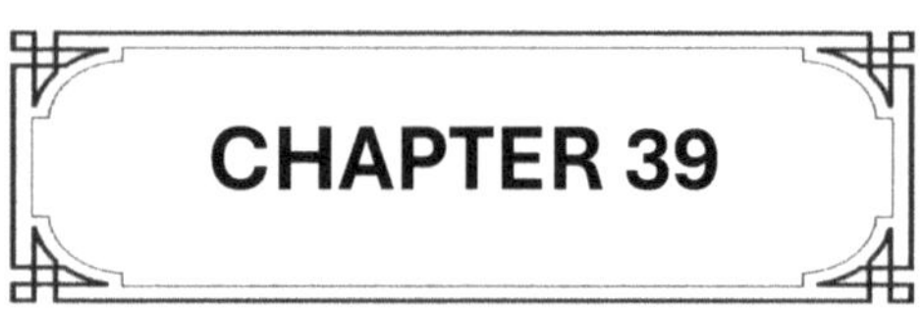

Dinner was delightful and delicious. Afterwards, they all adjourned to pool-side. Jesús picked his teeth, then lit up a cigar. Jesús, "I have never heard of this Rabbi Dylan character. I want to hear his prophecy."

Fidel went inside and put on "Blood on the Tracks" and switched on the outside speakers.

They all sat quietly and listened to the entire CD.

Jesús laughed, "Strength is in the words, truth is in the and sparkle is in the eyes. But I cannot see his eyes. Therefore, there is no truth, only words, and words are deceptive except in song. He sings a mean song. I'll meet him if he wants to pay a visit." Fidel, "Jesús, are you serious?"

Jesús, "What a ridiculous question. You've been catching this woman's disease, Fidel. She's rubbing off on you."

Abby, "Oh, man, you've got me in stitches."

Fidel. Pedro, Lolita and Jesús laughed along with her. Abby, "Could we possibly put all of the double-talk and puns aside and ask a few realistic questions?"

Jesús, "You mean 'bubble-talk' and 'pus.' I see all of your questions oozing from your mouths and floating like a bubble. But then the bubble falls, bursts on the ground, and the questions- like pus-leak all over the soles of my shoes."

No one could stop laughing. Even Abby was laughing while she stooped over and took Jesús' leather sandals off his feet and threw them into the pool. The laughter burst any question that might have been floating in a bubble. Abby quickly lunged from her seat and grabbed the slippers before they sank.

Jesús said, "Thanks. They needed a bath. Now, if you would, wash my feet."

Abby decided that that was a good idea and began to give Jesús a foot massage.

Abby was remembering how she and Stephan used to get massages when they traveled to special hot springs spas in Virginia and West Virginia. Abby especially liked her reflexology sessions. She even practiced on Stephan a few times after she read a few how-to pamphlets on the ancient Chinese art of foot massage and reflexology.

Now she began with Jesús' right foot, working all of the target zones and trigger points that she could recall. He was on Cloud 11. You could tell by the way his body let go and from the moans he released with every out-breath.

Fidel, Pedro and Lolita were lounging around Jesus and Abby, watching Jesús give in to the relaxation mode.

It was the perfect exercise for peace and quiet, but the silence was broken with Jesús stating, "All right, you may ask questions. There is a time and a place for everything. There is even a time when the movie has played through it's reel and should be rewound and placed on a shelf."

Abby, "Your intuition never ceases to amaze me."

Jesús, "I suspect chewing gum amazes you." Abby, "Now, what brought that up?"

Jesús, "The way you used it on my friends as a means to win their friendship. They swallowed it. That was a great compliment paid to you. That's why they brought you to me. The invisible people see right through the facades. They intuit their entire existence. That's why you may never see them again. And as the jungle becomes smaller due to development and the dominance of the white man, the invisible people will continue to recede until they disappear like the buffalo. How do I know this? I see with my own eyes. That which is obvious will blind those who see nothing but dollar signs. It is the way of the new world. I may live in the old world, practicing old ways, but I see what's going on around me in a global sense. I do not wear blinders. I choose to stay off the new path because it is heading to the end of the world. My world continues onward with my passing. It is what I believe. I love the way you make my 'souls' feel."

Abby, "You still amaze me."

Fidel got up and went inside to put "Blonde on Blonde" on the outside speakers. Everyone listened as Dylan wailed on "Like a Rolling Stone." Abby then asked Fidel to fast-forward the CD to "Sad-Eyed Lady of the Lowlands," which he did. Abby caressed Jesús' right foot, putting it to rest as she picked up his left foot and repeated the process. Jesús slipped back into orbit and opened his ears to "with your mercury mouth and your missionary bells and your magazine husband who one day just had to go." Jesús was circling Pluto.

Pedro, "Oh, mama, can this really be the end?""

Lolita, "To be stuck inside Jesús' head and there's no way out but in."

Fidel, "Nice ad-lib, Lolita."

Lolita, "Just a little fill-in-the-blank when you're reaching for a verse."

Abby, "We've got the makings of a rock opera starring Jesús and Dylan."

Pedro, "Wait a minute. I thought this was going to be a play in real life at the Theater of All Possibilities, starring double-trouble Jesús and the Rabbi, smoking cigars, sitting around a campfire drinking jungle nectar."

Fidel, "That sounds most real, but is it possible?"

Jesús, "Only the absurd is possible. The more absurd, the more likely. Is this guy Dylan a man of his word? Does anyone know him?"

Abby, "Oh, God, what real questions. 'Is he a man of his word," and, 'Does anyone know him?' The world knows him, but no one here has met him one-on-one. Woody Guthrie might have, back in 1960."

Jesús, "So bring him forth to the big campfire this month." Abby, "I'm afraid Woody's passed on."

Jesús, "Oh, well, bring him back."

Abby, "How?"

Fidel, "The same way Dylan does, with words."

Pedro, "Yeah. Let's contact Dylan and tell him we've got a channeler in Guatemala who can communicate with Woody."

Jesús, "Don't even say things you can't be true to. False promises are corrupt.

Lolita, "Why don't we just suggest we have someone we want him to meet. No fanfare, no special billing, just a campfire chat with an old friend he hasn't seen in a long time."

Abby, "Great idea. How do we go about contacting Mr. Dylan?"

Jesús, "It will unfold just the way it is supposed to with a little help from the gods."

Fidel, "Meaning, start praying."

Pedro, "Prayer helps, but I suggest we make a more aggressive effort."

Abby, "You know, when I went to B.U. I often heard of Arlo Guthrie playing around Boston, and I think he lives in the Berkshire Mountains somewhere in Tanglewood. He appears to be somewhat approachable, so maybe I could try to visit with him and tell him we'd like to attempt to gather himself, Dylan and Jesús in Guatemala to conjure up his dad. That's not suggesting Jesús is a channeler and that he can communicate with the dead. But just maybe it might pan out that Arlo and I have a contact transmission and that way there may be an attraction, an incentive to get him to come. It's a long shot, but it might be worth it."

Pedro, "Dylan seems to be constantly on tour. He could probably use the break, but the timing of the contact and request must be perfect."

Jesús, "That's where the prayers come in. The spirits will tell us when to move. Until then, I ain't going nowhere because my feet are stuck in Abby's hands, and the stars are twinkling just for us tonight. Let us enjoy the moment."

Lolita, "Play the Dylan CDs again."

Fidel, "Okay. First, I could use a brandy and perhaps light up a cigar."

Abby was just putting the finishing touches on Jesús' blissful state by gently resting his left foot on the ground. She requested what Fidel was drinking, and Jesús put in a request for a cigar only.

Pedro and Lolita were perfectly content gazing at the stars.

Fidel went into the house and a few minutes later returned with the goods. There was no more discussion about "Jesús Meets the Rabbi." Instead, Abby asked, "Jesús, where did you learn to speak English so well if you've never left the jungle?"

Jesús, "The parrots speak fluent English in the jungle. They told me anyone who claims to be a healer fixes the heels on the soles of my shoes or commands a dog to heel at his side."

Everyone laughed, including Abby.

Jesús, "All these parrots sitting here tonight taught me. I mimicked their every word, sometimes silently- just listening-- and other times listening, then repeating. Monkey see, monkey do. Parrot speak, parrot repeat. I catch their words in a Playtex living bra, 36-double D, and sling them at people like you. Both cups can yield volumes of bullshit."

Abby, "Interesting."

Pedro and Lolita expressed a desire to head for home. They rose from their chairs, stretched their arms toward the sky, bent at the waist and exhaled a sigh like a gust of wind. Arm in arm, they bid adios to all.

Fidel said, "You know the way. Until we see you again."

In a moment, they were on their way back home.

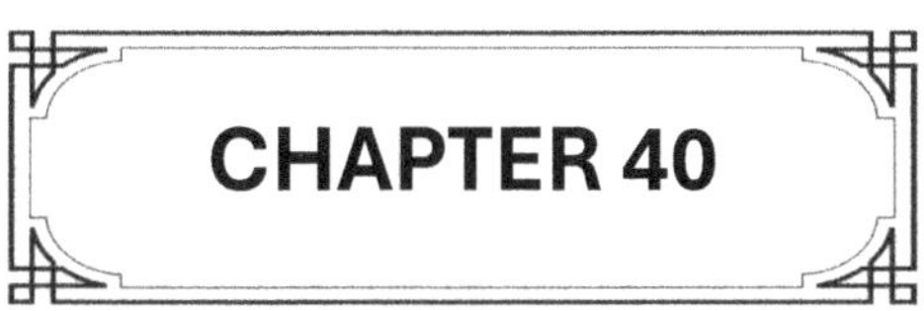

Jesús stripped naked and was in the pool faster than a lightening bolt. Abby was startled at his quickness and fluidity. On entering the water, he hardly made a splash and there was almost no sign of ripples.

Abby and Fidel followed suit. They all stood in the 4-foot depth of the water close to each other, no motion and no chatter. The night was alive with moon reflections on the still water and wild animal noises surrounding them as if in stereo. The night air was filled with supernatural energy, and there was a peacefulness that felt like a narcotic. It lasted until Jesús moved through the water to exit the pool. He announced he was going into the jungle, and Fidel knew to simply leave it at that. Abby watched his slender, wer body as he stood in the night air to dry before dressing. She wanted to touch him. She felt her libido rising and wanted to catch a glimpse of his penis, but that didn't happen, so the urge to seduce him subsided.

She and Fidel stood silently in the pool as Jesús wandered off roward the darkness of the jungle. Fidel reached out to Abby and she welcomed his caress. She was most definitely falling in love with his charm, but she wondered about his heart. sex."

Fidel said softly, "This could become habit-forming."

Abby, "Most good things are-like candy, jimson weed and

Fidel, "Let's go to the zen garden, create something, ring the gong, and allow the sound waves to carry us to infinity."

Abby, "Naked or clothed?"

Fidel, "Nude."

They exited together at the south end of the pool, closest to the garden.

Fidel picked up the formal wooden rake which had a broad head and about 20 wooden prongs attached. He gracefully dragged it across the top of the sand, smoothing out the design from the day before. He handed Abby the other rake, which had a much smaller head and five pointed prongs. She held the rake in the moonlight glow, then gently pressed the prongs into the sand and dragged the rake in a wide, swooping motion to form a meandering river of sand. She then placed a large rock in the middle of the river and walked over to the edge of the bamboo and picked up a fallen branch. She stripped the short branch of its bamboo leaves and placed it across the sand river at one of its bends to form a bridge. Then Abby found the largest bamboo leaf and placed it in the middle of the river downstream from the bridge and the rock to form a floating Chinese boat.

Her task completed, she walked over to Fidel's naked body and hugged and kissed him. He broke away and picked up the mallet and struck the gong.

He whispered to Abby, "Hop on the wave... let's surf to bed." He swept one arm behind Abby's knees and made a chopping motion. As she collapsed into his grasp, his other arm rested behind her shoulder blades, and she was gently carried up to the Passion Pit.

Fidel laid Abby on top of the bed and splayed her legs like opening the pages of a sacred text. When he sensed that she was ready, he went down on her, slurping his dessert like a hot fudge sundae. He was in her garden of sacred joy for minutes which, to a nymph, seemed like seconds--but her orgasms were multiple when Fidel harvested her joy and came up for air.

Abby, groaning, said, "Come in me-now! Make passionate love to me! You're a sex god, Fidel! I love you."

And he did the deed until they were both satisfied and exhausted.

Sleep came quickly after that.

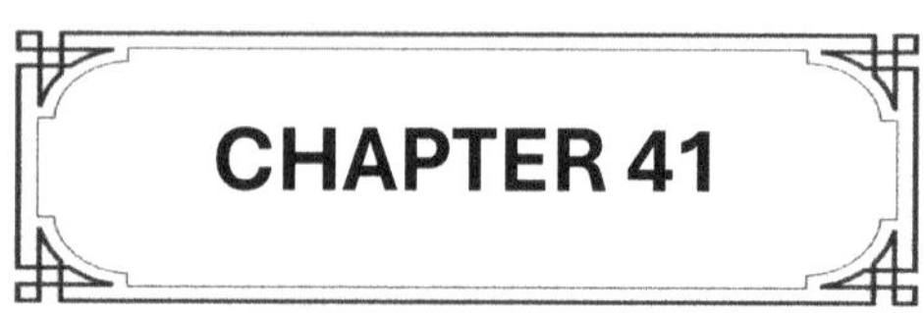

The next morning. Abby asked Fidel if he would drive her to the Salvarez farm. She wanted to check up on Carlos and see how he was getting along. Fidel agreed, and they set out after breakfast.

After the 2-hour drive, they pulled into the long Salvarez driveway and passed under the timbers of the gate with its steel trademark.

Abby found herself reflecting on Pedro's heart attack in the field there and how Jesús pulled him out of it by pinching his big toes.

Fidel glanced over at Abby and said, "What? Where did you just go?"

Abby said, "I was recalling the magic healing Jesús performed on Pedro when we were last here."

Fidel, "Don't refer to it as magic around Jesús. He is a clown and performs tricks, but he's not a magician. He wouldn't take offense at it--he'd simply deny it because magic is different than clowning around."

Abby, "All right. Boy, I sure do have to be on my P's and Q's around him."

Fidel, "He just calls you on your stuff and won't let you get away with anything. He sees leaks in your energy field and then forces you to fix them yourself because only you caused them and only you can fix them. People are tools, and time is the work table." Abby, "And earth is the arena, the stage."

Fidel, "You're catching on."

They parked in front of the porch to the main house where horses used to be tied to the hitching post. There was even a water trough in front of the rail to the right where, they assumed, horses would still be tied. It was high noon and lovely aromas came wafting through the screen door. Margarette, inside at the kitchen counter, looked up and exclaimed, "Fidel! Abby! Set two more places, Angela. We have very special guests joining us."

She came rushing out to greet them both with heartfelt hugs and kisses on the cheeks.

"Fidel, it has been too long since I last saw you." Margarette said. "We must catch up before the chocolate melts."

Fidel, "Oh, you are so funny. You still remember that. Abby. Margarette is talking about the time Pedro and I hadn't seen each other for maybe five years. He was off to Harvard, and I was in Mozambique. When we finally reunited, in this very kitchen, Margarette was melting down 10 pounds of solid chocolate to make chocolate sopapillas for the Festival of the Dead celebration. It took three hours of slow cooking and stirring it at a very low temperature for that block of chocolate to melt just right, without burning. We stayed in the kitchen the whole time talking, catching up on old times and smelling that aphrodisiac aroma for the entire three hours. Margarette called it her 'chocolate buddha of enlightening conversation reuniting old friends. And now she wants to do it again!" And aside to Abby, "But I'm afraid it will make me horny for you again."

Abby, "And what could be so wrong with that?"

Margarette, "So you two have met and become sweet on one another. Could not have happened to two more deserving people. You must have met after you left here with Pedro."

Abby, "Si. Pedro introduced us on the way to his home that day."

As lunch was being served, bridges of conversation were built, spanning the gap of time. Pictures were drawn and visions portrayed on the invisible canvas from the transparent palette of speech.

Margarette could clearly see where this was going. This would call for a visit to the community kitchen to see Carlos and a stroll through the orchards to see if Jesús might appear. Abby was pleased to hear such glowing reports about Carlos' first few days cooking on the farm, making friends with everyone, and, she assumed, romancing Juanita (although it wasn't revealed that bluntly, it was certainly obvious in Margarette's motherly, discreet way). Carlos' Cuban Spanish was slightly different than the local dialect, but certainly smooth enough to blend in with the general conversations, so it sounded as though he wasn't having problems communicating. Margarette and Fidel went to visit Juan and then Carlos. Abby then ventured off on her own to seek Jesús.

Suddenly, she heard these words, "There is a real fine line between fantasy and reality when it is show time, and dreams are conjured into the potion of everyday life and how you want things to be. You walk down the path and a rattlesnake appears and strikes at your throat. You withdraw. You are either stricken, with venom flowing in your system, or the strike misses and you walk past the striker. It's either being normal, reacting to an abnormal scene, or it's being normal reacting normally to a very normal scene. It is all in your head and how you conjure things. You walk on and no one dies from a rattlesnake strike."

Abby heard Jesús whisper this to her like a horse whisperer to a rogue horse, taming its wildness.

"Jesús, where are you?" Abby whispered back.

"Up here, as always-over there-under here-no, over here. Now here. Here, now. Be here now," Jesús said first from his perch in an orange tree, then from the ground behind a tree trunk, then from under a burlap sack used to gather fruit.

Abby finally caught up to him and said, "Why do you always do this to me, Jesús?

Jesús, "Why not? You invite it. It irritates you and you grow from it. You still have a stupid leak to fix. Open up and receive the gift. Now, change and fix the leak."

Abby, "Come join the others back at the community kitchen." Jesús, "No. You go play with Carlos. You have things to catch up on. I'll see you when it's my turn."

Abby. "Okay. I've got to run then." Jesús, "Don't let me stop you."

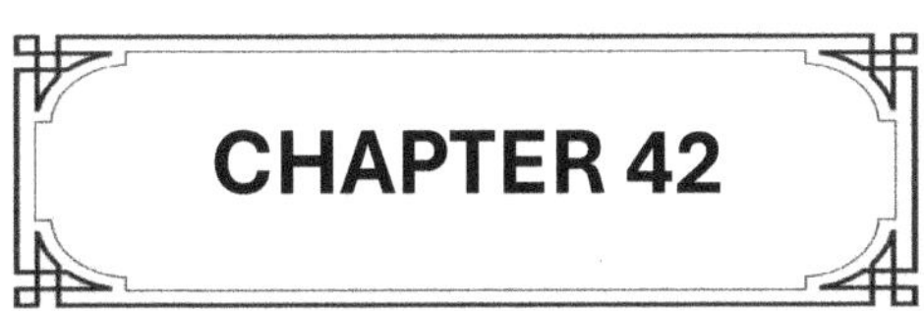

Abby jogged through the path between the fruit trees, breaking into the open after a quarter mile where she slowed to a walk to catch her breath. Her blouse was wet from sweat as she opened the door to Carlos' new residence and place of employment. She saw him behind the counter talking to Margarette and Fidel. This was the first time Fidel and Carlos had met. Carlos and Abby exchanged glances and his quick look into Abby's eyes said, I know what's going on and I'm happy for you. What we had was a happening. What I'm left with is a memory and a psychic debt I owe you for saving my life.

Amazing what a glance can say. Image a stare with daggers; imagine fire in your eyes; imagine a blank look, void of form; imagine dollar signs. Abby thought these things and felt relief that Carlos cared enough to send her his signals of loving friendship. Fidel was quite aware of the look Abby and Carlos exchanged. He smiled at Abby and said, "Ah, there you are."

Margarette asked, "Did you find Jesús?"

Abby, "No, he found me as always. How does he do those things?"

Fidel. "No magician reveals his slight of hand, and no clown reveals his secrets."

Carlos, "I can tell you this, Abby. In the few days I've been here, I've seen Jesús everywhere. He's in the cracks and crevices of the earth, he's in the bark of trees and the rinds of fruit and, for sure, he's in the clouds. I've fed him a few meals and he's spoken to me. When he speaks, Abby, listen. Do not question him. Listen. He is amazing. He is the brujo you were looking for, and you found him and walked right by him. He tells me things so simple I can't understand them. Sometimes I glance into his eyes and see crucifixes, and other times I see crosses and helixes. He is a figure of geometric design, and certainly a creation of mysticism. He is the most spiritual enigma I've ever come across, which makes him totally inexplicable. Therefore, don't ask."

Abby, "Geez, why does everyone keep telling me that?"

Margarette, "Because there's a lesson there, and it appears you're not getting it. You ask too many questions. Try listening instead. Simple as that."

Abby, "But every time I try that, I always ask myself, 'Why can't I ask questions?' How am I to learn?"

Carlos, "Like you did at B.U., by listening during lectures." Abby, "But what if I don't understand something?"

Fidel, "Study, be attentive, and listen some more. Meditation is not what you think. You must learn to distinguish between the crackling noise within, the quest for silence of the mind, and clouds passing by. No one can teach you that. You have to listen and then turn in by giving yourself up.'

Abby, "Oh, boy. You guys got it, and I keep missing it."

Margarette, "It takes time. You get it, and then you let it slip away. Go 'fix the leak,' as Jesús would say. Then when you get it, perhaps it will stay."

Abby, "I hear you."

Fidel, "There, you listened instead of asking. Listening is your greatest tool. Questioning is just a shovel of dirt. Smoke signals tell stories and offer warnings without speech. Hand signals, sign language, make deals and bring peace. Seeing is better than looking. It's the difference between 'visions of grandeur' and 'sight of danger." Would you have fear of Frankenstein if you didn't have sight?"

Carlos, "I've learned a lot since I've been here, Abby. This farm is just what I needed for my soul, but I still have a lot to learn and process."

Abby, "Carlos, let's go for a walk."

Margarette, "That's a great idea. Fidel and I have much to catch up on while the chocolate melts and I am sure Juan wants to see him."

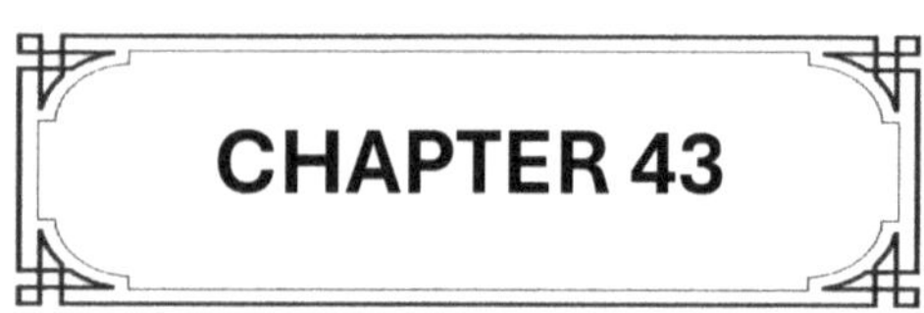

CHAPTER 43

Margarette and Fidel walked next door to Juan's lab. Abby and Carlos walked across the courtyard, behind the Salvarez house, to the common barbecue arena. They sat on bales of hay and talked about the past couple of days.

Carlos asked, "Abby, may I go in?" Abby, "Sure. Let's see where this goes."

Abby turned and looked directly into Carlos' eyes. The contact transmission worked, and Carlos was gone. He went back to the hovel in Rome. Abby opened up and allowed the entry into her movie-reel mind and made herself free of obstacles or distractions.

Carlos became Artemus as a young man. Felicia was a mature woman. It was now 10 years after Argos had died. She was raising Artemus to be an oar-maker like his father.

Artemus was very close to his mother, and to his dismay. watched her take ill. She was battling scarlet fever and not doing well. During her high fever, she experienced hallucinations. She had visions of how she,

Argos and Artemus would reunite. Artemus was by her side every moment possible. She gained consciousness but was fading in and out of delirium in her final days of life. She knew she was dying and wanted to pass on as much information as possible to her loving son. Artemus tended to her every need, feeding her, helping her drink herbal tea and water, and even changing her clothes and undergarments. Artemus was even able to find a person knowledgeable in herbs who knew what to do for Felicia to bring her some comfort and cool her fever with golden seal and comfrey. Felicia told Artemus to learn and remember everything about herbs, teas and potions. She reminded him to fill his empty pockets full of wisdom. This was, of course, the saying Argos had said on his deathbed when referring to the future. Felicia also reminded Artemus that they would all meet again after being washed ashore on some foreign land, and that it would be up to that "new" person possessing their spirit and soul to find the cord and reunite, "some other place, some other time." Felicia suggested that Artemus would find her on a big bird that streaked across the sky and screeched like a peacock and that their eyes would help them find the spiritual cord of kinship. But, alas, she could not tell him who these people would be, because she did not know. The lesson would be in remaining perceptive and open to energy waves, to be willing to accept the unknown and receive it as a blessing.

Felicia passed her spirit and soul while she lay in Artemus arms on the fourth day of her fever. He breathed in her last exhalation and then exhaled and released her entire soul to the spirit world, blessing the wind, that someone else might breathe it in and be transformed in another life.

Artemus gave up oar-making and took to walking, traveling, listening and preaching. He saw himself as a dry sponge longing to be moistened from other people's knowledge, even if it was just from an eye dropper of experience. His wanderings then took him back to the Holy Land. He had heard of tribes and bands of religious nomads spreading the word of God as the Sole Creator. These preachings were not yet organized. Many zealots and orators who spoke against the state were executed, imprisoned or crucified.

As Carlos sat on the bale of hay, deep in his trance, he viewed Artemus and all of the goodness he was doing in helping others he met on the path who were more desperate and destitute than he was. He possessed the Midas touch of healing. There were others like him who believed.

Carlos twitched, Abby blinked, and it was over. Carlos, immediately composed, marveled at what he had seen and where he had traveled.

Abby confessed she had held nothing back, but was not there with him.

"Where did you go, Carlos?" she asked.

"Well, I saw you die in Artemus' arms just the way Pedro described it when you, as Felicia, saw Argos die in your arms. Then I observed the remainder of my adult life, and I was just getting to the place where I was absorbing everyone else's energies and ways of the world when I came out of it. But just before I did, I heard of this young man-younger than I was at the time-who was born in Bethlehem and declared to be the Son of God. The Roman soldiers were in pursuit of him for blaspheming against the state. And, Abby, I never got to meet him because I died. I don't remember how I died. Maybe I came back too soon. But I know now, I must learn everything I can from Jesús and others as ! 'fill my empty pockets full of wisdom.' Felicia reminded Artemus how vitally important this would be so we could meet again, 'some other place, some other time.' Abby, we did that together on our flight from Miami to our destiny. That was the big bird Felicia mentioned that screeched like a peacock."

Abby said, "You know, Carlos, I think I'm starting to see the big picture here, and perhaps I'm starting to 'fix the leak.' I need more time here. It's all about acquiring, learning, experiencing. filling up and spilling over-nor leaking it out, but spilling it over."

"Eortal," Jesús whispered from behind a tall mound of baled hay. Abby and Carlos turned and saw Jesús come out from hiding. Abby asked. "Jesús, you no longer startle me, but what did you say?"

"Eortal is an ancient Greek word of mythology. I love inventing words and feelings. Some are invisible, and some you cannot touch-like love. Eortal is the formula for life, the recipe for 'head food. It means experience, observe, reason, theorize, analyze and learn. Put each beginning letter together and you have 'eortal.' It's what I practice with every breathing moment, breathing in air from others, and releasing air for others. In and out, in and out, in and out. Practice it long enough and you will know the precise moment the exact breath-when you won't have to breathe in again, and then you become one with the weather upon that final exhalation. And that, my friends, is what it's all about. It's not really about past lives. It's about eternity and oneness-cortal.

Today is today, and tomorrow never comes because suddenly it is today again. Walk with that, become that, own it. Own yourself and you won't need me anymore. Then we will be able to play. You are too much work for me now, Abby. Go play-dance- screw around jump up and down-fly-swim and do better things for others now. Be more kind. Gentleness fixes leaks." Abby, "You blow my mind, Jesús." Carlos, "Mine, too."

Jesús, "Then it is time for me to leave."

Jesús walked away from Abby and Carlos, whose jaws were gaping in wonder. They were stunned and amazed-so stunned that they simply stared and watched Jesús walk into the orchards, with not a word spoken. They looked at each other and shrugged their shoulders, then exhaled two gigantic sighs simultaneously.

"Let's go find Fidel and Margarette," Abby said to Carlos.

They hopped off their bales and landed on the ground like paratroopers landing on a battlefield, but not before Abby informed Carlos that their contract transmissions would be limited henceforth. She asked for his understanding because she needed to relieve the pressure of constantly projecting the movie in her eyes. Carlos got the message and agreed not to ask her for a while.

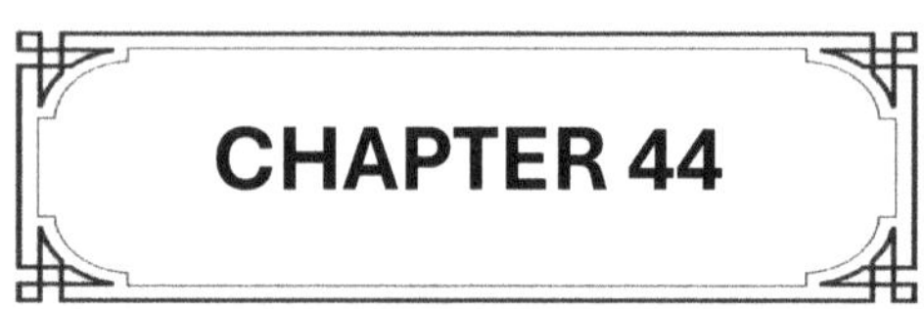

CHAPTER 44

Fidel and Margarette were just walking out of Juan's lab. They all waved to each other from across the courtyard. Abby and Carlos turned and waited on the porch of the main house. Juanita stepped onto the porch and Carlos and Juanita's eyes met in a look of erotic passion. No one else noticed. Fidel asked Abby if she was ready to go just at the same time Margarette invited them to stay for dinner. Abby, "We really should get going. I have to prepare to start work with your son and Lolita."

Margarette, "So you've made your decision, a wise one at that." Juanita, "There's always something for you here anytime, Abby."

Abby. "Well, thanks. That's so generous and reassuring to hear." Fidel led Abby to the safari buggy and they were off, leaving the Salvarez farm in a cloud of dust- "hi-o Silver!"

Juanita followed Carlos-innocently enough-into the community building for an "afternoon delight" in Carlos' room. She was so anxiously hot for him that she peeled off her blouse, like a stripper in a New York club, just inside the empty foyer. By the time they got to Carlos' room, her bra was off and her shorts unzipped.

Carlos was naked in a flash, and Juanita was on her knees sucking him. Carlos had hold of her head as it moved up and down on his wildly hard erection. She suddenly stopped and licked her way up his belly to his mouth and French-kissed him as she pushed him backward onto the bed. She mounted his penis like a cowboy putting his buffalo rifle into its sheath on his saddle. The smoking guns erupted in a duel of orgasms. She was riding her wild brahma, taming his bucking ride to a fine, well-tuned cantor, swear pouring from their bodies.

When the ride was over, Juanita dismounted and lay beside Carlos, staring at the ceiling. Their sweat dissipated and the breathing from the snorting bull and rider returned to normal.

Juanita, "You are delicious, Carlos. A marvelous Latin lover. I am happy you are here, but don't go getting any romantic ideas like falling in love-yet-at least don't tell me yet."

Carlos, "I think we had this conversation once before, and I'm willing to play the game. I don't want to blow a good thing. I'll leave the romance up to you."

On that note, Juanita got dressed and left Carlos naked on his bed in his room.

Satisfied, Carlos got dressed and went down to his kitchen to prepare dinner for the workers. He decided on stuffed peppers and refried beans and rice with a green salad. Employee dinners on the farm were always served buffet style, and diners could sit anywhere at the picnic tables in the community room.

Carlos blended right in with his new environment. He made friends easily. And to think he was going to hijack a plane just a few weeks prior to the changing of his life because of Abby. Amazing how a fleeting glimpse into someone's eyes of perception can open doors into a new and enlightened world. This was a complete turn- around for Carlos. Abby and all of the unknowing, innocent passengers on Flight 305 out of Miami to Guatemala would never know how their destinies were changed by fate and a glance into her eyes.

Carlos reflected on all of these events of the past few weeks and found that he was in love with life itself. Now he was settled into a job, had a place to live and eat, and many things to learn from Jesús and the other people with knowledge. Carlos now had a purpose. Yet the greatest gift was looking into Abby's eyes, getting a contact transmission and being transported back in time to view the movie starring himself as someone in a previous lifetime on this earth, and he knew they were going to be few and far between according to Abby.

Carlos continued to stuff his blanched red, green and yellow peppers with a combination of ground beef and beans. He knew that everyone would eat well at the farm. Happy, healthy people make for prosperous productivity, and the Salvarezes were extremely generous to provide such a pleasant work environment.

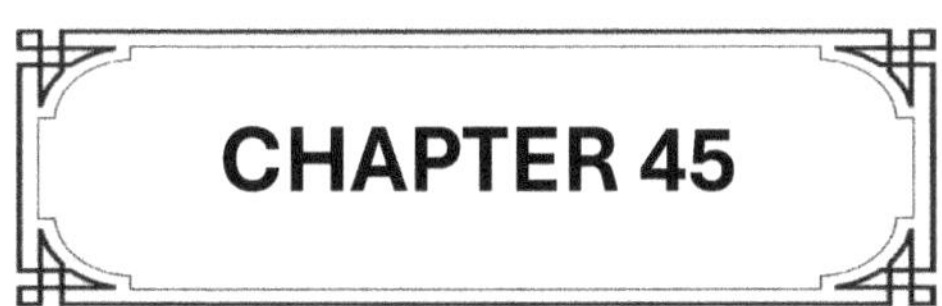

CHAPTER 45

The ride back to Phantom Fantasy was quiet and uneventful for Abby. Fidel asked her to stay over, and she graciously-and happily accepted.

After pulling into the driveway and parking Voyager in the barn, Abby asked to use the phone to call Pedro, and then to call her in-laws in Salem, North Carolina, and her parents in Florida.

Abby called Pedro first and learned that she could start work next week when the two part-time employees' kids were heading back to school. Abby let Fidel know about that great news. Now they had a week to play.

Then Abby called Bob and Pat Schumaker, Stephan's parents. She informed them of all the good news and exciting adventures she had had, leaving out much detail, but emphasizing how right she felt about her decision to return to Guatemala and the clinic where she had recovered from their tragic accident.

Abby made one more phone call to her parents, and bridges were built all the way from Callebocca to North

Carolina and Florida. All was well across the spanning structure of this spiritual architecture.

Abby asked her father if he still had contacts with people from Dupont. She remembered that one of her father's friends had a son who taught English Lit. and folklore at Clark University in Williamstown, Massachusetts. Her father told her that he knew the son personally and gave Abby his name and phone number. She wanted to call him and find out if there was any way of contacting Arlo Guthrie. Abby's father offered to assist, but Abby refused, and so he gave her all the information she needed. She had a real desire to go forward and pursue all available avenues to bring Arlo and Dylan to Callebocca to meet Jesús.

The professor's name was Dr. Jeffrey Noore. Abby called him and they spoke for about half an hour. It turned out that the guy was an old Dylan fan and played in a band, writing original music and lyrics. He even cut a few CDs at his own expense using studio musicians at a local recording studio where, lo and behold, Arlo had done some recording. Jeff and Arlo had jammed together at a few impromptu sessions. They got drunk once and Arlo cold Jeff a story about the time Bob Zimmerman came knocking at their door in New Jersey looking to meet his father, Woody, who was in the Brooklyn State Hospital, never to come home again. Arlo went on to say that this young punk named Bob taught him how to play the harmonica that day. Arlo was 11 and Bob was 19. The year was 1960.

Abby told Jeff about hoping for Dylan and Jesús to meet, and Jeff was quite impressed with this serendipitous plan. He invited her to his home when, and if, it could be arranged to meet Arlo.

The stage was set. The only thing that remained was the cast of characters. All Abby could do was wait, hopefully without worrying herself out of it. She ruminated on Jesús' mantra to "give up, turn yourself in, and fix the leak." In order to pull this off, Abby knew she'd have to sit on a fence post and begin repairs. Fidel could help, and so could Pedro.

Abby could smell something delicious that Fidel was cooking in the kitchen. She had just hung up the phone with Jeff and now related the conversation to Fidel.

Fidel, "This would be the perfect week to go to America before you start working at the clinic. The timing is just right. When did this guy say he was going to look into it?"

Abby, "I'm thinking right away."

Fidel, "Well, let's not lose any sleep over it."

Abby, "I don't plan to. I gave him two contact numbers where he could reach me. It's all up to him now."

Fidel, "Shall we eat?"

Abby, "God, it smells great. I'm famished. What's for dinner?" Fidel, "Crab cakes and rice."

Abby, "My all-time favorite!"

Fidel, "Would you like a little Chardonnay with your meal?" Abby, "Yes, please."

They slept warmly together that night like two bagel halves in a toaster perpetually set at "warm"-or "toast," depending on the moment.

The next day, Jeff called Abby at Fidel's house. It was 7 a.m., and they were silently enjoying their coffee before their walk around the grounds when they would make a change in the zen garden.

Jeff had good news. He'd called Arlo immediately after hanging up with Abby. Arlo had informed Jeff that it was the anniversary of his Dad's 80th birthday coming up in three days. Arlo had never celebrated the anniversary of Woody's passing on his birthday. A morbid thing to remember, but who could forget when it's your Dad? Nevertheless, it would be a day of celebration. Arlo wanted it to be a grand party for his father's 80th birth-day, not death- day. He invited Pete Seger, Buffie St. Marie, Joan Baez, Leonard Cohen and Bob Dylan as special guests, and more friends who had been at Woody's deathbed. Jeff explained Abby's idea about the play, "Jesús Meets the Rabbi." Because Arlo really liked the idea of going to Guatemala, he invited Jeff and Abby to the party in remembrance of his dad, but he didn't tell them who was on the "special guest list." He wasn't sure if any of them would be able to come. Besides, Arlo loved the element of surprise. So as far as Jeff and Abby were concerned, Arlo simply invited them solely on Jeff's proposal. It was a potential business venture and, most definitely, a spiritual uplifting-right up Arlo's alley.

It was Wednesday morning when Jeff called. The party Arlo was throwing was on Saturday, and Jeff and Abby were now invited. Could she swing arrangements to get there? She told Jeff she'd call him back later in the day.

Abby's work at the clinic was to start one week from the time of the call. "I'm sure Pedro would understand if I asked for a few more days or it's feasible I could be back here by Wednesday of next week. I could leave as late as Friday, travel all day, go to the gig on Saturday, meet whomever I'm supposed to meet and come back on either Monday or Tuesday." She was thinking out loud to Fidel.

Fidel, "Forgive me for butting in and being so presumptuous, but would you like some company? I've got about a million frequent flyer miles, and I'd love to see the Berkshires this time of year. The last time I was in Boston was when Pedro was going to med school at Harvard in 1986. The trip will be on me."

Abby, "My God, what more could I ask for? I'll start making reservations right now."

Fidel, "I use a bush pilot to fly me in and out of dark, secret, hidden places. He has his own airstrip on his farm about 20 minutes from here. Let me call him first and see if he can fly us to Guatemala City. It's about a 45-minute flight. He'll do it for a hundred bucks."

Abby, "Then let me call some airlines and see who's flying out of Guatemala City to either Miami, New York or Boston."

Abby called around and discovered that Continental flew every day to New York, leaving at 11:45 a.m. and 5:20 p.m. Once there. they could hop a commuter shuttle to Logan Airport in Boston. Seats were available on both flights on both Thursday and Friday. Now Fidel could call Philipp, and see if his plane was available either of those days and times.

Philipp, answered on the third ring, and, yes, he was available Thursday, but not Friday. Fidel booked his services, and Philipp. said they should be at his dirt airstrip by 8 a.m. tomorrow.

Abby called Continental and booked two seats on the 11:45 a.m. flight to New York. It was set. They were going to a party at Arlo Guthrie's place in Tanglewood, Massachusetts! Abby was dazzled by the spontaneity of how it was all falling into place, especially Fidel's accompaniment and the free tickets.

All of the technical arrangements had been made.

Abby called Jeff back and told him the approximate time of arrival into Boston. They would rent a car and drive 2-1/2 hours west. Barring any delays with connecting flights from New York to Boston, and considering layovers, baggage claim and car rental, they should be checking into a motel in Stockbridge, Massachusetts. around midnight. They would meet Jeff for the first time the next day, Friday. They agreed to rendezvous at Alice's Restaurant in Stockbridge, an easy place to find.

The remainder of that Wednesday was spent calling Pedro and Lolita, then Carlos. Their itinerary was given to everybody. Pedro reassured Abby that it would be all right to stay an extra day or two. Considering the play they were about to produce and direct, the future looked bright. Abby wondered if Jesús required any forewarning of this production, which was to star himself, and Pedro said, "Absolutely not! Jesús will appear when the time is right. You shouldn't brief him or have him prepare for this meeting." So that was that.

Carlos was thrilled at the theme of the production and the characters playing in the "Theater of All Possibilities." He just wanted an invitation to that special campfire. And so it would be.

Abby and Fidel packed their things and went to bed early, without making love-that would have been too much excitement. Fidel's house was self-sufficient when he had to be gone for long periods of time, so a 1-week absence required no real preparations on his part.

They awoke on Thursday to the clanking of bamboo in the morning breeze. It looked like they could expect a beautiful travel day.

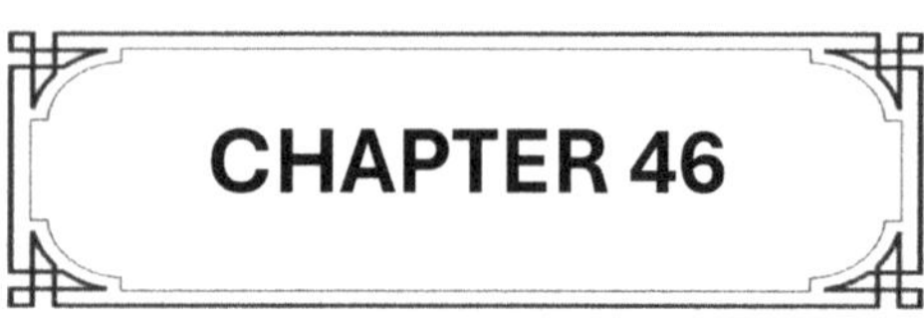

Philipp, revved up the twin engines on his plane, and before they knew it, they were full throttle running down the dirt strip waiting for the big lift everyone prays for at takeoff.

The second flight, from Guatemala City to New York took off on time. It was scheduled to be approximately a 9-hour flight. Abby and Fidel slept and woke, slept and woke, read and slept some more.

They even went to the bathroom together and joined the Mile High Club! Who would have thought that that tiny cubicle of a bathroom could be converted into a sex parlor? Abby sat on the sink and lifted her skirt. Fidel pulled her panties off and she conveniently nestled backside into the sink while Fidel pulled his pants down. She whispered in his ear, "I hope the 'Occupied' sign is visible." The door was locked-Fidel had checked-as they rhythmically pumped their way to mute and mutual orgasm.

And so they secretly joined that prestigious club without anyone else knowing. They thought there must be a million anonymous members.

They landed at LaGuardia Airport in New York at 9 p.m. The next air shuttle to Boston was at 9:20. How perfect! They raced to get on it. The plane touched down in Boston at 10:30. They got their bags, rented a car and decided to find a motel on the Mass. Pike off Route 128 west of Boston. They were in the Holiday Inn and asleep by midnight.

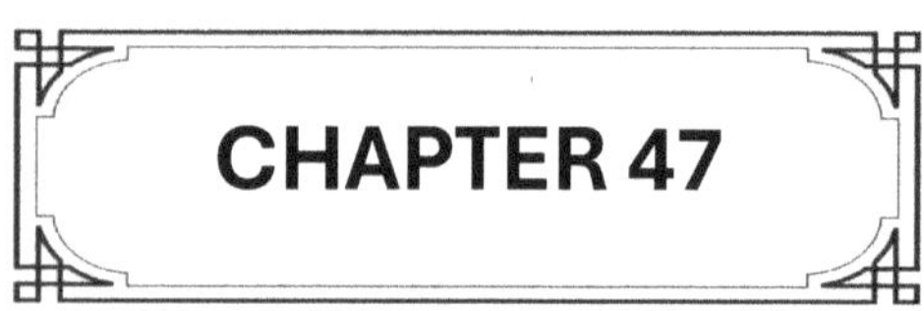

CHAPTER 47

The next morning they rose, air-battered and road-weary. They mustered the energy to shower, eat breakfast and push on to Stockbridge, another two hours west on the Mass. Pike. Their excitement escalated in the car as they anticipated meeting Jeff and looked forward to that special birthday party on Saturday.

It was late May and New England was doing its typical spring thing that it had done since the sun started its daily rise and God made butterflies. Wildflowers were in full bloom in the median of the highway, separating east- and westbound traffic. Trees were leafing and meadows were meadowing. As they say, this part of New England was "greenin' up fastah than up north." The temperature was a mild 73 degrees by high noon, and there wasn't a cloud in the sky. The Berkshire Mountains began to rise like big goosebumps on the horizon.

Abby reminded Fidel about what Jesús and Pedro had said about goosebumps, that they appear in times of fear or feelings of sensual pleasure. "When the earth makes goosebumps, we call them mountains," Abby said, and her words fell onto the dashboard of their Saturn rental car.

Just as Jeff had said, they had no problem finding Alice's Restaurant. They parked the car half a block away at a little past noon and strolled into this famous eatery.

Abby had met Jeff a few times maybe 10 years before when her Dad took her to the Dupont Company parties on the holidays and had seen him at summer picnics. Jeff's Dad's name was Peter, and Abby specifically remembered the co-ed, parent-child softball games they had played in. Could she recognize Jeff 10 years later? Would he have 10 years' worth of hair and facial growth? Would he be bald with a beard? Would he be heavy or skinny?

Alice's was crowded when Fidel and Abby walked in. They scanned the tabletops looking for perhaps someone waving at them. to get their attention. Sure enough, Jeff was motioning for them to join him on the side by the window. He rose to embrace Abby. who then introduced Fidel, and the three sat down.

Jeff, "Abby, you've changed. You are more beautiful than I remembered when you were standing on second base waiting for your Dad to get a hit. You beat us that day."

Abby, laughing, "Gosh, I can't believe you remember that from so long ago."

Jeff, "My mind is maybe on the petite size, but I remember every finite, minute detail of every beautiful event. All others! forget."

Abby, "You're a philosopher, too."

Fidel, "He'll get along well with Jesús."

Jeff, "Who's Jesús?"

Abby, "Well, you know, I can't answer that exactly. He's like an anchovy if you want to know what one tastes like, you have to put it in your mouth. He's the guy we want you, Dylan and Arlo to meet." Jeff, "Well, I can tell you, Arlo is excited, but apprehensive about you two being here as unknown outsiders, but he likes the prospects."

Abby, "Understandable--and to be expected."

Jeff, "And as far as Dylan being there, there's no way of knowing. I've gotten to know Arlo through our jam sessions, and the one thing I've learned is not to ask questions to a famous person about another famous person. What rises to the surface bubbles like stew and secrets are revealed in the steeping, not the stirring. So Arlo has really respected me for not asking, and he's offered little tidbits during our breaks. It's a blending of all the right ingredients, not too much heat, and plenty of simmering to reach the palette. That's why you've been invited to his party." Fidel, "A privilege and an honor."

Jeff then asked Fidel, "What do you do for work?" Fidel. "I escort beautiful women to their destinations." Abby, "Fidel is a jokester."

Fidel, "Yes, I teach people to laugh by forcing them out of their serious skin."

All three began to laugh.

After lunch, Jeff invited them back to his place. He lived about 15 minutes from the restaurant with his wife, Bev, on five acres with a nice cabin they had built themselves.

Abby and Fidel followed Jeff in their rent-a-car. Jeff's beautiful, large, modern log cabin was nestled in a forest that opened onto a clearing, with rolling fields in back which comprised the remaining four acres. Nothing was fenced in, and two black labs came bounding from the porch, barking, "Welcome home, Dad! You brought us some new friends to drool on and love! Now pet me... no, pet me... no, pet me! Woof, woof."

Abby's arms encompassed both dogs as they licked her cheeks. Fidel patted their rumps.

Jeff introduced them, "That's Fido, and this is Play-do. They're brothers and one becomes the other when you call them, so you can't go wrong with identifying them. They are inseparable. And this is Bev, my beehive of honey and nectar." Jeff gestured to the porch where his wife was standing. Abby climbed the three steps to greet her. They hugged and then Fidel approached and reached out to shake Bev's hand. She disregarded it and hugged him tightly, too, to let him know he was welcome.

Fidel, "You good white woman. You got red blood. A Blackfoot medicine man once told me that upon our first meeting in Montana."

Bev, "How interesting!"

"I like greeting people for the first time with a hug, but one must be careful and respectful of different cultures. Hug a chief in the middle of the Amazon, or a warrior in the heart of Mongolia, and you will never get any closer than their flesh, for they feel you don't know them well enough for intimacy, and then you have instantly built an invisible, impenetrable wall of psychic fear. It will take a lot of trust and building of confidence for you to ever hug that person again. That's why I naturally reach out for a handshake. Thanks for the hug."

Jeff, "Sounds like you're a world traveler."

Fidel, "It's in my blood."

Jeff gestured for everyone to come inside. Abby immediately spotted a book of photography on their coffee table. It was Manhole Covers of the World, by Fidel Hernandez.

Abby, "Fidel, look! My God, this is your book!"

Jeff and Bev both exclaimed together, "This is your work? You shot all of these manhole covers? This is one of our most treasured possessions." Jeff continued, "This is amazing. You won't believe this, but I give this photo book as a gift all the time. In fact, I gave one to Arlo two years ago. Geez, I had no idea."

Fidel, "Well, like that stew, all things surface and bubble. I really don't like to sound like I'm bragging about it. So if the pot is right, the heat is right and you don't over-stir, eventually the ingredients begin to merge."

Bev, "Well, this is certainly going to be interesting tomorrow. Did you bring your camera, Fidel? I'm familiar with your other famous accomplishments as well. You've won a lot of awards."

Fidel, "Yes, I brought my other little traveling companion. If the time is right and the lighting perfect, I'll take a few shots. Cameras can be like filthy tongues dipped in vinegar. If you pull it out at a most inopportune time, it sours all who experience it." Jeff, "Especially with the guests you might see at Arlo's tomorrow."

Fidel, "I will become invisible, like unexposed film, until someone chooses to expose me. Then I'll turn a negative into a positive."

Jeff, "Well, I can tell you, Arlo loved that Manhole Covers book for its creativity and uniqueness, so be ready to accept a compliment."

All four spent the rest of the afternoon wandering the grounds, pausing here and there to tell a story, and eventually worked their way to the barn where Jeff and his band rehearsed. The barn was nicely refinished and quite cozy. The drums were in place, and a few acoustic guitars had been left in their stands. An upright bass was standing there as if it was looking for Burl Ives.

"What's the name of your band, Jeff?" Abby asked.

"We're called The Berkshire Boys," Jeff replied.

Abby, "But you're teaching full time at Clark, aren't you?" Jeff, "Yeah, English Lit. and folklore. It feeds my love of oration. But my true love is playing live on stage and entertaining big groups of people. It's either an audience of students filling their ears with Billy Shakes or, depending on the crowd, me wailing Blind Lemon Jefferson's "Southern Blues." Open thy mouth and something is bound to spew forth, either words or song."

They left the barn musically deprived, echoing the unsung tunes left behind on the unplayed strings of the Martin D-28. Fidel was questioned further by Bev about his photographic expeditions.

Abby and Jeff talked about their parents and Dupont.

Eventually, Abby told them the story of the trip to Central America and how she lost her husband, Stephan. As she was recalling the details, she patted the hip pocket of her jeans and psychically whispered a silent breath to Stephan. Contact transmissions were discussed and defined. Bev and Jeff were intrigued and obviously curious to jump into the movie in Abby's eyes. They wanted to "fall." But Abby already knew from when they would stare at her while she had been speaking that it wasn't meant to be. They were on different wavelengths. She did manage, however, to enlighten them to look into someone's eyes with a different perception from then on. William Blake was discussed, and Jeff decided to put on The Doors "Morrison's Hotel." That led to a discussion about Jim Morrison.

The afternoon rolled into dusk, and stomachs began to growl.

Dinner was homemade pizza and salad. Fidel loved it, and so did Abby. Three empty bottles of wine stood looking lonely on the coffee table-no longer drunk, but the partakers were. They finally retired to bed. Two beds rocked that night as the walls were engraved with new, invisible sex graphics, and the observing ghost of Stephan moaned to Abby's gyrations. He rested contentedly in Abby's back pocket on the floor by the bed and wondered: Was his cord being washed ashore in the next room also?

Saturday morning, everyone gathered in the kitchen to have coffee and discuss what lay ahead that night. So Jeff brought them up to date about the day's events, including the 45-minute drive to the Guthries'. He then placed a call to Arlo and was heard talking privately to him about Fidel and Abby and asking what time the party started. "We'll be there by 5 tonight," he said. hanging up.

Jeff, "Well, it's set. We're on."

Abby, "Do you think there will be live music?"

Jeff, "Only if it's impromptu. I don't think he'll have a band playing. There won't be that many people there. It was invitation only, and only to those few who had a personal connection with his father."

Bev, "It'll be fun, I'm sure, and lots of good food. Arlo and Theresa have four kids. I know they'll be there. Jeff and I are about 10 years younger than Arlo and Theresa."

Abby. "That puts us all about the same age, except for Fidel. He must be Arlo's age."

Fidel, "Maybe a few winks older, or a few blinks younger-all depends on how you look at it."

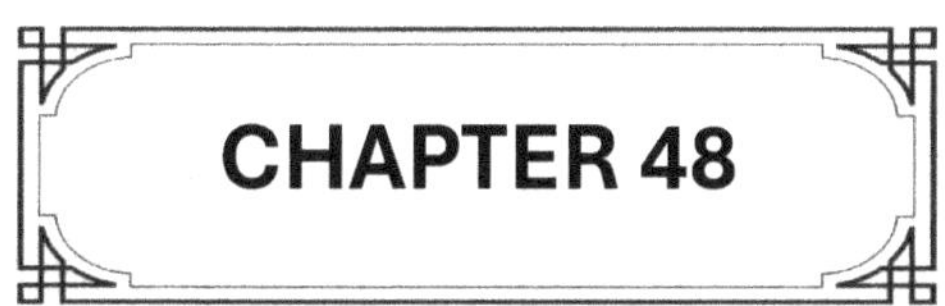

CHAPTER 48

Jeff, Bev, Abby and Fidel piled into Jeff's Suburban at about 4:15 and they were off to Arlo's. Three quarters of an hour later, they pulled off the road and onto a private driveway. Within a hundred feet, there were a couple of pick-up trucks parked with six guys sitting on the tailgates. They hopped off their asses and stood there to stop the car. They were checking people to make sure they were on the guest list. The Guthries wanted no party- crashers. The lead spokesman had a clipboard and checked "Noore party of 4" off the list.

Jeff proceeded a half mile down the drive and came upon another person standing by a pick-up directing people where to park. There were about 20 cars and trucks parked on the grass by the barn. Many guests were mingling outside. Arlo was outside and spotted Jeff's car. He came strutting over as they were getting out. His long gray curly locks flowed from his head down his shoulders and halfway down his back. His beard was gray and straggly.

"Hey, far out, man! You made it past the guards. I guess you were invited. Come on up. Who are your friends?" Arlo jovially asked.

"Abby and Fidel from Guatemala," Jeff said.

"Hey, far out. You're the folks who want to take us on a spiritual trip. Hey, far out, man. I love tripping. Hey, come on up, man. It's my Dad's 80th birthday. Happy Birthday, Dad," Arlo sang, looking up into the beautiful May sky.

Arlo gestured to the open barn doors and told them they could head on back there if they wanted--that's where the food and the bar was but they decided to go up into the main mansion. On the way, they saw a huge banner flying between two trees about 30 feet apart that read, "This land is your land." On entering the house, they saw people mingling everywhere. Abby and Fidel heard someone playing a guitar off to their right in the living room. They couldn't see who it was, but they heard a woman's voice, in perfect pitch, and knew it had to be Joan Baez. Abby recognized her voice and felt goosebumps, a sign of pure sensual pleasure. Abby knew she was in the presence of something very powerful that night.

Arlo spotted Theresa and called to her. She came over and hugged Jeff and Bev. When everyone else was introduced, Jeff told them that Fidel was the author of Manhole Covers of the World.

Arlo, "Hey, far out, man. I love that book. You showed us where all the shit hides. Hey, will you sign my copy?".

Fidel, "Yeah. That's funny. Sure I'll sign it."

Just then, Arlo glanced over Fidel's shoulder and fell into Abby's.

"Good God! Where'd you get those piercers, Abby? You have some depth to your perception--reminds me of a movie I saw once starring Sophia Loren."

Abby, "I was born with these. They have shown me the way."

Arlo, "Well, it's a beautiful movie, and it seems ancient to me. Perhaps we were lovers! Hey, far out, man. Hey, Theresa, Abby and I were ancient lovers. I can feel it in my bones and see it in her eyes."

Theresa, "Are you trying to make me jealous?"

Arlo, "No, that was then, this is now. It's not like she's a girlfriend from high school and I asked her to take a ride in my GTO. I really saw a glimpse of old London and the Bowery-- whores and stench. Wow, I love your eyes, Abby."

It was obvious there was some compatible DNA mixed in with that contact transmission. Abby got what she wished for, a connection to Arlo.

Arlo looked at Jeff, Bev, Abby and Fidel and said, "Hey, man. you're on your own. Mingle, nibble, dribble and fiddle."

The four of them wanted to stay together, so they grabbed beers and worked their way into the living room. Joan Baez was just finishing up her rendition of

John Prine's "Say Hello in There." It was wonderful and chilling. There were about a dozen people circling Joan-no real applause, just recognition of her greatness. This was not a concert. Joan passed the guitar over to a dark-skinned woman with long black hair streaming down her back like waves of angels. It was Buffie St. Marie who they recognized as a songwriter and singer from the '60s. She took the guitar and strummed "Blowin' in the Wind," her voice reverberating like steel wheels thundering down a cyclone track. Her voice was as melodic as hearts in love. Abby's arms looked like a gaggle of geese had been walking on them leaving bumps. It was the most sensual rendition of "Blowin' in the Wind" she had ever heard but no applause, just words of appreciation.

Jeff, Bev, Abby and Fidel meandered outside. The trees blocked most of the sunset, so it appeared darker sooner than they would have expected. Arlo was making announcements from inside on the PA system. He could easily be heard from the outside speakers mounted in the trees and on the barn about 200 feet from the house. He was suggesting that people gather in the barn for a dedication in memory of Woody. White lights came on and adorned the tree trunks, the rooftop of the barn and its big sliding doors.

The four were almost at the barn as they heard Arlo announce, "Grub is on the table and the brew is in the barrels," as they heard a dinner bell being run.

There were already about 50 people mingling in the huge open space of the barn. Long banquet tables were arranged buffet style so that a line could pass on either side.

The barn had a second story that was open, and a balcony overlooked the ground floor like an observation stage for med students to observe a surgical procedure. People were sitting on the edge with their legs dangling down.

The idea was to serve yourself and find a place to sit and eat. There were barrels of ice cold beer over by the bar where there was plenty of liquor and wine, and you had to be your own bartender. Abby said, "Let's go get a drink first."

"Good idea," said Jeff.

The four of them strolled past the buffet line to the far end of the barn where there were opposing open barn doors on a pulley track system exposing a gorgeous meadow and wildflowers on rolling hills. Darkness was descending quickly.

Abby bent down to grab a Heineken from the barrel. She happened to look behind her and there sat two older guys on bales of hay shooting the shit. At the same time, Jeff was reaching for his Heineken and saw the same two guys. It was too dark for Abby to recognize them.

Jeff said, in a whisper, "Do you know who they are, Abby?" Abby, "I can't tell."

Jeff, "That's Bob Dylan and Leonard Cohen."

Abby gasped, "Holy shit!"

Jeff, "Don't approach them. Don't say anything. Just leave them alone. Arlo will make the introductions if he feels like it."

Just then they heard Arlo on the loudspeaker again, but now he was holding a microphone and standing on a wooden barrel over by the food.

"Please, can I have everybody's attention? Today-tonight we're here to honor my father. He's 80 years old in heaven and he's here with us in spirit. I wanted as many of his good friends to be here today to celebrate with us in remembrance of him. I don't want this to be a long, drawn-out speech, so have fun tonight. Grab something to eat, drink whiskey and share the spirit of Woody. There won't be any performances, but you can strum a guitar if the spirit moves you. We'll have music on the loudspeaker. Enjoy yourselves--Dad always did."

Arlo hopped down from the barrel to the sound of thank you's from the crowd and made his way over to the bar. He approached Abby and Jeff, Bev and Fidel, who were slugging down Heinekens and sipping wine. Arlo grabbed a Corona from the icewater in the barrel and looked over toward the two men who were still speaking in the darkness on the far side of the barn.

"Hey. Bob, excuse me. I want you to meet the people I was telling you about-from Guatemala," Arlo said loudly. Leonard had started to head over to get some food.

Arlo led the four over to where Bob and Leonard had been sitting. Bob rose and mumbled something like, "Oh, yeah. Hey-yeah- ah-oh-well, um, yeah, Arlo, I remember. Hey, who are you?"

Abby reached out and shook his hand, then Fidel, Jeff and Bev did the same.

Dylan said, "There's a lot of you. You must be big people. Yeah well-ah-um-tell me more about this guy you want me to meet. What's his name?"

Abby, "His name is Jesús and he is one of the people with knowledge, a brujo. He's never been out of the jungle-or Guatemala, for that matter."

Dylan, for the first time, looked into Abby's eyes and staggered backwards.

Arlo laughed and said, "Yeah, they got me, too."

Dylan, "Whoa, man, what's in there? I just saw a huge fire and many people gathered around it. An Indian was walking in circles around the rim of the fire pit. Sparks were going up in the air. dancing with the stars. Whoa, lady, take me there. I want to go."

Arlo, "Are you diggin' that, man? If you go, I go."

Fidel, "I grew up with Jesús. He knows things you wouldn't believe. But before last week, he'd never heard of Bob Dylan. We played "Blood on the Tracks" and "Blonde on Blonde" for him. He loved your music and words, but said he needed to see your eyes to know the truth."

Dylan, "Why didn't you bring him with you?"

Fidel, "He is forced to live in the New World, but he doesn't participate in it. He certainly won't fly on an airplane."

Abby, "Yeah. He has other means to get around."

Dylan, "Well, Ms. Abby, if your eyes tell the truth, I must gather 'round a fire and spill my guts to Jesús."

Arlo, "Is anything really expected of us at this campfire?"

Fidel, "Absolutely not. In fact, expect the unexpected. He may not even show up if the timing isn't right. But I can tell you, if you're there, he'll be there in due time."

Arlo, "You don't expect us to play or anything?"

Abby, "Oh, God, no. This ain't no concert. We just thought it would be interesting to see how this unfolds if we could get a few of you down there for a fireside chat. We're sort of calling it 'Jesús meets the Rabbi' and Friends'-she thought she'd better throw that in to make Arlo feel like a part of the play.

Arlo. "I'm free next week. How 'bout you, Bob? Wanna truck on down to Central America to meet this brujo?"

Dylan, "I could swing it. The sooner the better for me. Let's go tomorrow."

Arlo, "All right with me."

Jeff, "Bev and I are definitely in. We wouldn't miss this for anything on earth."

Abby said to Fidel, "I can't believe this is happening. Pedro's going to freak."

Fidel, "Well, this certainly gives us cause to celebrate. Happy Birthday, Woody."

Dylan, raising his glass, "Yeah. Here's to you, man. Thanks for being there for all of us."

Dylan walked away, and then turned and nodded, saying, "Call me tomorrow. I'm staying in Arlo and Theresa's guest room. We'll make plans to travel. And bring your eyes with you, Abby."

Abby, "Better believe it."

Arlo caught up to Bob, and they adjourned to the buffet table. Abby, Fidel, Jeff and Bev were left standing there in a daze. "What just happened? Was that for real? Are they going to Guatemala with us tomorrow? How are we going to handle the publicity and fame of these guys?" Abby fired off these questions like bullets.

Jeff, "Well, I presume they have traveled before at their own leisure and avoid the press by not raising a fuss or perhaps they travel incognito. So they'll probably board the plane as regular passengers on vacation."

Fidel, "If you don't want the attention, don't look up. Keep your eyes to the ground and no one will recognize you. Wear normal clothes-nothing outlandish or flamboyant."

Abby. "We'll get them there unnoticed and untouched with the help of Jesus' prayers."

Bev, "Jeff, we should get something to eat and then head for home to pack."

Abby, "Fidel and I will make all of the flight arrangements to get us all to Callebocca."

Jeff, "How are we going to handle the financing of this little escapade?"

Fidel, "Well, I have a lot of frequent flyer miles that I'm willing to use for everyone. Once we're there, we have friends who can each put up a few folks, and we can have a few at my home. Abby. don't you think Jeff and Bev should stay at Pedro and Lolita's?"

Abby, "Absolutely. Bob and Arlo and Theresa can either stay at your place or the Salvarez farm where Jesús will hopefully be found."

Fidel, "Let's call Pedro and let him know we are bringing the 'Theater of all Possibilities' to Callebocca."

Abby, "Yes, we should do that. But first let's give Jeff and Bev a heads-up of what's in store for them. You two will be staying with Pedro, a childhood friend of Fidel's. Pedro is a doctor who runs a local clinic in his hometown. He's a genuine heart-soul healer. My husband and I had a terrible automobile accident in Guatemala several months ago. My husband died in the crash. Fidel stopped on the side of the road, after being flagged down, and transported me to Pedro's clinic. I was unconscious. That's where I recovered. Trust us, you'll be safe and in good hands at Pedro's."

Jeff, "We trust you implicitly. You guys came this far to see if you could put this gig together, and you did. Arlo and Bob are committed and, Lord knows, Abby, our parents have been best of friends. We trust you."

Abby, "Enough said, except I just love you both for making this happen."

Jeff and Bev said good-night to Fidel and Abby and were off to thank Arlo and Theresa. Suddenly, when they were halfway out of the barn, they shouted back to Fidel and Abby. "Hey, you two are coming with us, remember?"

They all laughed hilariously and couldn't believe Jeff and Bev had almost left without them.

After bidding adieu to all-Dylan, Leonard and Joan were not to be found Jeff drove them back to his home. The excitement that ran through the Suburban was like their own private electrical storm. They marveled at how this was unfolding the same way Peter Pan found his way to "never-never-land" with Tinkerbell's magic dust and the wonders of flight, the same way Jesús appeared in places where he couldn't be seen and then popped up in the jungle or some strange bar or perching on a fence post posing as a raven. The world in all its wonderment had sprinkled some glitter on the stage tonight. It was one of those rare performances that, if you missed it, you weren't supposed to be there. There was no dress rehearsal for this 1-act play and no seconds, fill-ins or walk-ons. The curtain was about to go up and everyone come to life-real life, alive with electric current.

(Author's note: Where there is electricity, there are poles, north, south, east, west, plus and minus. The Zen Buddhist would say, "Go with the flow." The Jungian would say, "Don't push the river." The Native American would say, "Thank the four directions of the wind, the great grandfather in the sky, and mother earth." Gandhi would say, "Remain a beacon in your lighthouse guiding the deaf on foggy nights." And Tinkerbell would say, "If you can't please yourself, then please someone else."

Fidel would say, "Be a light, not a lamppost. Illuminate the way for others to see."

And Jesús would say, "Fix the leak."

This experience could never be repeated. Yet tomorrow night, sitting around a campfire just might be a different story. Tomorrow never comes in "never-never-land." It's always today. Now do you know why? Finally tomorrow comes and, lo and behold, it's today.)

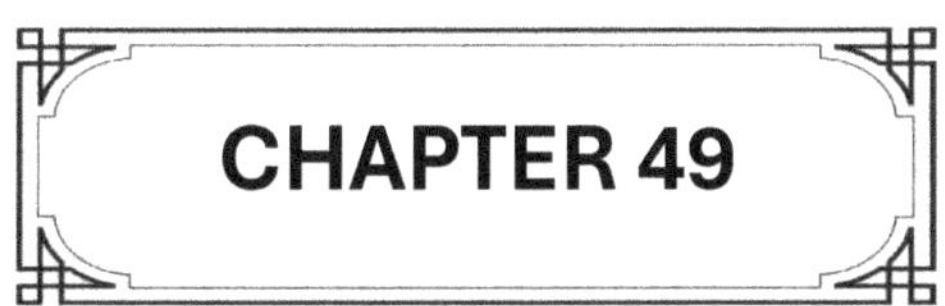

CHAPTER 49

All the flights were arranged for seven reserved seats leaving at 4 p.m. from Boston.

En route to Miami on Flight 1214, Dylan sat beside Abby, and Fidel was on the aisle. Arlo, Theresa and Bev sat across the aisle, and Jeff was right behind Bev.

Abby shared with Bob the details of her adventure in Guatemala. She tried to explain the characters in her contact transmission- who they were and where they fit in-including Jesús.

Dylan was enthralled with Abby's eyes. He wanted to fall into them, and Abby allowed it, since Dylan seemed to have seen something in them last night when they had met at the party.

Abby concentrated on looking at the back of the seat in front of her, then turned sharply and stared into Bob's eyes. He fell. Abby's eyes were wide and allowed no obstacles and no resistance. Bob became part of an Indian tribe somewhere in North America. He seemed to be apprenticing with a shaman. It was cold and there was lots of snow drifting around the teepee. There were hot coals in the center of the teepee on the bare ground in a fire pit and five Indians were seated cross-legged, around the fire, wearing bear hides on their backs. Bob saw himself as one of these braves. It was a positive identity because he heard the brave he perceived as himself say, "To all of creation and all of my relatives." Then he saw a mark on the brave's hand like a half-broken arrow. Bob carried a similar zig-zag birthmark, like a lightning bolt, on his same hand. He realized it could be the other half of this arrow he saw on the brave.

Bob twitched, almost like a spastic jerk, and he was back on Continental Flight 1214.

He was now in the present-but mystified.

Abby said, "Welcome back."

Dylan said, "All my relatives and all of creation.' That's what I bring back with me from the movie I just saw in your eyes. Did you go there? Do you control this?" He rubbed his birthmark on his wrist and thought of "Half-broken Arrow," his Indian name.

Abby, "No, I'm not a channeler or past-life regressor. If the energy is right and the DNA code finds its cord washed up on the shore, then my eyes act as the movie projector and allow you to see yourself as another being from a past life. But I don't program it. Psychic bridges are built and then disappear with a blink. For Pedro, Carlos and me, the most rare contact transmissions occurred, and I was part of the act. For Pedro, I was his lover, and for Carlos, I was his mother. 'Ancient Lovers entwine as one and one becomes the other, some other place, some other time.' Lives were shared, then death, and our breaths were washed ashore in some distant land only to be breathed in and absorbed by some lucky person."

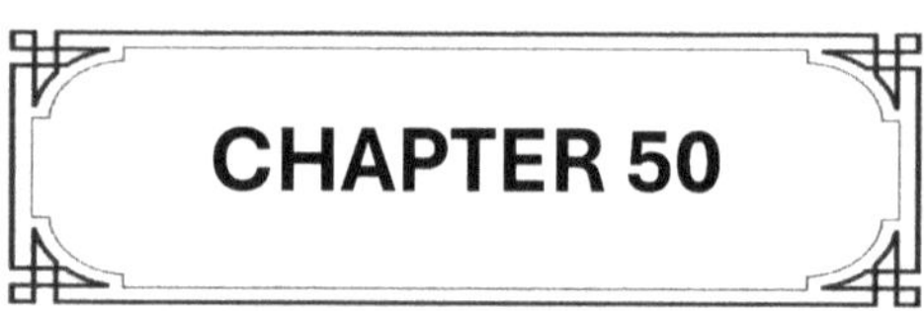# CHAPTER 50

rlo, believe it or not, had his huge mane of hair rolled up into a bun and tucked under a cap that said "Boston Bruins" on the front. Certainly no one would recognize him. It was the perfect disguise.

And since Dylan was known as a master of change, disguise for him was a sports jacket and shirt with jeans and boots and sunglasses no hat and no disheveled hair.

(Author's note: If you don't want attention drawn to you, don't attract it.)

Bob kept his eyes to the ground. The flight was smooth and time passed uneventfully. They landed in Miami at 8:30 p.m. Fidel phoned his bush pilot buddy, Philipp., to meet them at the Guatemala City International Airport tomorrow morning at 9:30 a.m. Once again, not a hitch. Philipp, was available, tuned up, fueled and ready to go. He had no idea who his passengers were going to be. It didn't matter. Fidel had commissioned his services so many times in the past, and had brought in such strange-looking characters that Philipp. had learned not to ask.

The flight from Miami to Guatemala City took eight hours, and they flew through two time zones. Time change in jet travel did not phase Dylan, Arlo, Theresa or Fidel. They were seasoned international travelers, but Abbey, Jeff and Bev were certainly weathered and sleep-deprived which made their moods as jagged as razor blades and as lethal as arsenic and old lace-nothing a little adrenaline rush and a dose of Jesús couldn't remedy.

Philipp, was there on time to greet them after their long ordeal at customs. Everyone was asked the nature of their business. Dylan was heard to say, "We're explorers looking for all my relatives."

The customs person didn't react, just stamped his passport, and Dylan passed through the turnstile into another world.

The flight to Callebocca was bumpy. They passed around some storm clouds to avoid the rain. Philipp, was quite the experienced bush pilot with only two crashes under his belt-no mortalities- but a number of barn roofs shaved off. He certainly knew how to navigate around nimbus and cumulus clouds, but a few times the drop in altitude from hitting an air pocket sent everyone's stomach up to their eyeballs. Gravity always wins and pulled their stomachs back into place. Before too long, they landed on Philipp's dirt airstrip with a pullback on the throttle to help their descent into a soft landing.

(Author's note: After all, when you reduce power, gravity always wins. It holds true with your heart, too.

Loss of power can pull you to the ground, dead, that's when your spirit gets airborne and becomes one with the weather-and eternity.)

They were on the ground, walking away from yet another successful flight. The few bags they carried were thrown into Voyager, which Fidel had left parked near Philipp's hangar, and soon the safari buggy was rolling down the road toward Phantom Fantasy. All but Abby fit comfortably in the front and back seats. In the back with the luggage by the periscope Fidel had mounted for photo shoots, Abby stood holding on for dear life.

The weather was clear, the temperature a balmy 95 degrees, and the time was 1 p.m. Timing is everything.

They checked into Fidel's hacienda and he gave a tour of the house and grounds. After their nude swim in the skinny-dipping pool, everyone felt refreshed, as though the road grime had been washed off. Dried and clothed, Fidel suggested he'd drive Jeff and Bev to Pedro and Lolita's if Abby would call and let them know they had company coming.

Dylan, Arlo and Theresa scrounged around Fidel's library and found some amazing books of ancient times.

Upon Fidel's return two hours later, dinner was waiting. When Fidel had a private moment with Abby, he told her Jesús couldn't be found.

"Oh, great. This is unbelievable. We get these folk heroes down here in the jungle and Jesús decides to disappear. My God, what are we going to do?"

Fidel, "Relax is the first thing. Give up is the second. And trust is the third, which is the same as the first."

Abby, "Don't double-talk me, Fidel."

Fidel, "You'll see. He's always somewhere. You'll see. Where he is is where he's supposed to be. If the spirit moves him, the energy will call to him and he'll be a flame dancing in the fire."

They joined Dylan, Arlo and Theresa on the deck. Twilight had eaten the sunlight and digestion had begun with the stars.

Fidel informed everyone that they would gather at the Salvarez farm tomorrow night for the regular community dinner and campfire that was held every month at full moon. Pedro had told Fidel that his parents were expecting additional friends. There were no further details given of who their guests would be.

Everybody wanted to hit the hay early as travel had thoroughly drained them.

"To all of creation, and all my relatives," Dylan said as all adjourned to their designated bedrooms.

Tomorrow would become today as today had become tomorrow yesterday.

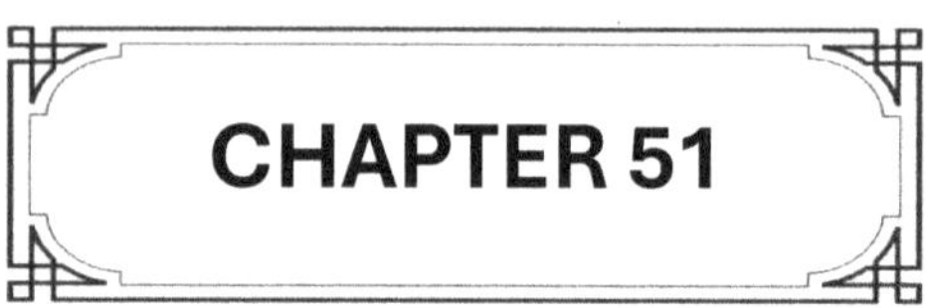

CHAPTER 51

They arrived at the Salvarez farm at sunset and the cloudy horizon exploded in full color as God made love to another angel, and van Gogh dipped his brush into his pallet of color, then his mouth, then onto the canvas sky. There was no greater spectacle than the colors of orgasm during a religious sunrise or sunset. This must have been what led to the belief of creation.

A roaring fire was ablaze and many people gathered around it, all falling into trances. Jesús was nowhere to be found. Dylan asked his new friend Pedro if there was a guitar around. Pedro quickly produced one from his childhood bedroom. No one knew who Dylan was, and those who did didn't care. Arlo was a little taken aback, but he listened. Dylan whispered to him. "It's okay. I wrote this for them on the plane. They deserve it."

Dylan's opening lines were spoken in ballad form while he strummed his guitar to Frankie Lee and Judas Priest. "Ancient lovers entwine as one and one becomes the other... some other place, some other time. We all get washed ashore on a distant land... a cord is found, the rope pulled, and you find you've been in love before. They say there's only one soul mate in this life for everyone. Well, souls get worn like the leather on your sandals, and sometimes you need to get 'em re-'souled. Find another soul mate, walk another path."

Just then, Jesús appeared barefoot walking across the fire. He came out of the flames and approached Dylan looking into his eyes, saying, "I thought so. What is real is actually what is not, yet remains a question. Come with me. We should talk."

Dylan replied, "When I close my eyes, I see lightning storms and thunderbolts exploding in my head."

Jesús said. "That's just your God playing tricks on all of us. Sometimes he threatens us with storm clouds, but they are empty. Other times, he delivers messages full of wind and tears. You are no different. Come, follow me. It is time we talked."

Jesús continued, "There was in my heart once a permanent bleeding interrupted only by the interference of some odd passerby scoffing because I was appearing to be having too much fun."

Dylan said, "And what if we had met 17 minutes later?"

Jesús, "Then we'd be 17 minutes off schedule for the bus, and right on time for this."

Dylan, "You're right. I reckon it's time we talked. So is there any more to this story than just firewalking?"

Jesús, "There is a lot more. This is just the tip of the iceberg." They walked off into the darkness.

The remaining embers glowed and made burps of light in hiccup fashion onto the crowd which seemed not at all concerned about where Bob and Jesús had gone off to.

Abby and Fidel held onto each other like an octopus making love to a conch.

(Author's note: What do you want from life? And the conch said, "Just a little more.")

Arlo and his wife were left twiddling their thumbs trying to hitch a ride to the next conversation.

Juan and Margarette approached them and offered them their genuine hospitality. Juan suggested that this could take some time, depending on how Bob responded to Jesús.

Margarette said, "Ah, yeah. And what about Jesús' disappearing act if he senses Bob is not paying attention?"

"Then they will both be gone, arm-in-arm. Jesús leading the way." Juan interjected.

Arlo, "Man, this is too far out. Here we are in the jungle of Guatemala, and Dylan goes traipsing off with some medicine man." Margarette, "He could not be in better hands. This is the only place on earth for him to be right now."

Conversations dwindled like the fire, and eventually the lights smoldered and went out.

(Author's note: Not all things are as they appear. Sometimes the water flows in reverse, causing an eruption of fluids. Psychiatrists say, "Don't make waves-go with the flow." Yet paddling upstream fighting the currents is sometimes the only way to escape the clutches of inevitable doom downstream. One must be present to know the difference. It is a learning experience.)

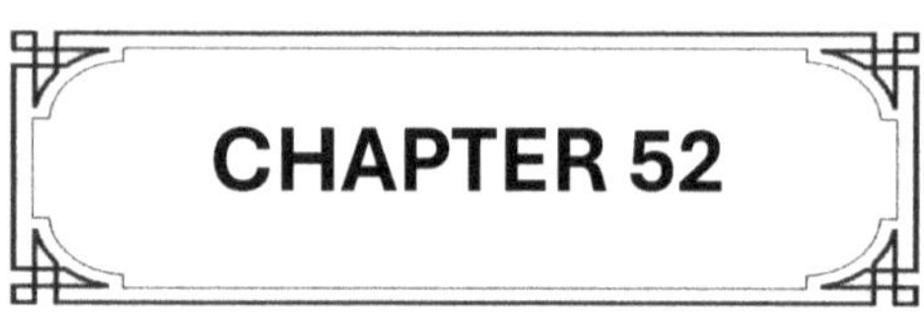

CHAPTER 52

Jesús and Dylan were off on an adventure. Jesús at the helm and Dylan tagging along with the utmost confidence and wonder, in a circle of trust. No one had gotten this close to Dylan since his divorce from Sarah. Even his kids kept their distance. But Jesús had this mesmerizing charm that enchanted those lucky enough to be in his presence.

The remaining family members standing around the fire pit watched Jesús and Bob get into the '48 Ford pick-up over by the Ponderosa building and heard the engine revving.

Dylan, in the passenger seat, looked over and saw Jesús step on the starter pedal by the accelerator. The old engine turned, hissed, and turned some more until it finally cranked over and purred like a satisfied cat. Jesús shifted the gears on the column into reverse and the vehicle went into back-up mode. He moved the lever into "D" and they went chugging forward, leaving everyone else behind.

Engine noises had a trance-like effect on Dylan, and in an instant, he dozed off.

Suddenly he awoke, feeling groggy, looked over at Jesús and then waited for the Fruit Flows gate to automatically open. When Bob looked over at the gate, he saw Jesús sitting on a rail. He snapped his eyes over to the driver's seat, and there perched a raven on the steering wheel. Bob blinked. The raven was gone, and Jesús was sitting there calmly with a cheshire grin on his face. Bob said, "How'd you do that?"

Jesús replied, "I didn't do anything. I'm not a trickster or a magician. What did you see?"

Bob told Jesús, and Jesús said. "Ah, for once. Now you are seeing! When you looked at me, you saw what you wanted to see.

When you begin to use your spiritual vision as eyesight, the hallucinations become rational. You will see more, trust me."

The engine revved, Jesús passed through the gate, and Bob entered his own dream world once again.

Close to dawn, Bob awoke, just as he had before, and saw Jesús driving the Ford and humming a tune.

(Author's note: Those who hum are either content or curious.) Bob asked, "Where are we going?"

Jesús said, "I'm taking you to see a medicine woman."

They pulled onto a rutted, dirt road and drove another hour, bumping along, bouncing out of their seats at 20 miles per hour, the old pick-up leaving a dusty trail, like Bob rewriting "Visions of Johanna." They passed a small cabin and stopped at the stables and riding ring just ahead.

Jesús and Bob got out of the truck as a vibrant old cowgirl approached them. She was radiant in an ancient kind of way. Jesús said, "Dona Soul searcher, this is Bob. Bob, this is Dona Soul searcher, your riding instructor."

Dona Soul searcher said. "So you are here for your riding lesson. Go pick a horse."

Bob looked over at the barn just as five horses were released to prance around the arena.

Bob carefully approached them and they scattered, shyly, not familiar with this stranger.

Jesús said, "Let them get to know you as you get to know them. One of them will pick you. They judge you by touch, sight and smell, so I want you to see with your hands."

Bob wasn't too successful at making equine friends. Minutes passed like hours and Bob was getting anxious.

Dona Soul searcher and Jesús watched the scene intently. Dona Soul searcher finally told Bob. "Let go and fix the leak." She told him his eyes were leaking and that he must close them. and trust that the horses would sense a change in his attitude, a desire to become approachable. "My mother is your mother as your mother is my mother," she said.

Bob came over to Jesús and Dona and said, "What do you mean? I don't get it."

Dona said, "You need some soup. Come inside and have some mush with us."

Dona and Jesús led the way. Bob followed, looking over his shoulder at the horses.

Once inside, Bob could smell the aroma of mushroom soup steeping in a cauldron on the old flat-top wood-burning iron stove. He also caught a whiff of the burning wood that smelled like a forest on fire. It was hot inside the cabin, but the chilly Guatemalan dawn made this seem like a warm sanctuary of relief, like a security blanket to a young child.

They sat on stools at a wooden table.

Dona said, "This mush will make your insides tingle and you will see my friends differently."

Jesús said, "It will even fix the leak. There's another storm coming. You will mount the horse that picks you, and she will take you for a ride as the world gets sucked into your brain."

Bob said, "Well, something's got to change. I feel like thunder is exploding in my head." Bob turned away and vomited.

After the soup. Jesús offered Bob a smoke. Bob took the hand- rolled cigar and puffed a big drag on it. He exhaled and left his feet.

The next thing Bob knew, he was on the horse he chose-or who chose him-galloping through the jungle. He came upon a clearing where his horse came to a stop.

There were native people mingling with one another as if in slow motion. Some were rolling in the sand; others were swinging their arms in the air. Bob stroked the horse's neck and whispered in her ear, "What's next?"

Bob dismounted and held his horse's muzzle, looking into her globe-like eyes.

"You'll see," the mare said.

Dylan just stared.

"What did you say?" he asked numbly, looking straight into her eyes.

There was no response.

The villagers took no notice of Bob or the horse. Bob watched them all, mesmerized at their nonchalance and their indifference toward him. He felt at home. No one spoke. The trance seemed to last forever.

Bob thought his eye caught something moving toward him in the air. It was a gasp. His mare whinnied. Bob looked into her eyes once again and heard her say, "Go ahead."

He took a step forward and melted into the earth. He looked down and saw that he was knee deep in dirt. He couldn't move. Panic struck like lightning. Then he immediately settled down and said to himself, "Well, I guess I ain't goin' nowhere till I fix the leak."

He relaxed his mind, opened his eyes and fell asleep standing. His horse became Buddha and advised him to "go in," breathe, and go with his exhale, ride on his out-breath.

Bob looked down and took a step. He was freed from the earth and able to move.

It was then that he realized each person around him was creating his own world, dancing in the wind and writing things in the sand. Bob knelt in the dirt, picked up a twig and began to create a verse of his own.

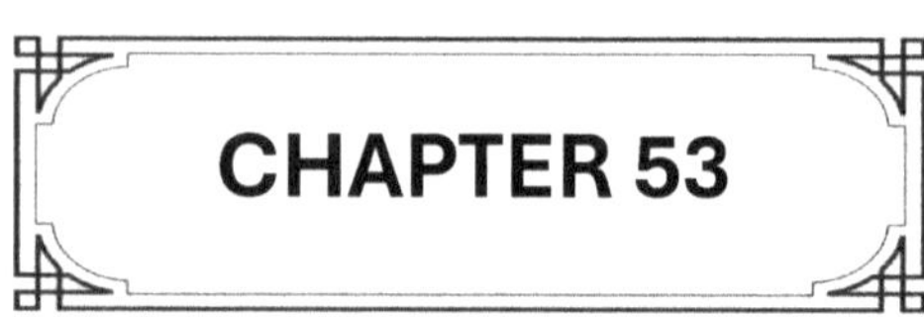

CHAPTER 53

When Jesús and Dona Soul searcher found him, Bob had scribbled words in the riding ring that read, "Sacred heart, useful hide, killer idea, smoking brains, hungry gut. One foot dancing. the other walking. Hands telling stories, one orchestrating, the other conducting: mouths eating, drinking, kissing and forming words. Eyes seeing visions-dreams or reality?- stirring life and shaking grapevines."

Bob looked up at them and asked, "What just happened? Where am I?"

Dona said, "You don't know?"

Bob exclaimed, "That was some kind of smoke!"

Jesús said, "Not to mention the soup. Now you know what we are talking about. There are many here among us who share this earth, but no one shares your space, sees what you see, or dreams like you. It is all in your head. You are on your own."

Dylan answered, "We don't sleep, we just climb the walls while the tea steeps."

Dona and Jesús looked at one another and said simultaneously. "He got it! He's there!"

Jesús helped Bob to his feet and said, "It's time to go. Dona, a divine pleasure as always."

Dona said, "Anytime. I'm always here-wherever that is." Jesús chuckled and said, "Me, too."

Bob asked Jesús as they were driving away, "Where are we going now?"

Jesús said, "Loco-wanna go? The truth stands before; you and me in a mirror, me beside you and you beside me, watching each other. You reflect upon those who see you, those who touch you. those who hear you. You are but a mere reflection of your own image, and I stand before you, the mirror, and we are the faces of cracked mud."

Dylan, "The faces of cracked mud."

-The End-